PRAISE FOR LEE GOLDBERG

Malibu Burning

"The author of the Eve Ronin mysteries returns with a fast-paced, over-the-top caper that entertains while keeping readers guessing."
—*Library Journal* (starred review)

"Goldberg returns to the wildfire he memorably chronicled in *Lost Hills* (2020) from a strikingly new angle . . . A businesslike thriller that shows how rewarding it can be to revisit the same story from a new point of view."
—*Kirkus Reviews*

"Goldberg's well-drawn characters will keep readers rooting for both crooks and cops, and he hangs everyone's fates on a clever, complicated con. The result is as explosive as a wildfire."
—*Publishers Weekly*

"Action-packed and captivating, *Malibu Burning* is a scorching-hot and fast-moving thriller that will have you sweating as if you're in the middle of a five-alarm fire. Once again, Lee Goldberg delivers a fast-paced, entertaining novel with well-constructed characters and an intriguing plot."
—Best Thriller Books

"Both fans and newcomers to Goldberg's work will enjoy the fast-moving, at times terrifying, tale and its close look at firefighting and arson-investigation techniques."
—'LUE

"Hilarious and touching, exciting and endearing. Highly recommended."

—*Deadly Pleasures*

"Lee Goldberg is one of the best thriller authors in the business and proves it again with *Malibu Burning*. He keeps things racing along at such a pace, and in such smooth prose, that it's almost impossible to stop reading in this novel."

—Rough Edges

"If *Malibu Burning* were a wine, we'd describe it as rich and full-bodied, with tasty top notes of humor and lightheartedness, a robust blend of experience infused with enormous heart."

—The Thriller Zone

"Lee Goldberg writes a scorching-hot thriller with his *Malibu Burning* that delivers on all the heat. Fast paced, the plot moves relentlessly to an unexpected climax."

—*Montecito Journal*

"Lee Goldberg knows how to write entertaining novels. His latest thriller, *Malibu Burning*, is a prime example. He creates a diversity of characters, throws them into some impossibly dangerous situations, and ratchets up the tension and suspense. Like a wildfire storming through the woods, I was racing to get to the novel's ending."

—Gumshoe Review

"This splendidly entertaining tale unfolds at a cinematic pace. Goldberg blazes new ground in his already storied career, treading on the territory of the great Don Winslow. Not to be missed for crime-thriller aficionados."

—BookTrib

"*Malibu Burning* is a blistering thrill ride full of Southern California thieves, cops, and firefighters, all facing high stakes and imminent danger. Superbly researched and told, fast-paced, and downright fun, this is Lee Goldberg at his best!"
—Mark Greaney, #1 *New York Times* bestselling author of the Gray Man series

"By turns tense and rambunctious, wildly entertaining, and breakneck-paced, Lee Goldberg's splendid *Malibu Burning* is pure storytelling pleasure from beginning to end."
—Megan Abbott, Edgar Award–, Anthony Award–, Thriller Award–, and *Los Angeles Times* Book Prize–winning author of *The Turnout*

"A well-written, fast-moving crime novel. Highly recommend. Lee did his work, and it shows. The plotting is perfect, the characters are fully drawn, and the dialogue is leavened with Lee's wicked sense of humor."
—Brendan DuBois, #1 *New York Times* bestselling author

"*Malibu Burning* is classic Lee Goldberg at the top of his game: a fast-paced, funny, and deeply satisfying page-turner."
—Jess Lourey, Amazon Charts bestselling author of *The Quarry Girls*

"An inventive, twisty, and funny caper from one of crime writing's true pros. Elmore Leonard and Donald Westlake would've loved this wild heist."
—Ace Atkins, *New York Times* bestselling author of *Robert B. Parker's Bye Bye Baby* and *The Heathens*

ASHES NEVER LIE

The Ian Ludlow Thrillers

True Fiction

Killer Thriller

Fake Truth

The Fox & O'Hare Series (coauthored with Janet Evanovich)

Pros & Cons (novella)

The Shell Game (novella)

The Heist

The Chase

The Job

The Scam

The Pursuit

The Diagnosis Murder Series

The Silent Partner

The Death Merchant

The Shooting Script

The Waking Nightmare

The Past Tense

The Dead Letter

The Dead Man Series (coauthored with William Rabkin)

Face of Evil

Ring of Knives (with James Daniels)

Hell in Heaven

The Dead Woman (with David McAfee)

The Blood Mesa (with James Reasoner)

Kill Them All (with Harry Shannon)

The Beast Within (with James Daniels)

Fire & Ice (with Jude Hardin)

Carnival of Death (with Bill Crider)

Freaks Must Die (with Joel Goldman)

Slaves to Evil (with Lisa Klink)

The Midnight Special (with Phoef Sutton)

The Death March (with Christa Faust)

The Black Death (with Aric Davis)

The Killing Floor (with David Tully)

Colder Than Hell (with Anthony Neil Smith)

Evil to Burn (with Lisa Klink)

Streets of Blood (with Barry Napier)

Crucible of Fire (with Mel Odom)

The Dark Need (with Stant Litore)

The Rising Dead (with Stella Green)

Reborn (with Kate Danley, Phoef Sutton, and Lisa Klink)

The Jury Series

Judgment

Adjourned

Payback

Guilty

Nonfiction

The Best TV Shows You Never Saw

Unsold Television Pilots 1955–1989

Television Fast Forward

Science Fiction Filmmaking in the 1980s (cowritten with William Rabkin, Randy Lofficier, and Jean-Marc Lofficier)

The Dreamweavers: Interviews with Fantasy Filmmakers of the 1980s (cowritten with William Rabkin, Randy Lofficier, and Jean-Marc Lofficier)

Successful Television Writing (cowritten with William Rabkin)

The Joy of Sets: Interviews on the Sets of 1980s Genre Movies

The James Bond Films 1962–1989: Interviews with the Actors, Writers and Directors

ASHES
NEVER
LIE

LEE GOLDBERG

THOMAS & MERCER

Text copyright © 2024 by Adventures in Television, Inc.
All rights reserved.

Published by Thomas & Mercer, Seattle

www.apub.com

Amazon, the Amazon logo, and Thomas & Mercer are trademarks of Amazon.com, Inc., or its affiliates.

ISBN-13: 9781662512384 (hardcover)
ISBN-13: 9781662512391 (paperback)
ISBN-13: 9781662512377 (digital)

Cover design by Shasti O'Leary Soudant
Cover images: © Stu Gray / Alamy; © albertgonzalez, © Tverdokhlib / Shutterstock

Printed in the United States of America

First edition

To Valerie & Madison

CHAPTER ONE

The charred, steaming hulk of a Toyota Camry sat in a burned-out patch of scorched brush in the middle of what was now the Chatsworth Nature Preserve, which had previously been a sacred Chumash Indian ceremonial ground, a limestone kiln used by Spanish settlers, a movie studio back lot, and the dry lake bed of the long-abandoned Chatsworth Reservoir.

But to Los Angeles County Sheriff's Department arson detectives Walter Sharpe and Andrew Walker, who'd just arrived in their modified Chevy Tahoe SUV, the place was Hellmouth, a jurisdictional, bureaucratic, and political nightmare situated on the northwest edge of the San Fernando Valley.

The unincorporated land was bordered by the Simi Hills in Ventura County to the west, the Santa Susana Pass State Park to the north, and Los Angeles urban sprawl to the east. Los Angeles County was responsible for handling any fires at the preserve, a job that was significantly complicated by the interests of the bordering municipalities and the strict oversight of the Los Angeles Cultural Heritage Commission.

"I will shoot the son of a bitch who burned this car," said Sharpe, grimacing in the passenger seat, watching the firefighters gather up the hoses and other equipment that they'd used to battle the fire.

"The last time I checked," said Walker, switching off the ignition and tipping up the brim of his Stetson cowboy hat, "torching a car isn't an executable offense."

"It is when you do it in Hellmouth." Sharpe's grimace seemed to deepen the crags on his jowly, droopy face that made him look constantly weary. If Sharpe ever had a facelift, Walker thought, they'd have to pull the skin over his head, down his back, and to his heels before it tightened up. "We are going to have so many heads up our asses that our colons will be officially designated convention centers."

"Thank you for that vivid image."

"If the arsonist set fire to that car anywhere else in the county, we could do our walk-around, have the wreck towed away, file our report, and be done with it," Sharpe said. "But here, where everything is under historical and ecological protection, we'll have to justify every move we make, starting with why we drove in here and ran over a rare snoot-whistle flower instead of dropping in by parachute."

Walker had been Sharpe's partner for only a year and still had a lot to learn about arson investigation, but he knew it was pointless trying to change the man's dour mood. Walker's job here would be damage control, which mostly meant keeping Sharpe away from the firefighters.

"You take the torched car," Walker said. "I'll handle the pleasantries with the firefighters and run the plates."

Sharpe nodded, grabbed his investigation bag from the floor, and got out. He didn't have a problem working a scene alone. In fact, he preferred it.

Walker got out, too. He was six feet tall and twenty years younger than his partner but in worse physical shape. He had a bum knee and there were buckshot pellets in his back that the doctors weren't able to carve out. The injuries were painful reminders of his eleven years as a US marshal. Even so, he still craved the action and independence that he'd left behind to save his marriage.

Both Walker and Sharpe wore the LASD's standard tactical uniform—a dark-green shirt with hidden buttons over a black tee and matching cargo pants, held up with a black utility belt holding their Glocks, cuffs, and Maglites. There were no Velcro clasps anywhere on their uniforms or on the bags they carried, because the static electricity that the fasteners could spark might ignite flammable gases or explosives.

Walker adjusted his hat, flashed his most winning smile, and strode out to meet the local LA County fire captain, who was easy to identify. The man stood beside his gleaming red-and-chrome fire engine and wore a scuffed yellow helmet with a plate labeled CAPTAIN mounted above the brim. His name, GUYETTE, was written on a patch on his heavy coat.

Captain Guyette was as linebacker big and wide as Walker was, but with some lines on his brow and gray in the buzz-cut stubble of his sideburns that marked him as being perhaps a decade older than the detective.

"You put that out quick, Captain," Walker said, holding out his hand and introducing himself.

They shook hands. "Only because our station is a half mile away. We saw the smoke and were rolling before we even got the official call." Guyette watched Sharpe warily circle the burned car and avoid the firefighters cleaning up around him. Somehow, Sharpe's aggravation was obvious in his body language, though Walker couldn't identify exactly how. "What's up Shar-Pei's ass?"

"Nothing now," Walker said, "but soon it'll be the head of every bureaucrat with an interest in the Chatsworth Nature Preserve. He hates getting called out to Hellmouth."

"Imagine how we feel being stuck in the middle of it," Guyette said. "I'd prefer to fight a major structure fire than even douse a lit cigarette in here or up in the state park. I'll have to file reports on this incident to sixty different agencies and write a heartfelt eulogy for the endangered globby twizzle gnat that hit our windshield as we drove in."

"Sharpe thinks we ran over a snoot-whistle flower."

The captain turned and looked at him. "Oh God, not a snoot-whistle flower."

"Is that bad?"

"It's the only nesting place of the globby twizzle gnat." Guyette laughed and clapped Walker amiably on the back. "Hope you weren't planning on joining the Sierra Club."

"Did you get a license plate off that car?"

Guyette dug into his pocket for a notebook and read off the number to Walker, who thanked him and went back to the Tahoe to run the plate on the computer.

The details on the car came up on the screen in a split second. What he learned from the information fit the truism that there were only three motives for an urban arson: revenge, profit, or covering up a crime. This one ticked off two of those boxes.

Walker got out and tried to avoid stepping in the thick mud as he joined Sharpe, who was peering through what had been the driver's side window of the Camry.

"The interior was doused with gasoline and then ignited with a road flare," Sharpe said, then nodded to a clump of weeds behind them. "The empty gas can was tossed over there. Even you could have solved this arson."

"I'm flattered."

"Let me guess—you ran the plates and discovered that the car was reported stolen by the owners."

"First thing this morning."

Sharpe sighed. "I understand the regret of buying a car for $1,000 over sticker and paying double-digit interest on the monthly payments. But reporting it stolen and then setting it on fire is a stupid way of getting out of the contract. Thieves either sell the cars or strip them for parts. They don't burn them."

Walker said, "Unless the car is used in the commission of a crime."

"How often does that actually happen?"

"Two hours ago, at a bank robbery in Canoga Park. The plates on this car match the getaway vehicle."

"Well, there's a first time for everything."

"I'll bet the bank robbers had another stolen car already stashed here," Walker said. "They set this one ablaze, got into the other one, and kept on going, probably up the 118."

Walker was referring to the freeway a few miles north of them, also known as the Ronald Reagan or the Simi Valley depending on who you asked, that ran along the upper boundary of the San Fernando Valley and the base of the Santa Susana Mountains, from Interstate 5 to the east into Ventura County and the 101 freeway to the west.

"They are long gone now," Sharpe said. "Not that we're going to be chasing them."

"If I was still a US marshal, I could catch them by dinner," Walker said. "We still could if we wanted to."

"It's not our job."

"Why not? We're supposed to identify and apprehend arsonists."

"They committed a bank robbery first. It's an FBI case now." The instant Sharpe said it, his entire attitude changed, as if he'd had a revelation. He smiled with delight. "In fact, we're going to walk away from this car and leave it for the Feds. They can deal with the regulation-crazed bureaucrats, the animal spirit–channeling medicine men, the stoned and unbathed ecologists, and the tweedy, bifocaled historians."

Walker liked that idea, too, but couldn't resist ribbing Sharpe anyway. "You'd be lost without your stereotypes."

"Says the sheriff's deputy wearing a Stetson."

Walker looked past Sharpe and noticed the firefighters were hurrying back to their trucks. Something was up. Captain Guyette came over to the detectives.

"We're out of here," he said.

"Where's the fire?" Sharpe asked.

Guyette pointed north, to the mountains above the freeway, where a thick spiral of black smoke twisted into the sky. "Just got the call. There's a new, unoccupied house ablaze in the Twin Lakes housing development."

"That's a million-and-a-half dollars of real estate up in smoke," Walker said.

"Much more than that is at risk if we don't stop the fire from spreading," Guyette said. "Twin Lakes is in the middle of nothing but bone-dry open space and plenty of fuel."

And with that, the captain hurried back to the fire engine and jumped inside, and they sped out, sirens wailing, with absolutely no regard for any snoot-whistle flowers or globby twizzle gnats they might flatten.

Walker understood their urgency. If the blaze ignited the dry, highly flammable brush in the Santa Susana Pass State Park that bordered Twin Lakes, it could generate an insatiable wildfire that would quickly rage southwest through Box Canyon and Calabasas, over the 101 freeway, and into the Santa Monica Mountains in a relentless charge to the sea.

He knew all that from terrifying personal experience. A year ago, after he'd worked with Sharpe for only a few days, they were both caught in a massive firestorm in the Santa Monica Mountains, the biggest in the state's history, and had barely escaped with their lives. Their partnership was truly forged in fire.

Sharpe said, "How do you know about the home prices in Twin Lakes?"

"We looked at the models a couple of weeks ago."

"You can afford that?"

"Of course not," Walker said. "Carly likes to visit model homes and fantasize."

"Is that how you two spend your weekends?"

"It's what you do when you're living with a toddler in a tiny, sixty-year-old, two-bedroom shack in the armpit of Reseda."

"What do those homes up there have that yours doesn't?"

"Three more bedrooms, a kitchen island the size of my pickup truck, and a casita for the in-laws."

"Are you planning to have more kids and invite your in-laws to live with you?"

"It's Carly's dream and my nightmare."

"Does she know that?"

"She's a psychologist," Walker said. "If she doesn't, she should turn in her license."

"You have my sympathy." Sharpe clapped him on the back and headed for the Tahoe. "Let's go."

"To lunch?"

"To the fire."

Walker hurried after him. "Why? We're detectives, not firefighters."

"Exactly. All firefighters know how to do is spray water on flames and wash away evidence. They don't know anything about criminal investigation." Sharpe got into the Tahoe and slammed the door.

It was that opinion, which Sharpe never hesitated to express to firefighters, that forced Walker to spend most of his time at arson scenes running interference. But he also knew that there was a lot of truth to Sharpe's viewpoint—he just wished the man could keep it to himself.

Walker opened the driver's door and climbed into his seat. "What makes you think it's arson?"

"Nothing. Arsons rarely occur in broad daylight at a busy construction site."

Walker started the SUV, backed up, and then headed out of the preserve. "So why are we going?"

Sharpe flipped on the siren. "It's a fire. We're arson investigators. It's what we do."

"Only after a fire captain notifies us that there's something suspicious and potentially criminal about the blaze. That hasn't happened yet."

Walker fishtailed the Tahoe in a hard right onto Plummer Street and sped east through a residential neighborhood toward Topanga Canyon Boulevard, which they'd take north to Twin Lakes on the other side of the 118 freeway.

"I think an unoccupied new home bursting into flames is obviously and unquestionably suspicious," Sharpe said, one hand on the dash to brace himself.

"You just said you don't think it's arson."

"That's right, but do you see any storm clouds?"

"No," Walker said.

"So if the house wasn't hit by a bolt of lightning, then the fire was caused by accident or intent. Which is it?"

"I don't know."

"I can guarantee you the firefighters won't, either," Sharpe said. "I'll figure it out for them."

"They are going to love you for that." Walker charged into the intersection at Topanga, running the red light and nearly clipping two cars going in opposite directions as he made a sharp, tire-screaming left and continued speeding north.

"I am not doing this job to be loved," Sharpe said.

Walker swerved around a slow-moving pickup truck full of lawn mowers and gardening tools. "Then you're succeeding brilliantly."

CHAPTER TWO

There hadn't been any lakes at Twin Lakes in nearly eighty years, back when the area was developed as a Mayan-themed resort community and subdivided into five hundred parcels for homes, campsites, and a country club.

The Great Depression killed the project, and over the following decades, the man-made lakes dried up, the Mayan arch over the entrance road crumbled, and nature reclaimed the undeveloped parcels. By the 1970s, the empty land was slated to become a trash dump before community uproar got the idea scrapped.

Now the hillsides north of the 118 had been graded, and the portion of Devil's Canyon that ran between them was packed with landfill, to create the Twin Lakes housing development, the future site of two hundred 4,000-square-foot "modern ranch estate homes" offering a "a warm, rural lifestyle" and "spectacular city views" for "sophisticated, nature-loving, middle-class urbanites."

Forty homes were already sold and occupied, another twenty were completed and either awaiting sale or residents moving in, and a dozen more were in various stages of construction.

Walker drove through the entrance, past the cul-de-sac of model homes ringed with promotional flags fluttering in the smoke, and up to a two-story home that was fully engulfed in fire, flames licking out the windows. Firefighters were firing jets of water into the burning house from multiple directions, but they seemed to him to have succeeded only in containing the blaze rather than diminishing it.

He parked behind a crowd of construction workers and a trio of well-dressed people—two women and a man—that Walker pegged as sales staff.

"They're drenching the house with water," Sharpe said, scowling at the firefighters.

"Maybe because it's on fire."

"They're obliterating all the evidence of what went wrong and washing it into the street."

Walker had heard this rant from Sharpe at least a hundred times before. He gestured to the framed-out houses in various stages of construction on the cul-de-sac uphill from the burning house. Behind those construction sites were more graded lots and, farther on in the hills above, the state park, where the ground was parched and the brush was dry after two years of drought.

"It's better than those framed houses catching fire and the embers igniting the dry hillsides," Walker said.

"All I'm asking for is a little more care and precision."

They got out of the Tahoe and Sharpe glowered at the water and mud streaming into the dirt lots and down the asphalt street, watching his investigation literally go down the drain.

Walker approached one of the salespeople, a potbellied man in his thirties who sported a curly hairpiece that looked like he'd bought it at Burt Reynolds' estate sale. He wore a polo shirt, slacks, and leather loafers with tassels, which might have belonged to Burt, too.

"Are you in charge here?" Walker asked him.

The man turned, saw that Walker was a cop, and said, "I'm Ed Bell. I'm in charge of the sales office, not construction."

"That'll do," Walker said, then introduced himself and Sharpe. "Can you tell us how the fire started?"

"I have no idea. One minute the house was fine, the next it just burst into flames. When I say 'burst,' I mean it literally," Bell said. "It was the construction workers framing the house on the next cul-de-sac who noticed it first. It scared the crap out of them."

"Did they see anything suspicious before it happened, like someone hanging around the house?"

"They didn't see anybody over there."

"Was anyone working inside or outside the home, like a painter or welder?"

"Like I said, there was nobody. There's nothing to work on. The house was finished and completely empty. The cleaning crew hadn't even been in there yet."

Sharpe frowned. "So there's no furniture or anything else inside that house?"

"There's nothing," Bell said, perspiration escaping from under his toupee. "All the rooms are empty. The new homeowners weren't supposed to move in until this weekend."

Sharpe stared at the fully engulfed house. The fire was intense. Walker knew what he was thinking.

What was the fire feeding on if there were no couches, beds, bookcases, or other flammable objects to burn?

Sharpe looked back at Bell. "Have the utilities been activated?"

"They were turned on today so the cleaning crew could vacuum the carpets tomorrow and power-wash the windows outside," Bell said. "But that just involved flipping a switch downtown. Nobody had to come out here and do it."

Sharpe shifted his gaze to a finished house across the street that appeared to Walker to be the same model as the one on fire.

Walker pointed to it and asked Bell, "Is that home identical to the one that's burning?"

Bell nodded. "Yes, it's the Montecito. It's the same, except for some minor designer details, like the style of kitchen backsplash tiles, the stone on the bathroom countertops, and the carpet color."

"Can we walk through it?"

"Sure, it's unlocked. But the model is much nicer." Bell gestured to the cul-de-sac of model homes down the hill. "And it's air-conditioned."

"This one will do," Sharpe said. "But I'd appreciate a copy of the floor plan."

"Of course. I'll go get you each a copy." Bell headed down the hill, carefully avoiding the mud streams created by the firefighting effort.

Sharpe watched him go, then made a show of taking out his phone and glancing at the screen. "I just got a text. William Shatner wants his hair back."

Walker grinned. "You noticed the toupee."

"I don't miss any details at a fire scene." Sharpe started walking toward the unoccupied Montecito, which stood in the center of a naked, graded dirt lot.

Walker walked beside him. "I'm surprised you don't want to watch the fire."

"That won't tell me anything. But a peek at this house will. We'll see exactly what that house was like before the fire, which is a rare opportunity. Usually, we have to take our best guess."

That often meant using Google Earth images of the street or, if they were lucky, recent photographs that the owners had kept in the cloud instead of their house.

They walked through the front door, which opened into a two-story entry hall framed by a curving grand staircase. The hall led to the "great room," with giant windows that looked out over a tiny backyard and a bare hillside.

The windows were overkill, like using a 150-piece orchestra for a doorbell chime, Walker thought. A totally wasted effort.

They moved silently through the empty house, glancing at the dining room, laundry room, guest suite, and finally chef's kitchen, with an array of professional-grade appliances and a central island that was bigger than Walker's living room. The island contained a bread-warming drawer, a microwave drawer, a freezer drawer, and a second sink and stove.

All the windows downstairs were closed. The house smelled of new carpets, fresh paint, and new wood, a pleasing bouquet that would disappear within hours of people moving in, bringing with them the odors of their furniture, belongings, bodies, pets, and later their first meal being cooked.

A staircase behind the kitchen also led upstairs, making it easy to sneak down for a midnight snack without using the grand staircase.

The two detectives went upstairs and walked around, peeking into the spare bedrooms and then into the massive main bedroom that was an apartment unto itself, with a wet bar, a deck, and a built-in entertainment center.

The adjoining bathroom was outrageously large, with a freestanding bathtub in the middle of an enormous glassed-in shower with multiple his-and-hers showerheads. The showerheads struck Walker as more ornamental than useful since the water pressure in Los Angeles County was so weak lately, thanks to the flow restrictors mandated by law to conserve water. Taking a shower now was like being peed on by someone with a serious prostate problem.

Sharpe wandered over to a window that was left half-open, as if someone had taken a shower and wanted to clear the steam from the mirrors.

"All the windows downstairs are closed and locked, but up here, they're mostly open."

"It makes sense," Walker said.

"It does?"

"There's no electricity to run the AC or any fans, so the painters or carpet layers who were working in here probably opened the windows to get some fresh air flowing."

"Why didn't they do it downstairs, too?"

"They didn't want any critters or crooks to get in."

Sharpe nodded, apparently accepting the explanation. "They might've done the same thing at the house that's on fire. Open windows upstairs would help explain how the house became fully involved in fire so fast, especially without any furnishings for fuel. The airflow fed oxygen to the blaze and drew it up through the house."

Sharpe walked over to the giant shower, which was essentially a glass room, and stared at the bathtub with obvious disapproval.

"What's wrong with the tub?" Walker asked.

"This bathroom is big enough to hold weddings. I don't see the point of putting a freestanding bathtub inside a huge shower stall when there's plenty of room for it out here."

"Because it looks cool in there," Walker said. "It's a contemporary take on the common bathtub-shower combo. It's a conversation piece."

"If you like dull conversation."

Walker didn't, so he changed the subject. "What else have you noticed during the walk-through?"

"It's too much house, bordering on ridiculously, grotesquely indulgent. You're paying for a lot of wasted space you don't need, like most of this bathroom."

"I meant things that might relate to the fire across the street."

"I don't see any ignition sources. Do you?"

"Nope. But maybe a painter left a pile of dirty rags on top of some cans of paint and thinner in a room over there and it spontaneously combusted."

They'd had a case like that a few months earlier. The homeowner, who was behind on his house payments, was accused of arson until Sharpe came in and proved it was an accident, that the man's only crime was trying to save money by repainting a room himself. He'd left the paint and rags near the window, in direct sunlight, and closed the door.

Sharpe shook his head. "Bell said the house was empty, that it just needed a cleaning."

"He could be wrong. Or maybe some disgruntled worker, on his way to take a crap at the porta-potty on the lot, poured gasoline all over the first floor and tossed a match inside."

"Bell said that the construction workers didn't see anybody around before the fire."

"They were busy hammering nails," Walker said, "not watching the neighborhood or the crapper."

Sharpe went to a window and looked outside at the burning house. The fire was gone, leaving behind blackened stucco where flames had licked out the windows, reaching for the edges of the still largely intact roof. Some of the stucco was gone, too, exposing the home's charred wooden skeleton. The house was bleeding black water from the ground floor, the flow carrying soggy drywall, chunks of stucco, and pieces of broken wood out into the mud lot and onto the asphalt road.

"Looks like they've drowned the fire and everything else," Sharpe said. "We can go in there now."

They walked out of the house and went to their truck, where they started suiting up.

Walker swapped his Stetson for a hard hat with a miner's light on it, put on his work gloves, and was reaching for a shoulder bag full of metal canisters and plastic baggies for evidence collection when Bell approached them with two sets of floor plans and sales brochures.

"Here you go," he said, handing the material to Sharpe.

"Thanks, that's very helpful, but we only need the plans," Sharpe said, and held the brochures back out to him.

Bell waved him away. "Keep the brochures. We give an active-duty military and first responders' discount."

Sharpe didn't argue. He tossed all the papers into the truck's cab, pulled out his tool kit for examining and extracting evidence, and headed for the house, where the firefighters were mopping up.

Walker walked beside him, keenly aware that he was functioning now more like an assistant than a partner and he was bored just thinking about the hours ahead bagging bits of burned this and charred that. It wasn't why he became a cop.

Captain Guyette noticed them for the first time and clearly wasn't pleased by their arrival. "What are you two doing here?"

Sharpe said, "We were in the neighborhood."

"I know, but this isn't arson."

"What is it?"

"An accident," Guyette said. "Bad wiring."

"We'll see," Sharpe said.

"I've seen," Guyette said. "It's obvious."

This wasn't starting off well, Walker thought. But he decided to keep quiet. The conflict might be entertaining and keep him from nodding off.

"Tell me," Sharpe said.

"There wasn't a single origin or ignition source but rather multiple spots all over the house, all near electric sockets, light switches, or lighting. That's how the fire spread so fast. It was already everywhere," Guyette said, then looked Sharpe in the eye. "I know what I'm doing."

Walker was convinced, and ready to go back to the truck, but not Sharpe, who held Guyette's gaze.

"So do I," Sharpe said.

"I've fought hundreds of fires over the last twenty years," Guyette said. "How many have you fought, Shar-Pei?"

"None."

Guyette grinned, but not with amusement. More like disdain. "You're like a virgin telling an experienced lover how to satisfy a woman. I rest my case."

"You haven't made a case yet. You'd know that if you'd spent those twenty years as a cop instead of fucking around."

Guyette glared at Sharpe for a long moment, then went back to his truck.

Walker watched him go, then looked at Sharpe. "If I'm gonna hang out with you old vets, I'm going to need to up my metaphor game."

Sharpe and Walker walked slowly around the exterior of the house, doing their best to avoid the thick, sooty sludge while they surveyed the damage.

The first thing Walker noticed was that any windows that hadn't been broken open by firefighters were still closed, though the glass in some had been shattered by the flames. Otherwise, the land around the house was barren, wet muck, except for a porta-potty at a far corner of the lot. There were no flammable materials, spark-emitting machinery, or power lines around that could ignite a fire.

The two detectives entered the house from the attached garage, which was intact and undamaged, at least by fire. There was plenty of soot on the garage walls and water on the concrete floor.

Sharpe and Walker moved methodically through the house, looking for fire patterns—the smoke trails and charring on the walls, doorways, and ceilings that charted the course and intensity of the fire. The patterns could also serve as a reliable chronology of the event, but this time Walker couldn't read the clock, which in itself was a clue.

As the detectives silently studied what the patterns told them, and were rained on by filthy water dripping from the second floor, they ignored the nasty looks from the firefighters who were still going through the house checking for hot spots and who'd probably overheard Sharpe's argument with their captain.

The firefighters would have been shocked to learn that Walker agreed with Guyette. It sure looked like the fire had erupted in the walls, the ceilings, and the floors at roughly the same time.

Sharpe surveyed the kitchen, then headed up the back staircase to the second floor. Walker followed him and noticed again that all the windows were closed. They stopped together in the main bedroom, which was the least damaged space in the house. It felt to Walker like the right time to share his opinions with Sharpe, out of earshot of any firefighters who might still be in the house.

"I know you don't want to hear this from me," he said, "but I think Guyette is right. Faulty wiring started this fire."

Sharpe gave him a stony look. "You've been doing this for what, a year? And now you're an arson expert?"

"I've picked up a few skills along the way and refined some that I already had."

"Like what?"

"I'm a manhunter, that's what I do best. Bad guys leave tracks. They can't help it. Same with fire. The burn patterns might as well be footprints. Bad guys chase money. Fires chase fuel—oxygen and flammable materials—but these flames didn't run toward open windows or fat couches, because there weren't any. The fire was already everywhere, in the walls and ceilings. Bad wiring makes sense."

Sharpe nodded. "That's all true. But you're missing something."

"What's that?"

"All the windows in the house were closed. If the fire wasn't getting oxygen, and there was nothing in the rooms to burn, what was feeding it?"

"The house itself."

"The walls are filled with fiberglass insulation, which is practically fireproof."

"But they are wrapped in paper," Walker said, "which isn't."

Sharpe smiled. "Very observant."

"I've had a half-decent teacher."

"But the paper lining isn't enough fuel to generate all this heat, and some of the insulation is melted," Sharpe said, pointing to an example visible between the exposed studs on a wall. "The melting point of fiberglass is 1,300 degrees. A blowtorch can do that. Do you see one around here?"

"Burning wood can do it, too."

"What got the wood that hot?"

"The fire," Walker said.

"Just when you were starting to impress me, you had to say something incredibly stupid."

Sharpe's phone buzzed in his pocket. He pulled it out with his dirty gloved hand, getting soot on his phone, and answered the call. He listened for a moment, grim-faced, and told the caller, "We can be there in ten minutes." He wiped the phone on his shirt in a futile gesture to remove the soot and then pocketed it. "That was the lieutenant. A house burned down in Calabasas this afternoon. The firefighters say the entire place reeks of accelerants."

"That makes our job easier," Walker said.

"There's also a body inside."

And that made it many times more difficult.

CHAPTER THREE

Walker told Bell to not let anyone inside the burned-out house, that it was an active crime scene until they determined otherwise, and that they'd be back soon to continue their investigation.

They got into the Tahoe and sped southwest, siren screaming, down across the valley floor to Calabasas, a small community on the foothills of the Santa Monica Mountains that relied on the county for all of their law enforcement and firefighting.

Calabasas began as a lawless, often deadly stagecoach stop ruled by a ruthless Mexican rancher. Later it became known for Park Moderne, an artists' colony nestled in the hills. Now it was famed for its celebrity-packed gated communities and its garish town center, a Disney-esque re-creation of an Italian village with a clock tower topped by the world's largest Rolex.

The house fire was in old Calabasas, on one of the so-called bird streets, where the art deco bungalows of Park Moderne once stood. Most of the bungalows on the narrow, oak-lined, bird-named streets were long gone, replaced over the years by ranch-style homes, which were now being razed in favor of bloated Spanish-Mediterranean mini-mansions crammed onto lots far too tiny to hold them.

The presence of the fire engines and LASD patrol cars forced the closure of Black Bird Way, which was not much wider than a single lane even when there were no emergency vehicles parked on it. A uniformed deputy waved Walker through and they drove along the wet asphalt to a fire-scarred one-story ranch house. It wasn't as badly burned as the Twin

Lakes home, Walker thought, but it would be a total teardown anyway. What wasn't burned was damaged by smoke and water.

The firefighters were wrapping up their work, dragging charred furniture and other rubble out of the house and piling it into heaps on the front lawn, where they soaked it all with more water. Seeing them doing that provoked a string of colorful profanity from Sharpe, some of it new to Walker, who considered himself well versed in swearing. He was tempted to take notes.

The two men got out of their truck and spotted two plainclothes LASD detectives, a man and a woman, standing on the driveway, watching the firefighters work.

The male detective was easily in his sixties and overweight, a heart attack–in-waiting clothed in an off-the-rack suit. The slim woman beside him seemed too young to Walker to be a detective, more like a teenager accompanying her father on "bring your kid to work day." But there was no mistaking her cop posture or the badge and the Glock clipped to her belt.

Sharpe approached the man and reached out his hand. "Donuts, I thought you'd retired."

The man smiled warmly and shook Sharpe's hand. "I tried but it didn't stick. Besides, she still has a lot to learn." He tipped his head to the woman beside him, who had piercing blue eyes that studied Walker warily.

"I know the feeling," Sharpe said, tipping his head in kind to Walker.

Walker said, "You're saying that you're sticking around just to educate me in the fine art of arson investigation?"

"Of course not," Sharpe said. "I'm staying because without me, most of the arsonists in this city would never be noticed and the few that are would never get caught."

The fat man turned to the woman, who was still watching Walker. "As you can see, Eve, my old friend Walter Sharpe suffers from a crippling lack of self-confidence. So, you two already have something big in common." Now the man turned to Walker. "I'm Duncan Pavone, and my partner is—"

Walker interrupted him. "Eve Ronin." He met her gaze. "I know who you are."

Eve was in her midtwenties and the youngest female homicide detective in the history of the Los Angeles County Sheriff's Department. She'd won her promotion thanks to her off-duty arrest of Blake Largo, the star of the *Deathfist* action movies. She'd spotted him smacking his girlfriend in a parking lot. Eve swiftly overpowered him, planted him face-first on the ground, and read him his rights. The stunning encounter was caught on camera by onlookers and the video went viral at a time when the sheriff's department was plagued by scandals and needed any good PR. She shrewdly leveraged her fame, which was distracting the public from all of the sheriff's other woes, to get the transfer to homicide, which kept her in the news cycle even longer.

Eve's rapid ascent to a top detective position, based solely on publicity and not experience or merit, was reason enough for her colleagues to resent her. But then she got even more glowing media attention by exposing corruption within the department while also solving several major homicide cases. The public loved her, but the same couldn't be said of her fellow cops.

"I'm Andrew Walker. Why are you looking at me like you're about to draw your Glock?"

"The last deputy I met who wore a cowboy hat tried to kill me," she said.

"That's not saying much," Walker said. "Most of the deputies you meet want to kill you."

Duncan nodded in agreement. "That's the other reason why I couldn't retire."

Walker smiled at her. "Don't worry, I'm a big fan. My wife loves your TV series."

Eve's exploits had inspired *Ronin*, a fictional crime show that had recently premiered on a streaming service.

"I like your show, too," Eve said. "How's your spin kick?"

"I've never tried one, and it's too late now with my bum knee." Because of his name, his profession, and his hat, lots of people wrongly assumed that he'd modeled himself after *Walker, Texas Ranger*. He didn't. "I've also never worked in Texas, and the only black belt I have is the one that holds up my pants."

"So why the hat? Hiding a bald spot?"

"I'm an LA County deputy sheriff," Walker said. "I'm respecting our legacy."

Sharpe said, "You wore it when you were a US marshal, too."

"It's also part of their legacy," Walker said.

Duncan grinned. "And you wear it because it makes the bad guys think you're a redneck, gun-crazy, cowboy maniac."

Walker nodded. "That's the main reason."

"Are you?" Eve asked.

"You'll have to wait and see."

Duncan said, "Let's hope it doesn't come to that. We're here because of the body in there." He waved his hand at the house. "We believe the victim is Patrick Lopresti, who resided here with his wife and kid."

Walker looked at the house more closely now and saw the fire-blackened skeleton of a car in the heavily burned garage. He also saw several white, oval cameras, some of them melted, mounted in the eaves of the roof and in the trees around the house. An ADT security sign was posted in a flower bed.

"Where's the family now?"

"We don't know yet. But we can tell you when Lopresti got home," Duncan said. "Calabasas has license plate readers and traffic control cameras at all the major intersections, so we were able to track his Audi from the Valley Circle off-ramp of the eastbound 134 freeway at 4:15 p.m. all the way to the corner of Park Ora and Old Topanga without incident or anybody tailing him."

Walker had driven that same route and knew the intersection was only a few blocks away.

Eve said, "ADT says he deactivated the security alarm by entering his code on the keypad inside the garage five minutes later. The smoke alarm was triggered twelve minutes after that."

Walker gestured to the cameras around the house. "What about those? Can we see the video?"

"While we were waiting for you to show up, we called a judge for a warrant and it's being electronically served to Arlo now."

Sharpe looked at Eve. "Who is Arlo?"

"That's the brand of these cameras and the name of the video recording, streaming, and storage service that goes along with them."

"When we get the videos," Sharpe said, narrowing his eyes at Eve, "are we going to see you charging into the house to look around?"

"No, of course not," Eve said. "We wouldn't dare contaminate your crime scene."

Sharpe glanced at Duncan, who said, "I had to physically restrain her."

"I appreciate it," Sharpe said.

"Why?" Eve gestured to the pile of furniture on the lawn. "What harm could I possibly do in there that the firefighters haven't already done?"

Walker looked at Sharpe. "She has a point."

"No, she doesn't. We'll suit up now and do our initial walk-through." Sharpe turned and started to walk toward the truck.

Eve said, "What we need to know from you is if we're dealing with a homicide, a suicide, or an arsonist who accidentally got himself killed."

Duncan groaned. Sharpe stopped, turned around, and gave Eve a weary look.

"Thank you for reminding me what my job is, Detective Ronin. Otherwise, I might have forgotten."

He managed to say it without any anger or reproach, which somehow made it even more devastating.

Eve flushed with embarrassment. "Sorry."

Duncan said, "You'll have to forgive her, Sharpe. She's chronically impatient."

"You can join us once we've documented the scene and finished our preliminary examination," Sharpe said. "If CSU and the ME get here while we're inside, please keep them out."

Eve gestured to the uniformed deputies keeping onlookers away and directing traffic. "The deputies can do that. I'm going inside with you."

"We don't need your help."

"I'm not offering any," Eve said. "If it's a homicide, I don't want you contaminating *my* crime scene. It's bad enough that house has already been hosed down and gutted. I'm astounded that the firefighters didn't drag the corpse out onto the lawn, too."

Well played, Walker thought. Eve definitely scored big points from Sharpe with that last remark. But was she genuinely airing a gripe or shrewdly manipulating his partner?

Sharpe said, "What about you, Duncan? Do you also want to go in?"

Duncan tugged on a pant leg. "These are new pants and my favorite shoes. I'll stay out here, work on getting a couple more warrants, and chat up the lookie-loos for information about Patrick Lopresti."

Sharpe turned to Walker. "Get Detective Ronin suited up while I have a word with the fire captain."

"Don't make me break up a brawl," Walker said.

Sharpe glowered at him and headed to the fire engine while Walker led Eve to their Tahoe.

Eve said, "Sharpe doesn't play nice with others?"

Walker thought that was an interesting question coming from her. She had a reputation for irritating people. "He's only got a problem with firefighters."

"What is it?"

"Same as yours." Walker unlocked and opened one of the equipment storage units that ran along the sides of the Tahoe.

"It doesn't bother you that they're careless about preserving evidence?"

Was she trying to play him, too? Walker rummaged through the stuff in the truck to find her an extra hard hat, gloves, and gas mask.

While he did that, he said, "They have one job to do, which is putting out fires, and they do it well. I respect that. It just makes our work harder."

"Why did they drag everything out of the house?"

He turned to look at her. "Is this your first fire death investigation?"

"Yes, it is," she said. He was startled by her honesty and it must have shown, because she added: "I'm a big believer in admitting what I don't know."

"You aren't worried about looking dumb?"

"I'm more worried about getting things wrong."

Walker was impressed that someone with so much to prove was willing to confess any lack of knowledge or skill.

"The firefighters are afraid they'll leave and then some smoldering couch or bed will rekindle the blaze. So, to cover themselves from liability and embarrassment, they drag out anything that might reignite," Walker said. "But there's a practical purpose, too. It also gives them a chance to make absolutely sure nothing is still burning in the walls or floors behind all that stuff. So they'll walk around with pike poles, poking the floors and opening walls for a peek."

"Further destroying possible evidence."

"Or saving any remaining evidence from burning up."

"You like to look at the bright side."

"I don't want to become a bitter, angry guy. It's not healthy for my stomach lining or my marriage." Walker tossed his Stetson in the truck and put a hard hat on instead.

"No bald spot," Eve said. "That's a surprise."

"I'm full of them." He handed her a hard hat with a miner's light on it, a pair of goggles, leather gloves, and a gas mask. He took the same equipment for himself.

Eve put everything on but held on to the mask, holding it out to him as a question. "There's no more smoke."

"That doesn't mean there isn't cancer-causing toxins in the air. Think of all the different materials and chemicals that burned in there.

But hey, it's your fertility and your life, not mine." She kept the mask. "You want a Tyvek jumpsuit to wear over your clothes? I've got one somewhere."

"Do I look like I care about my clothes?"

Sharpe stomped over to them, a scowl on his face.

Walker asked, "What did you get from the captain?"

"Acid reflux."

But Sharpe didn't offer any details. He got suited up and grabbed his kit.

Walker hefted his bag of evidence containers—baggies and metal jars that resembled unlabeled coffee cans—and slung the strap over his shoulder.

Sharpe turned to Eve. "We'll start by walking the perimeter."

"The body is inside," she said.

"It's not going anywhere." Sharpe turned his back on her and headed for the house.

Walker and Eve followed behind him.

"What he means," Walker said in a low voice, "is that we need to get a sense of the overall damage, then we'll go inside, starting from the area of the least damage to the most. Hopefully, that will lead us to the origin of the fire and reveal how it moved through the house."

"I'd start with the body and circle out from there."

Sharpe overheard her and said, "Because you're not an arson investigator."

"If there's an axe in his head, or noose around his neck, or a gaping gunshot wound in his chest," she said, "wouldn't that tell us more than burn and smoke patterns about how he died?"

"Not necessarily."

"It would if you're a homicide investigator."

Walker spoke up quickly to prevent a barbed retort from Sharpe. "Fire does some nasty things to bodies that makes how they died harder to see or that trick you into seeing something that's not there."

Sharpe added, "Or into not seeing what is there."

Walker touched Eve's arm to indicate she should stay back, and they let Sharpe march on ahead to examine the exterior without distraction.

Once Sharpe was out of earshot, Walker said, "But he sees it all."

"Is Sharpe good at his job?"

"Annoyingly brilliant."

"I've already picked up on the annoying part."

"The brilliant will come," Walker said. "And I'll realize yet again how little I know about what I'm doing."

"I'm sure you're better at this than you think you are."

"I'm okay," Walker said. "The way our partnership works is that he solves the arson, I catch the arsonist."

The three of them went into the backyard. There were eight bamboo-style tiki torches, the kind Walker saw stocked at Home Depot every summer, arrayed around the yard to give the place a tropical feel at night. Several strings of Christmas lights stretched from the house to the trees, creating a festive canopy over the picnic table and barbecue. A scattering of toys belonging to a small child were spread across the dying lawn.

Eve spoke quietly to Walker. "What are we looking at now?"

"We're getting a sense of the house, what condition it was in before the fire, and if there is anything outside that might've contributed to what happened inside."

"Like something going wrong with that string of lights, maybe igniting a gas leak from that propane grill over there . . ."

Walker nodded, but all of that looked fine to him. "We're also looking for things that aren't necessarily flammable or explosive."

"Like signs of a break-in."

Walker nodded again. "We're also looking at the damage, how the fire seeped out of the house, and how intense it was when it did. That will help us pinpoint the origin, the cause, and the chronology of events."

He was glad to play teacher, even though he didn't know much, because he liked Eve and wanted to help her. But he was still just doing damage control again by keeping her from annoying Sharpe.

This wasn't Walker's kind of police work.

There wasn't enough chasing for him to do in this job, which had started off so well with him and Sharpe getting trapped in a raging wildfire while hunting a team of professional thieves.

That was police work.

But in the months since then, the arsonists had been ridiculously easy for Walker to catch. The most dangerous thing he did lately was parallel park their truck.

He was so bored.

Eve asked, "Isn't the origin of the fire where the most damage is?"

"Or it's just where the most flammable, heat-generating stuff was located, like couches and beds."

"You mean it could actually be the last place the fire ended up."

"You're catching on."

They worked their way around to the front yard again. Walker noticed now that the front door was splintered, barely hanging from its hinges, after being broken open by the firefighters to get into the house.

Sharpe stopped outside the doorway and looked at Walker. "What did you notice about the windows?"

"There was one open in the back and this one in the front," Walker said, gesturing to the living room window.

Eve asked, "Did the firefighters do that?"

Sharpe shook his head. "They break windows, they don't open them."

"What difference does it make?"

Sharpe said, "Someone wanted to create perfect cross-ventilation for the fire so it would move faster through the house."

"Does that matter?" Eve said. "We already know it's arson from the gasoline the firefighters smelled."

"But now we know that whoever did it understands fire more than you do, which tells us something about the person we are dealing with," Sharpe said. "He's familiar with fire dynamics."

And with that, Sharpe put on his gas mask and went inside the house.

Eve glanced at Walker. "Ouch."

CHAPTER FOUR

Lopresti's house had been extensively remodeled in recent years. Walker assumed that because the entry hall and several walls appeared to have been removed to create the open-concept living room–kitchen that he and Eve stepped into as they came in the front door. He knew that ranch-style homes of this era in the valley typically didn't have an open-concept design. Not only that, but "open concept" was the gospel preached by all of those HGTV fixer-upper shows that Carly loved because it resulted in a dramatic renovation that was better television than something less extreme.

A short hallway to their right led to the garage, where the door was open and badly scorched, revealing the burned car beyond.

Sharpe was in that hallway, studying the burn patterns on the walls, floors, and ceilings, and then he walked past them into the living room as if they weren't standing there. It wasn't because Sharpe was rude—he was totally focused on what he was seeing and following.

That was obvious to Eve, too, who said, "What is he seeing that I'm not?"

"Fire has a flow, like water," Walker said. "The soot on the walls, the charred wood, the burned and melted stuff, it all tells a story, if you know how to read it."

"Do you?"

"I'm getting there," Walker said. "For instance, see the melted light-bulb in that table lamp?"

She followed his gaze. The lamp was on a living room side table, which was against a wall. The lampshade had burned away, and the bulb was misshapen, resembling a boxer reeling from a gut punch.

Walker said, "The melted-in portion of the glass tells you the direction the heat was coming from."

Eve studied the indentation, then turned to her right. "The garage."

Sharpe said, "Give that woman a lollipop."

It would be hard for her to eat with a gas mask on, Walker thought.

Sharpe did a quick visual survey of the room from where he stood, then turned and went past them again, down the short hallway leading into the garage. Walker and Eve followed him inside.

Walker nudged Eve and pointed to the walls. "See the V shape of the burn pattern on that wall? It's like an arrowhead pointing to the source of the fire."

The point was aimed at the burned hulk of the Audi. All four doors were open, the dashboard was melted, and the seats were burned down to their cushion springs.

Eve leaned into the driver's side, lifted the gas mask off her face, and sniffed. "It smells like someone burned a pile of lemons in here."

"It's citronella," Sharpe said. "Tiki torch fuel."

"You can tell that from the smell?"

"From the melted bottle of tiki torch fuel in the back seat," Sharpe said, and pointed to it. "I think the arsonist drenched the interior of the car with citronella, then tossed the bottle inside, too."

Walker asked, "What did he use to ignite the fluid?"

"I'm guessing he lit the end of a rolled-up magazine or newspaper and tossed it inside the car." Sharpe gestured to some paper ashes on the floor of the front seat. Walker hadn't noticed them.

Eve spotted something. "Is that a cell phone?"

She pointed to the passenger-seat bottom, where a small, misshapen plastic object was wedged inside the springs. Walker could make out the buttons of a numeral keyboard on the object, which had the familiar shape of a cheap phone. It didn't have the size or distinct form of an iPhone or an Android.

"You've got a good eye," Walker said.

"I wouldn't say that," Eve said. "I missed the bottle of tiki torch fuel in the back seat."

"That's because you're focused on smaller details."

Sharpe snorted at that, as if to say "kiss ass" to Walker, then walked around to the other side of the car.

"Look at this," Sharpe said.

Walker and Eve came over to his side. The gas lid was open and a ropelike object hung out of the fuel tank.

Eve leaned close to the tank lid and examined the dangling object without touching it. "Is that a piece of a garden hose?"

"It is. The rest is over there, along with a pair of bolt cutters." Sharpe pointed to a burned garden hose piled nearby. The hose looked like a black, coiled snake. "Somebody cut a section off the hose to siphon the gasoline out of the tank into a bucket or other container."

Eve said, "Why use tiki torch fuel to burn the car if you have a bucket of gasoline?"

"You're asking the wrong question," Sharpe said.

"What's the right one?"

"Why did somebody want to incinerate the interior of the car?"

"To destroy evidence," she said. "But of what?"

"That's an even better question."

Walker said, "He did a good job burning down the garage, too."

Sharpe said, "The cans of paint and thinner in the corner helped, taking out most of the back wall of the kitchen when they exploded."

"The fire started here," Walker said.

"You're right. You get a lollipop, too," Sharpe said, and walked back into the house, leading them all to the kitchen portion of the open-concept living room.

"Here's what happened. The arsonist set fire to the car, opened the door from the garage to the entry hall, then opened the front window to draw the fire in here from the garage . . ." Sharpe pointed to the dials on the stove. "He turned on the gas stove for the open flame, then doused the kitchen and all of the family room furniture with paint thinner." He pointed to some scorched metal cans on the kitchen floor. "He knew the flames would also eventually ignite the paint thinner fumes, but he couldn't wait for that to happen. So, he lit a roll of paper towels and tossed it on the couch to get the fire started, then opened the window to the backyard to create the cross-ventilation."

Walker was about to ask how Sharpe knew about the paper towels, but then he noticed that the charred countertop paper-towel holder was now on the living room floor.

Eve said, "What was he saving the gasoline for?"

"He poured some of it on the floor as he walked to create a fuse." Sharpe followed a burn line on the floor from the living room, down a scorched hallway, past a bedroom full of melted toys, to the main bedroom at the end. "And then lit it when he got here, where he saved the rest of the gasoline for this . . ."

Sharpe stepped cautiously through the doorway, careful not to disturb the burned, naked corpse on the floor beside the bed, or the melted bucket nearby.

Walker was sure the room reeked of gasoline and burned meat but didn't lift up his gas mask to find out.

The body was charred black all over and curled into a pugilistic stance, like a fighter preparing to take blows, his hands tightly fisted, his mouth gaping open in a silent, primal scream. But Walker knew it only indicated that the intense heat had caused the muscles to stiffen and sharply contract, creating the misleading posture.

The bed was burned to the mattress springs, but the firefighters had been smart enough not to drag this piece of furniture out of the house or to disturb anything else in a room that had a dead body in it.

Sharpe said, "The victim and the bed were doused with gasoline and then set aflame."

"But was it done by a murderer," Walker said, "or did this guy torch himself, intentionally or accidentally?"

They'd investigated several cases involving dumb arsonists who'd accidentally burned themselves to death while starting a fire. This looked just like one of them.

Eve said, "If it was murder, and if this is Patrick Lopresti, then the killer could have been in the car with him. That would explain why the car was torched. The killer wanted to erase any forensic evidence he might have left behind."

Sharpe crouched beside the body but didn't look at it. He examined the floor around the corpse instead.

Walker turned to Eve. "Do you have any video from intersection cameras in Calabasas to go along with the license plate reader data?"

"Not yet. But even if the video only shows Lopresti driving the car, that doesn't mean there wasn't somebody hiding in the back seat with a gun pointed at his head."

"Speaking of which," Sharpe said, "there's a gun right there."

He pointed to the melted remains of the weapon. It was on the floor beside the victim's right hand. Eve crouched next to Sharpe, but she studied the body, not the floor.

"That's a gunshot wound in his head," Eve said, pointing to a jagged hole in the skull, by the temple. "This is a murder."

Walker was inclined to agree. But they'd have to positively identify the corpse, then find the bullet and wait for the ME to confirm the cause of death before they could officially reach that determination.

Sharpe got up and went over to the remains of what had been the nightstand and looked around. After a moment, he said, "It's a suicide."

Walker didn't challenge his conclusion. He knew better than that. The explanation would come in due time. Instead, he asked, "Why set yourself on fire and then blow your brains out?"

"It was the other way around," Sharpe said. "Lopresti poured gasoline on the bed and then himself and, to avoid the agony of burning to death, shot himself in the head. The spark from the gun probably set him aflame at the same instant. The lighter he used to ignite everything else is on the floor."

He pointed his boot toe at the metal tube from the barrel of what was once a plastic gun-shaped fire-starter. Recognizing these melted remains as a lighter wouldn't have been obvious to most people, but Sharpe and Walker had seen enough of them at fire scenes to identify the parts on sight.

"Okay, even if I got it backwards," Walker said, "why would anybody kill themselves like that?"

Eve stood up. "They wouldn't. It's crazy. There's no evidence to prove any of that scenario."

Walker winced, knowing it was a big mistake to take Sharpe on directly like that, not when it involved his area of expertise.

Sharpe said, "The evidence is everywhere and definitive."

"I don't see it," she said.

Walker didn't, either, but he kept his mouth shut.

Sharpe sighed. "For starters, the reason Lopresti came in here was obviously to use the gun that he kept in his nightstand and so he could look at the framed photos of his family before he died."

"How is any of that obvious?"

Sharpe pointed to the floor. "The picture frames are in the ashes of the nightstand, along with exploded bullets."

Now that Sharpe showed him where to look, Walker saw the frames and the shell casings, too, and felt stupid for not immediately spotting them himself.

Eve said, "Exploded bullets?"

"The fire ignited the box of ammunition that he kept in the drawer," Sharpe said.

Eve shook her head. "That doesn't mean anything. The killer could have known where Lopresti kept his gun and ammo and purposely started the fire here so you'd assume it was suicide."

Walker winced again. Eve had foolishly doubled down on her mistake by insulting Sharpe.

But instead of lashing out, Sharpe replied with an overly patronizing tone, as if explaining a simple concept, like chewing or breathing, to a child.

"When arson is used to cover up a murder, the victim is almost always found where the fire started. That wasn't here. It was in the garage."

Eve didn't back down. "If the murderer knew enough about arson to open the windows to feed the flames through the house, maybe he also knew to place the body away from the fire's origin point so you'd reach the wrong conclusion."

Walker winced once more, but this time Eve noticed it in his eyes, and must have realized that she'd gone too far, so she quickly added: "I'm not saying that you're wrong, of course, only that I wouldn't rule out murder just yet."

Sharpe said, "How did the murderer get out?"

Eve looked over her shoulder at the door to the hallway, and Sharpe shook his head.

"Not possible," he said. "Going back out there would've been certain and immediate death, either from the intense heat or from carbon monoxide poisoning. The evidence clearly shows that the rest of the house was aflame and filled with smoke by the time Lopresti was soaked with gasoline and set on fire."

Eve looked past Sharpe to the cracked windows behind him.

Sharpe didn't bother to look over his shoulder because, Walker knew, he'd already seen the windows the instant he'd walked into the room and had factored them into his deductions. Instead, Sharpe kept his gaze fixed on Eve.

"The windows are still locked from the inside. The glass was shattered by the heat, indicating conclusively that they were closed during the fire."

"Okay," Eve said, lowering her head in concession, "perhaps it was suicide."

Sharpe said, "It *is* suicide."

A very bizarre one, Walker thought, and said, "But it still doesn't make any sense. If you're going to kill yourself, why torch your car and burn your house down first? And why pour gasoline on yourself before shooting your brains out? Did Lopresti want to save his family the cost of cremation?"

Sharpe shrugged, then gestured at Eve. "Maybe she'll let us know when she finds out."

And, with that, Sharpe walked out of the room, leaving Walker alone with Eve, her face flushed with embarrassment. She knew that Sharpe had made a fool of her and that it was her own fault.

Walker looked at Eve and asked, "Do homicide detectives investigate suicides?"

"This one does."

Walker was sure that Sharpe knew that, too.

And that made him wonder if Sharpe's parting shot was simply a snide, cutting remark, or if it was shrewdly intended to provoke Eve Ronin into action.

Perhaps it was both. It was hard for Walker to decide. Sharpe was a complicated man.

CHAPTER FIVE

Sharpe and Walker spent an hour diagramming and photographing the scene but waited to bag any evidence until the LASD Crime Scene Unit arrived and could document it all, too. And they didn't touch the body, though they would assist with the removal when the medical examiner got there to make sure that no evidence on or under the corpse was lost or damaged in the process.

When Nan Baker, head of the CSU, and deputy medical examiner Emilia Lopez showed up with their teams an hour later, Sharpe explained the situation to them and they discussed the delegation of duties.

Nan was a big-boned African American woman who'd worked with Sharpe for years, and they'd developed a shorthand for communicating. Emilia was a tiny woman who wore glasses that were too big for her soft, round face, and she didn't have a strong relationship with either Sharpe or Walker yet.

It was mutually decided that the arson detectives would collect samples of the victim's clothes and other items for accelerant testing but that Nan would actually take the evidence to the lab and oversee the work. The detectives would also lift the body with Emilia so they could examine and document what remained of the flesh and clothing, or anything else underneath, that might have been protected from the flames. With that and some other technical details worked out, Nan and Emilia went into the house with their crews.

Sharpe and Walker lingered outside a bit longer to confer with Duncan and Eve, who'd been doing some legwork and had some information to share.

Duncan said, "I spoke to Patrick Lopresti's neighbors. They say he's a microbiologist at Triax Biotech in Thousand Oaks. He's married and has a ten-year-old daughter, who has the week off for spring break. The neighbors say the wife and kid went to Houston to visit his in-laws, but he couldn't get away from work."

Walker said, "Lopresti has a ten-year-old and yet he kept his gun and ammo in his nightstand? That was a tragedy waiting to happen."

"It won't happen now," Eve said. "We got Lopresti's location data and calls for the entire day from the warrant we sent to his mobile phone provider."

Sharpe said, "His melted phone is still in his car. How did you find out who his carrier is already?"

Eve said, "He registered his Arlo and ADT apps on his iPhone. The companies gave us his mobile number."

Walker was familiar with the process from his fugitive-hunting days. "Anybody can take a phone number and find out the carrier."

Sharpe cocked his head. "Anybody? Really? You don't need a search warrant for that?"

"There are a bunch of sites that do it for free. It's totally legal," Walker said, then turned to Duncan. "What did you find out?"

Duncan said, "The GPS on his phone shows he spent the day at Triax, left there at 4:00 p.m., and came straight home. The last phone conversation he had was a call from Triax at 4:25, which was five minutes after he got home, based on when ADT reported that he deactivated his security system, and it was six minutes before the smoke alarm went off."

The timing all fit, Walker thought, but something didn't, and he didn't know what it was. He could feel it, though, a burr itching the back of his mind. "Did you get the videos from Arlo yet?"

Eve nodded. "They just came in. We were waiting to watch them until you came out of the house."

Sharpe glanced at Duncan. "I thought you said she was chronically impatient."

"She is," Duncan said. "The links showed up in our email as you were walking out the door."

Eve ignored the dig and held out her iPad so everyone could see it. "These are motion-activated cameras, so I'm not sure how much we're going to see."

Sharpe, Walker, and Duncan gathered around Eve and her iPad. The first video came from the camera in a tree that was pointed at the garage.

They saw Lopresti arrive in the Audi, wait for the garage door to open up, and then drive inside. He exited the car alone, talking on a phone as he tapped a code into the ADT keypad on the wall beside the door to the house. He was smiling and seemed happy.

Duncan said, "He's obviously alone, and we know that nobody is waiting for him in the house. Otherwise the first motion-activated video we'd be seeing is the intruder disabling the alarm and going in. And ADT would have noted the deactivation."

Sharpe looked at Eve. "More evidence that Lopresti wasn't murdered, as if we needed any."

Eve ignored this dig, too. "But he looks happy, not like someone minutes away from burning his house down and killing himself."

Yes, he did, Walker thought. Happy and talking to someone on his phone. But that wasn't possible.

"Freeze the video," Walker said. "Who was he talking to there?"

"His office," Sharpe said.

"It can't be Triax," Walker said. "That call came five minutes *after* he deactivated the alarm."

Duncan referred to something on his own phone screen. "This is odd. I'm looking at his phone records, and they show he didn't make or receive any calls other than the one from Triax."

"On *this* phone." Now Walker knew what didn't fit before. He pointed to Eve's iPad. "Can you back up and zoom in on his face?" She did. Walker studied the image. "You said that his Arlo and ADT apps were on his iPhone. That doesn't look like an iPhone to me."

"You're right," Eve said. "It's not, but it's the same size and shape, more or less, as the one in his car. I think it's a burner, no pun intended."

"If that's the phone he took into the house, how did it end up in his torched car?"

"He must have burned his burner," Eve said.

Duncan nodded. "How appropriate."

Walker said, "We'll probably find the iPhone on his body, along with his wallet."

Eve unfroze the video and they saw Lopresti hit another button on the wall as he went inside the house. The garage door closed behind him. "I wonder what he's hiding that he needed a burner."

"Maybe the secret is what drove him to suicide," Walker said.

Sharpe sighed wearily. "The phones didn't start the fire. I'd like to see what did. Can we please move on so I can go in the house? What's next?"

"Video from the front porch camera and one in a tree pointed at the house," Eve said. "Remember, these are motion-activated."

She pulled up videos and played them side by side in split screen. They saw Lopresti opening the living room window from inside the house at 4:32, according to the time code.

Walker tapped the screen. "Look at the time. This was right after the call from Triax."

The next videos were from the same cameras two minutes later. Lopresti opened the front door, unhooked the hose from the house, and brought it inside.

Eve froze the porch video, which was the closer angle, and zoomed in on his face.

"He's crying," she said.

Lopresti closed the door. There weren't any more videos until the arrival of the fire department activated the cameras again and the house was already ablaze.

Sharpe said, "Case closed. All that's left is collecting the physical evidence, confirming the victim's ID with the medical examiner, and writing the reports."

"I'd like to know what that call on the burner was about," Eve said.

"It's none of our business," Duncan said. "We're homicide detectives and this obviously wasn't a murder."

Walker said, "I'd like to know about the call, too, and the one from Triax."

Sharpe looked at him. "What does either call have to do with our arson investigation? We know how the fire was set and how he killed himself."

"But not *why*," Walker said. "I'm sure his family would like to know, too."

Sharpe looked at Walker and sighed. "We're going to be here for another couple of hours, supervising the removal of the body and sifting through the debris that's under it for evidence. I know you think it's tedious work and I don't need you whining while we do it. So, you'd be doing me a big favor if you'd find something else to do."

"Okay, if you insist," Walker said, grateful that Sharpe had decided, for his own mysterious reasons, to let him pursue what might be a pointless exercise without actually condoning it.

Eve looked imploringly at Duncan, who offered a sigh that matched Sharpe's.

"I can't leave until the body does," Duncan said. "But there doesn't have to be two of us stuck here."

Eve turned to Walker. "I'll drive."

Duncan spoke up quickly. "The only problem is, I won't have a chance to pregame before dinner."

"Pregame?" Walker asked.

Eve replied, "He likes to have a snack before dinner."

Duncan patted his belly. "To grease my digestive machinery before the workout."

"'Grease' being the operative word," she said.

"Swing by In-N-Out on your way back," Duncan said. "Bring me a Double-Double, fries, and a Coke."

Sharpe said, "Same for me."

Walker went back to the Tahoe, traded his hard hat for his Stetson, then called Carly to let her know that he'd be coming home late and shared with her some details of the case.

What he didn't say was that he finally had some police work to do.

Walker got into Eve's plain-wrap, department-issue Dodge Charger and they sped off toward Thousand Oaks, which was west of Calabasas.

Eve said, "While you were getting your hat, I googled Triax Biotech. They create biological defenses against highly pathogenic viruses and emerging infectious diseases. Prior to COVID, they worked closely with the Wuhan Institute of Virology."

"We should have brought our gas masks."

"Thanks for coming," she said.

"I wouldn't miss it."

"I believe that," Eve said as she took the on-ramp onto the westbound 134 freeway. "I get the feeling that you love the hunt."

"I do," he said.

"So why'd you leave the US Marshals Service to poke around in ashes all day?"

"Manhunting is hard on the body. I got tired of tearing up my knees and getting shot. You should try to avoid that, too."

"Too late," Eve said.

"Which part?"

"Both parts. I took a shotgun blast to my knee and then fell off a cliff," she said. "But I'm much better now."

Walker doubted that, given how much his old injuries still bothered him. He had a compression sleeve on one knee right now and wondered if she did, too. "Maybe you ought to think about transferring to arson."

"Sell me on it."

"You're still a lawman, but you keep banker's hours most of the time. You won't touch your medical deductible. The bad guys aren't that hard to find, you don't have to run after anybody, and nobody shoots at you."

"I'd miss the action and excitement."

So did he. "Your perspective changes when you get married and have a kid. I don't want to miss my family or for them to miss me. But I admit that it's not easy."

"If you really want to play it safe, you could be a mailman."

"Too much walking," he said, rubbing his knee. "And they get chased by dogs."

CHAPTER SIX

Triax Biotech was located in the craggy, boulder-strewn hills on the northern edge of Thousand Oaks, in an area where government bomb makers tested explosives during World War II, contaminating the soil with countless carcinogens. Hundreds of westerns were later filmed there, the action kicking up toxic dirt that all those actors and crew members breathed into their lungs, causing an untold number of Hollywood deaths.

Now, electrified chain-link fences topped with razor wire and, every few yards, tall poles crowned with an array of security cameras and motion detectors surrounded the property. The Triax offices and laboratory buildings were hidden somewhere behind the hills.

Eve rolled down her window as they approached the guardhouse at the front gate. An armed guard stepped out and she flashed her badge at him. "I'm Eve Ronin and this is Andrew Walker. We're detectives with the Los Angeles County Sheriff's Department."

"This is Ventura County," he said.

"Yes, we are aware of that," Eve said. "But thank you for the geography lesson. We need to speak to somebody in charge about one of your employees."

The guard nodded, stepped back into the guardhouse, and picked up the receiver on his desk phone.

Eve turned to Walker. "Can you feel the warmth?"

"I've never felt so loved."

The guard returned. "Drive up the road and park in one of the guest spots. Remain seated in your vehicle until you're met by our head of security."

The heavy gate slid open and Eve drove through, following the road between the hills to a vast parking lot full of cars and, farther ahead, a sprawling campus of rectangular cinder-block buildings with narrow windows. The buildings had the architectural charm of a prison, only without the guard towers. It was probably the weapons factory, Walker thought, but with a new coat of paint on the outside and big renovations on the inside.

He also noticed a helipad, with a black aircraft parked on it, and some structures embedded in the hills that resembled bunkers. He wondered if they were remnants of the old bomb facility and if, perhaps, they were now labs intentionally distanced from the offices and essentially buried for safety.

Eve said, "This feels more like a military base than a biotechnology company."

"It could be both. There are a lot of people who think COVID was a virus modified into a biological weapon that leaked out of a military-backed facility in Wuhan, China."

"Is that what you believe?"

Walker shrugged. "It's possible. I'd find it easier to believe if the great minds who were pushing that theory weren't fighting COVID by gobbling up animal deworming pills."

Eve didn't bother looking for a guest spot. She parked in the red zone, right in front of what appeared to be the main entrance. Walker would have, too, if he'd been driving. It was a cop privilege. They got out of the car, not bothering to "remain seated" until given permission to leave, and strode purposefully toward the lobby doors.

A man wearing a business suit rushed out of the main building to intercept them. There was a military bearing to his urgent stride, and his irritation was expressed with clenched teeth and clenched hands. Walker suspected he was clenched all over.

"I'm Dash Nolan, head of security. You were told to stay in your vehicle."

"We're claustrophobic," Eve said.

"What can I do for you, Detectives?"

"We're here about Patrick Lopresti."

"What about him?"

Something about the way Nolan asked the question told Walker that he'd been expecting them or at least some trouble.

Walker went with his instincts. "I think you already know, Dash, so spare us the bullshit. We don't have time for it and neither do you. This is urgent."

Walker's words, particularly the last few, seemed to startle Nolan, who took a quick breath before speaking. Whatever wasn't clenched before certainly was now.

"Has he started vomiting or hemorrhaging already?"

"It's gone way beyond that," Walker said.

Nolan grimaced. "That's unusually fast. I hope you have him isolated."

"We do."

"Thank God for that," Nolan said, relaxing just a little. His hands weren't fists anymore. "We're prepared to help in any way we can."

"Glad to hear it," Eve said. "You can start by telling us how this happened."

Nolan cleared his throat. "We don't entirely know, only that a few minutes after Lopresti left, our sensors detected that there had been a breach in the air systems in the laboratory where he'd been working." He glanced in the general direction of one of the bunkers, confirming Walker's earlier guess about how they were being used.

"Why didn't your system detect the leak while he was still there?" Eve asked.

"That's the part we don't know. But at that instant, the emergency anticontamination system immediately contained and cleansed the impacted facilities."

"So your call to Lopresti was to alert him that he'd been infected."

"Didn't he tell you why we called?"

Walker said, "He's in no condition to talk anymore."

Nolan took a deep breath, absorbing all of the horrible implications of Walker's response. "Did anybody come into contact with him?"

"We know from traffic cameras that he didn't stop anywhere between here and his home," Walker said. "And the few people who approached him after that were already in protective gear."

So far, Walker and Eve had told Nolan the truth, which made them seem convincing, even though they were speaking from an entirely different context than Nolan was. Walker didn't know how much longer they could keep up the charade and enjoy him volunteering information he'd otherwise withhold.

"Thank God for that," Nolan said. "But they still need to be quarantined and closely monitored."

That was an unsettling thought. Walker wondered if their gas masks had provided enough protection from whatever infection Lopresti had, even after he'd nearly cremated himself.

"We're on it," Walker said. "We'd like to speak to whoever made that call."

"That would be Colin Oxley, the system supervisor who monitors the labs when they are being used. He's the one who saw the delayed alert and is absolutely distraught, as you can imagine."

Nolan led them into the building and down some stairs into a basement corridor as sterile and unwelcoming as a morgue, their footsteps on the linoleum echoing off the empty walls. If anybody else worked in the basement, they were either hiding behind closed doors or gone for the day.

The one door that was open revealed an orderly little office adorned with *Star Wars* trinkets—a baby Yoda doll, a C-3PO action figure, and a TIE Fighter model shared the shelves with his books, binders, and manuals. Oxley himself sat on his couch, dressed in a lab coat and scrubs, elbows on his lap, face in his hands.

Nolan said, "Colin, meet Los Angeles County sheriff's detectives Andrew Walker and Eve Ronin. They're here about Patrick Lopresti."

Oxley looked up, forlorn, his eyes bloodshot. He was pale and prematurely balding, with a pencil-thin beard that started at his sideburns and provided some much-needed definition between his jawline and his chubby neck.

"How is he?" Oxley asked tentatively.

Eve said, "Not well, Colin. Tell us about the call."

"It's the hardest thing I've ever had to do . . . I told him about the leak, and that we'd incinerated the lab . . . but that he had to come back right away."

"Hold up," Walker said. "You're saying that you set the lab on fire?"

"That's what the emergency containment system does," Oxley said. "It was the only way to be certain the virus was totally eradicated."

It was a shocking method of cleaning, but the news was also a relief to Walker, because Lopresti's house was essentially incinerated, too, which meant it was safe for investigators to be inside.

Nolan got a call on his cell phone and stepped into the corridor to answer it, leaving them alone with Oxley for the moment. Walker took advantage of the opportunity to question him without Nolan's potentially intimidating supervision.

"I didn't see any smoke when we came in."

"The lab is mostly underground and we have an elaborate filtration system."

"What did Lopresti say in your call?"

"He assured me that he hadn't been in face-to-face contact with anybody and that he'd do what was necessary."

Eve said, "What does that mean?"

"I assumed he was on his way back here to be quarantined until . . ." Oxley got choked up, got a hold of himself, then continued: "Do you know what it's like to tell someone that they are about to die? That's essentially what I did. It's awful, it's sickening. And I had to do it twice."

"This has happened before?"

"No, never," Oxley said. "He wasn't the only one in the lab today. Justine Bryce was in there, too. She left here the same time he did."

"Where is she now?" Eve asked.

Before Oxley could answer her, Dash Nolan stormed in, everything clenched again, and gave the detectives hard looks that might have caused lesser individuals to lose control of their bladders. But Walker had to stifle a grin and he bet that Eve did, too.

"Our rapid-response biohazard containment team has eyes on Lopresti's house," Nolan said. "They haven't seen any biohazard personnel, just a crime scene unit and the medical examiner. You misled me."

"Not really," Walker said. "Everything we said was true. We just left out some key facts, just like you've been doing, Dash. You could have stopped Lopresti from killing himself."

Oxley gasped. "He's dead?"

Nolan ignored him and addressed himself to Walker. "The house was already burning when the biohazard team got there, and they didn't know if he was inside. He could have set it on fire before he left for somewhere else. So they stayed in the van, waiting to see what happened and, if given the order, to lock down the neighborhood."

"Exactly what were Lopresti and Bryce working on?"

At the mention of her name, Nolan glowered angrily at Oxley for revealing it, then looked back at the detectives. "Classified research for the US military. We could be arrested for treason if we tell you any details."

Eve said, "I'll arrest you both now if you don't."

"On what charge?"

"Manslaughter. Your call directly provoked Lopresti to kill himself. You might as well have ordered him to do it."

"It was *his* call." Nolan gestured to Oxley. "Not mine. The virus causes a truly horrific, indescribably agonizing death within a day, maybe two. Lopresti did the right thing for himself and the community."

Walker asked, "How contagious is this virus?"

"Extremely. Even in a corpse. Unless it's burned."

"Is the infection curable?"

Nolan shook his head.

Now Walker understood what Lopresti had done. His actions, which at first appeared to be senseless and bizarre, were actually a rational, courageous response to a dangerous situation.

"That's why he torched his house, the car, and himself," Walker said. "To make sure nobody else got infected."

"He's a hero," Oxley said, choking up. "Maybe that will offer some solace for his family."

"It's not over," Walker said, then repeated his earlier question: "Where's Justine Bryce now?"

Nolan said, "We don't know."

"She's infected with a highly contagious, incurable virus that causes a gruesome death," Walker said. "And you don't know where she is?"

"She was going home. We've got our biohazard team on standby outside her house."

Eve said, "What are they standing by for?"

"The authority to enter," Nolan said. "She's not answering her phone and we're a biotech company, not a government agency. So they're in the van, keeping an eye on the house, and making sure nobody goes in."

Eve and Walker shared looks of disbelief, then Eve turned to Nolan and said, "You're telling us that you haven't alerted *any* authorities about this potential disaster?"

"Of course we have," he said. "The FBI, Homeland Security, and the CDC are huddling now to figure out the best path forward. This has to be handled delicately. We don't want to start a panic."

So nobody is doing anything yet. Walker couldn't believe what he was hearing. "Do you want to decimate the population of Los Angeles instead? Bryce could be strolling through the Topanga mall right now, infecting everybody."

Oxley spoke up, a defensive edge to his voice. "She's not. Justine is a very responsible person and knows better than anyone what the risks are."

Eve said, "Does she have a family?"

"She's single and lives alone."

Eve turned to Walker. "Maybe that's why she hasn't torched her house yet."

"Maybe she's still working up the courage," Walker said, then looked at Nolan. "What's her home address and mobile number?"

Nolan gave him the information. Walker took out his phone and got to work on Justine Bryce's number using online databases.

Eve handed Nolan her card. "Call me immediately if you hear from her."

She walked out of the office and Walker followed her into the corridor, eyes locked on his screen. "Are you looking up Bryce's cellular carrier?"

"I've already got it. It's Verizon," Walker said, showing her the result on his phone. "We need to find out where she is and where she's been. How good are you at getting warrants in a hurry?"

"Not as good as Duncan." She tossed Walker her car keys. "You drive. I'll call him on our way to Bryce's house."

CHAPTER SEVEN

Justine Bryce lived in Encino, twenty-five miles east of Thousand Oaks and only a few miles south of Walker's home in Reseda. The proximity of Bryce to his family made Walker uneasy.

How fast can a viral infection spread?

Encino was deep within LAPD territory, but Walker and Eve didn't discuss jurisdiction because they instinctively knew that neither one of them gave a damn. Their shared priority was finding and isolating Bryce before she got sick or infected anybody else. They'd deal with the bureaucracy later, assuming the week didn't end with a zombie apocalypse.

As they left Triax on their way to Bryce's house, they informed Duncan by phone of what they'd learned.

Duncan called back just a few minutes later, as they sped east past Calabasas on the freeway, their siren screaming, in the day-end, rush-hour traffic, which in Los Angeles typically started at 3:00 p.m. and lasted until 7:00 p.m.

He'd managed to not only get and serve a warrant for the mobile phone data but also get the data itself, in record time because he'd stressed to the judge and Verizon that it was an urgent public health emergency endangering all of Southern California.

Eve put Duncan on speaker.

"After leaving Triax, GPS data indicates that Bryce headed east on the Ventura Freeway and received a call in Woodland Hills at 4:12 from a phone number registered to SmartCellTech, a disposable phone supplier for Walmart," Duncan said. "The call ended at 4:20. Then she got the call from Colin Oxley at Triax, then another call, for under twenty seconds, from the same unregistered number, at 4:36. Her phone went dead after that while she was still on the freeway, leaving Tarzana."

It was roughly where they were now. Eve thanked Duncan and told him she'd get back to him with whatever they found.

"The burner call had to be from Lopresti," Walker said. "The timing matches."

"They shared their death sentences with each other," Eve said. "That's why he was crying in the security camera video."

Walker sped down the fast-lane shoulder, within mere inches of sideswiping the concrete center divider to his left and cars on his right. He loved it. The adrenaline rush also sharpened his thinking.

"Lopresti was using a burner," Walker said. "But Bryce wasn't, meaning she wasn't worried about anybody seeing the calls on her phone."

"Because she's single and lives alone," Eve said. "Nobody is going to be checking out her calls."

"But Lopresti is married."

"I think we just deduced Lopresti's big secret," Walker said. "He was having an affair with Justine Bryce."

"That's the real reason he didn't go with his wife and kid to Houston for spring break."

"Nookie," Walker said.

"We are deductive geniuses."

"It's a shame there's no one here with us to be impressed," Walker said as he abruptly crossed four lanes of traffic to reach the White Oak exit, nearly causing a chain-reaction pileup in his wake.

They raced down the off-ramp shoulder, half their car tilted up on the weedy berm on his side, half still on the roadway.

Eve held on to the grab handle above the passenger door, anticipating his next move. "What do you make of her turning off her phone?"

He burst into the intersection and made a sharp right, heading north onto White Oak, and then roared up the paint-only median, leaning on his horn to underscore the siren. Traffic parted in front of their Charger like the Red Sea did for Moses.

"Either she didn't want any more calls, or she didn't want to be tracked, or both," he said. "She might've tossed her phone out the window on the freeway."

"That's something a criminal would do," Eve said. "She's not one."

"But she may be on the run."

"From what? She'll be dead tomorrow. There's no place she can go to escape that."

Walker crossed Ventura Boulevard into the residential area to the south, then turned off his siren as he made a left and snaked through several tree-lined streets of handsomely maintained homes.

An unmarked, dark panel van idling at the curb on a dark street indicated they'd reached Bryce's home.

Walker pulled up to the van from the opposite direction, driver's side to driver's side, and rolled down his window, flashing his badge at his reflection in the tinted glass.

The van driver lowered his window, revealing a grim-faced man and another equally grim guy in the passenger seat. They wore matching gray overalls.

Walker identified himself and said, "Are you the Triax biohazard team?"

"Yeah," the man said, introducing himself as Isaac Sturbin.

"Is that her house across the street?" Walker gestured to a yellow-and-white, one-story ranch-style home with a fake birdhouse built into the highest eave. Similar homes were everywhere in the valley. Walker himself lived in a smaller version.

Sturbin nodded. "Nobody has come in or out. We haven't seen any lights or movement inside, either."

"We're going to need two of your biohazard suits."

Without waiting for an answer, Walker made a U-turn and parked behind the van. He and Eve got out and were met by Sturbin.

"You can't go in her house," Sturbin said.

"You can't," Eve said. "But we can. We're the law."

"Do you have a warrant?"

"Are you a lawyer?"

Before Sturbin could reply, Walker spoke up. "We have exigent circumstances or you two wouldn't be here. So let's cut the shit and get to work."

Sturbin sighed and knocked on the back door of the van. His partner opened it up. Four biohazard suits hung on the side walls amid all kinds of equipment. "Let's suit up these two fools."

Sturbin and his partner got Walker and Eve into the bright yellow suits and used duct tape to reinforce the seals where their boots, gloves, and helmets were attached.

When they were done, Walker and Eve looked like astronauts. They had breathing units on their backs and their helmets had large, clear visors with internal microphones that allowed them to be heard.

Sturbin shook his head. "If people in the neighborhood see you two walk into her house dressed like that, word will spread faster than the virus. We'll have news choppers circling over us in five minutes."

"Film us with your phones," Eve said, "and tell anybody in the neighborhood who asks that we're USC students shooting a sci-fi movie. They won't call anybody."

"Good idea," Sturbin said.

Walker liked it, too. It would also double as a way to document their actions if it ever became an issue in court.

Eve went to her car, popped the trunk, and took out a small battering ram.

"I never leave home without it," she said, and slammed the trunk.

If he weren't married and deeply in love, Walker thought, he could fall for her.

They headed across the street to Bryce's front door, Sturbin and his partner filming them with their phones, probably to cover their own asses as well. Walker knocked insistently on the door.

"Justine, we're detectives with the Los Angeles County Sheriff's Department. We need to talk with you."

No answer. He leaned on the doorbell and called out to her again. Still no answer.

Walker looked at Eve. "Maybe we should knock louder."

She smashed the door with the battering ram. The door splintered open with the first, well-placed swing. The burglar alarm immediately went off.

The two detectives stepped inside and Walker saw the keyboard flashing on the wall-mounted alarm console.

Walker said, "Either she never came home, or she set the alarm again after she came in."

"Or she came home and left again before the biohazard team got here."

"You check the bedrooms," he said. "I'll look in the garage."

Walker went through the galley kitchen to the attached garage. There was no car parked inside.

He walked back into the kitchen and noted the cereal bowl, coffee cup, and spoon in the sink. She liked Lucky Charms. Soggy pieces of cereal were still stuck in the bowl.

Eve came in. "Nobody."

"No car, either, and the breakfast dishes are still in the sink. I don't think she's been back. So it's safe in here."

Walker peeled the duct tape from around his neck and twisted off his helmet. He didn't wait to see if he began bleeding from his eyeballs before he picked up the receiver of Bryce's wall-mounted phone, called his dispatcher, and identified himself. He told the dispatcher to alert the LAPD not to send a patrol car and to ask ADT to please turn off the alarm.

Eve removed her helmet, too, and then they looked around the house more carefully, their sense of urgency eased a bit, especially once the burglar alarm stopped shrieking. But they both knew the LAPD would send a car anyway. They'd want to know what two LASD detectives were doing breaking into a home in their backyard.

Walker noticed a bulging black garbage bag resting beside a tall wicker trash can in the kitchen. The bag was overstuffed with Baby Yoda toys in all shapes and sizes. There were a few more Baby Yodas on the kitchen table, too. He wondered what she was doing with so many of them.

He wandered down a hallway decorated with family photos to the main bedroom, where Eve had opened the walk-in closet, which was neat and orderly. The clothes hung on matching wooden hangers in a neat row, evenly spaced apart. There was a little OCD possibly at work here, he thought.

Her large collection of shoes was on shelves, like a store display. Two carry-on suitcases were in one corner. None of that meant she hadn't packed another suitcase, but there was no sign of disarray that might show she'd quickly sorted through her clothes and fled.

The dresser told the same story. Eve opened the drawers and found everything neatly folded inside, no indication of a hurried sweep to stuff a suitcase. The same was true in the bathroom with her toiletries and medications, though that didn't mean that nothing was missing.

Eve turned to Walker. "If she hasn't been back here, where did she go?"

"I don't know."

"I thought you were a manhunter."

"I am," Walker said, and he had nothing. "Justine Bryce could be anywhere."

CHAPTER EIGHT

The blackened remains of Patrick Lopresti's house were illuminated by several portable floodlights brought in by the LASD so the forensic team could continue to work in the darkness.

Walker and Eve arrived with plenty of In-N-Out burgers, fries, and soft drinks for themselves, Sharpe, and Duncan, and the four of them used the hood of the Charger as a dinner table. They ate standing while Walker and Eve filled their partners in on everything. They'd already informed Nan Baker and Emilia Lopez about the virus so they could take whatever precautions might be necessary while collecting evidence from the scene and examining Lopresti's corpse.

"Did the LAPD take a bite out of your ass?" Duncan asked when they were finished, his mouth full.

"They never got a chance," Eve said. "We left as soon as the first uniformed patrol officers arrived."

"You mean you *fled*." Duncan dabbed a napkin on the In-N-Out secret sauce that he'd dribbled on his tie but couldn't prevent the stain.

"That's what the biohazard team did," Walker said. "They didn't even stick around long enough to ask us for their suits back."

"What did you do with them?" Sharpe asked.

"They're in my trunk," Eve said. "They might come in handy. Justine Bryce is still out there somewhere."

"We got a call from the FBI while we were in line at In-N-Out," Walker said. "Special Agent Donna Leyland told us she is taking over the hunt for Bryce, and every other aspect of this case except for the arson investigation, which she's leaving to us."

"It's basically done," Sharpe said. "We found Lopresti's wallet and his iPhone in his pockets. Now all we have to do is wait for the dental records and other test results to confirm what we already know."

"It's a suicide, not a homicide." Duncan reached for his second double cheeseburger. "And since there's no robbery involved, either, Eve and I are completely out of it."

"Bryce still has to be found," Eve said.

"But not by us." Duncan took a big bite out of his burger, then waited until he was done chewing to say: "It's up to the Feds to find her—or her body."

Walker said, "If they don't, they'll know where to look soon. It'll be near where all the people are spewing blood from their eyeballs and every orifice."

"Doesn't mean it's the virus," Duncan said, devouring his burger in three bites. "I had a street taco that did that to me once."

Sharpe balled up the wrapper that his burger had been in and stuffed it in the paper In-N-Out bag. "I'm glad you waited until I finished eating to share that delightful anecdote."

Duncan ate a handful of fries, then washed the last of his meal down with a big gulp of Coke. "I'm full of great stories, Sharpe. You and your wife ought to come visit one weekend at our place in Palm Springs and I'll tell you more of them."

Duncan burped proudly and with satisfaction.

"Thanks, but the desert is not for me," Sharpe said. "I don't like the heat."

"You investigate fires."

"After they've been put out," Sharpe said. "Not when they're burning."

So, now it's over, Walker thought. There was nothing more for them to do except write their reports. They were out of the game.

He offered his hand to Eve. "It was a pleasure working with you today."

"Likewise." She shook his hand. "How frustrated are you that you aren't chasing down Bryce?"

"I might start chewing on the brim of my hat."

"If I had a hat, I would be, too."

"You ought to get one," Walker said. "It'd suit you."

"No thanks, I already draw too much attention."

Duncan snorted. "That didn't stop you from saying yes to a TV series."

Sharpe and Walker gathered up the garbage and walked back to their truck, where they had a trash bag set aside for on-the-go meals.

Sharpe said, "We have to go back to Twin Lakes in the morning and finish investigating the house that burned down."

Captain Guyette had probably filed his report by now, citing faulty wiring as the cause of the blaze, so Walker knew they had no *official* reason to go back. That case wasn't closed—it had never opened. But Sharpe never let that stop him, and Walker wasn't going to try.

"That's fine. Can you drop me at home? I live ten minutes from here," Walker said. Their office was in the sheriff's department campus in Monterey Park, thirty miles east of Reseda and a good hour away in traffic. "I'm not going back with you to HQ now just to get my truck, turn around, and drive back here. I'll take an Uber up to Twin Lakes in the morning and meet you there."

"I'd be glad to. You know me," Sharpe said. "I'm all about reducing our carbon footprint."

Sharpe got into the driver's seat and drove them at a leisurely pace east on the Ventura Freeway to the Reseda Boulevard exit, where they headed north.

"When you were talking to FBI Special Agent Leyland," Sharpe said, "did she mention anything about that torched car we left for them in Hellmouth?"

"As a matter of fact, she did."

Sharpe turned right off Reseda Boulevard into one of the many residential neighborhoods that were once valley farms, sold and subdivided in the early 1960s to mass-produce affordable housing for young families. "What did she say?"

"It's a toss-up whether they'd rather get infected by the virus or deal with all the bureaucracy involved with that car fire."

"So, no hard feelings?"

"I think she'd like to use our badges to carve out our eyeballs and eat them on toast."

Sharpe pulled up in front of Walker's 1,200-square-foot home with an attached garage. There were flower boxes filled with roses under the two front windows, which were bordered with fake shutters. The only thing that had changed on the house since it was built, besides new coats of paint, was the wood-shingled roof, which had been replaced with fire-resistant tiles.

Carly came out to greet them wearing a tank top and yoga pants. Physically, she was a lot like Eve Ronin—tall, slim, and athletic, with her hair cut in a stylish bob that didn't require much maintenance. Right after Cody was born, during her maternity leave, she began exercising hard every day to burn off the pregnancy weight, and now she was in the best shape of her life, making Walker feel fat and slovenly by comparison. But if he was being honest with himself, he'd felt that way since they'd met. She'd been able to continue her exercise regimen when she went back to work because there was a full gym, and a nursery for babies and preschoolers, at the Sherman Oaks psychology practice she'd formed with three other women.

Walker turned to Sharpe before they got out of the Tahoe. "Don't say anything to Carly about the virus."

"Why? You were never exposed. The fire took care of that."

"It doesn't matter. If she thinks there was a risk that I could have been exposed, she'll be furious with me for taking it and terrify herself with what might've happened. She believes arson investigation is safer than being on the street."

"We *are* on the street."

"It's Sesame Street compared to what I was doing before."

Carly still didn't know that he'd been trapped with Sharpe in the Malibu fire a year ago and he was determined that she never would.

Walker and Sharpe got out of the truck.

Carly smiled at them both. "Are you two carpooling now?"

"Just tonight, since we were working in Calabasas, so close to home," Walker said. "It would've been silly for me to go all the way back to the office tonight just to get my truck."

Sharpe said, "Where's Cody?"

"I put him to bed hours ago. He's fast asleep, clutching Sharpie."

"Sharpie?"

Walker winced.

"The stuffed animal puppy you gave him when he was born," Carly said. "He loves it."

The truth was that Sharpe had given Walker thirty dollars to buy something for Cody to celebrate his birth. Walker bought the plushy dog and told Carly it was from Sharpe, who now pinned him with a stony look.

"Why does he call it Sharpie?" Sharpe asked Walker.

"Because he can't pronounce Shar-Pei," he said.

"Isn't that adorable?" Carly said. "So, did you two figure out what happened in that fire in Calabasas? Was it a murder?"

"It's suicide," Sharpe said. "The guy set his house on fire and then shot himself."

"That's very unusual," she said. "I'd love to know the psychological motivation for that. There are so many possibilities. For instance, the enormous pressure of paying his mortgage might have been too much . . . especially if he'd just lost his job."

"He didn't," Sharpe said.

Walker wished Sharpe hadn't answered that question and was worried that Carly would now ask what Lopresti's profession was. So, he quickly spoke up.

"Thanks for the ride. Have a safe drive home."

Carly ignored her husband or had simply been lost in her thoughts. "Or it could be about what the house symbolizes, which is primarily family. Did his wife take the kid and walk out on him?"

"They are spending spring break with her parents in Houston," Sharpe said, continuing to engage Carly, to Walker's discomfort.

"And he stayed behind?" she said. "Well, there it is. You'll find the motive for the suicide in his marriage."

Actually, she wasn't far off, Walker thought. "I'm sure you're right." He turned to Sharpe. "You've really got to go. It's a long drive back to Pasadena and your wife is probably waiting."

"She's bingeing another strange Korean series on Netflix, so she'll be snoring on the couch by now. Happens every night," Sharpe said. "But yeah, I should get going. Good night."

Carly said, "I'd give you a hug, Walter, but you're all sooty. This will have to do."

She air-hugged him instead. Sharpe smiled, got in the truck, and drove off.

Walker reached his arms out to Carly. "What about me? I don't get a hug?"

She took a big step back, holding up her palms in a halting gesture. "You're all sooty, too. Strip before you come inside."

"What will the neighbors say?"

"I didn't say do it in the front yard. Come through the garage. I don't want you tracking soot through the house."

Carly went inside and used their remote control to open the garage door for him, revealing her shiny BMW parked to one side. She was the breadwinner in the family and he was fine with that. Access to the house from inside the garage was through their laundry room, so he undressed in there, shoved everything in the washing machine, and walked into the living room wearing only his Stetson.

Carly laughed when she saw him. "My God, it's like our honeymoon all over again."

And then she gave him that hug, and a lot more.

◆ ◆ ◆

At eight the next morning, Walker had the Uber driver drop him off in front of the Twin Lakes model homes. When he got out, he saw that their arson-unit Tahoe was already parked at the charred ruins of the house. Sharpe got an early start. But so had everybody else at the development.

There were already at least a hundred hard-hatted workers spread among the dozens of homesites in various stages of construction. Some houses were being framed, some were having their foundations poured, while others were just getting their finishing touches of stucco or paint.

A huge tanker truck drove slowly over the graded lots across the street from the scorched home. Water shot out in wide arcs from sprayers on the front and rear of the tanker, moistening the soil for compaction and keeping the dust from swirling into houses and yards that were already occupied by homeowners.

As Walker surveyed the activity, he was joined by Ed Bell, the salesman, who took a deep breath and hiked up his pants.

"It's a beautiful sight, isn't it?" Bell said. "I love the activity, the smell of wet dirt and fresh sawdust, and the sweet sound of nail guns firing and saws sawing."

"There are people who would argue it was more beautiful before the trees were cut down, the hills were graded, and all that asphalt and concrete was poured."

"Yes, there are," Bell said. "And those are the ones you should be talking to about the fire."

"Do you know something we don't?"

"After you two left yesterday, we thoroughly checked the wiring and electrical systems in several of the homes that don't have drywall up yet," Bell said. "We found nothing wrong. It couldn't have been faulty wiring that caused that blaze. It had to be arson."

"Just because one house is wired right," Walker said, "it doesn't mean there wasn't sloppy work done in another."

Bell nodded toward the occupied homes, their new landscaping gaunt and dry, struggling to survive in Southern California's heat and drought. "The same electricians worked on all the homes in phase one, which have been occupied for months without any electrical problems."

"Tell that to the homeowner of the house that burned and see how that argument goes over," Walker said. "Have they filed a lawsuit yet? I mean, let's be honest, isn't that what you're really worried about?"

"Worse than that. We have a customer moving into that house tomorrow." Bell pointed to a house at the end of a cul-de-sac a few doors downhill from the one that burned. "I'm afraid they are going to back out of their purchase agreement as soon as they hear about the fire."

I would, Walker thought.

Bell continued, "How many others who've put deposits down on homes will do the same thing? If that happens, we can kiss any future sales goodbye. Nobody will want to buy a house here if they think they'll burn to death in it." He looked over at the occupied homes. "And everybody who is already living here will evacuate and sue us, too. It will be an epic disaster. That's why you've got to announce today that it's arson and not a wiring problem."

"That's not how we work," Walker said. "All I can promise you is that we'll follow the evidence wherever it leads. Speaking of which, I better get to it."

Walker walked up to the Tahoe, swapped his Stetson for a hard hat, put on a pair of work gloves, and searched a bit for his bag of evidence containers before he realized that Sharpe probably had it. He didn't bother putting on a gas mask. The house was empty when it burned, so he wasn't worried about inhaling something deadly.

He went inside and found Sharpe crouched on the floor in the family room, examining the char on a wall stud.

"How's it going?"

Sharpe stood up and gave him a hard look. "You named the stuffed animal I bought your son Sharpie?"

"Of course not. What kind of man do you think I am? He named it."

"He's barely a year old, and he's your son, so he's got a vocabulary of maybe ten words, tops," Sharpe said. "How could he have come up with that name for the dog unless that's what you call me around the house?"

"Because the stuffed animal *is* a Shar-Pei."

"You must have looked long and hard to find that."

"Not at all," Walker said. "There's a million of them online under thirty dollars and they are all adorable."

"I guess I should be thankful my nickname isn't Dickhead or who knows what toy you would have bought him."

"You should be flattered. He loves Sharpie more than the little cowboy hat I got him."

"Then there's still hope for the kid," Sharpe said.

Walker gestured at the empty room. "What's the plan here?"

"A methodical, systematic investigation."

"Could you be a bit more specific?"

"I've made copies of the floor plans the salesman gave us." He pulled a clipboard with the floor plan on it out of his bag and handed it to Walker. "I want to identify every electrical outlet, switch, and lighting fixture you see in the house on one of these plans, and chart the path of the fire as you see it on another that we can use like an overlay."

"There is no path," Walker said. "The fire was everywhere all at once."

"That's what Captain Guyette says."

"Do you see something different?"

"Not yet," Sharpe admitted, surprising Walker. "But after this, I might. Ashes never lie."

"Wouldn't it be easier to get the blueprints, which will have the location of all the electrical stuff on it, or walk through one of those framed houses and see exactly how it's wired, rather than search for it all ourselves?"

"Easy isn't the goal. Understanding is."

"You should write fortune cookies."

"We're going to follow all the wiring and tie a ribbon around every arc we find, no matter what the likely cause of the arcing might be." Sharpe reached into his bag and held up a sack of ribbons. "You won't find the arcs on a blueprint. The ribbons will lead us to the origin of the fire."

What Sharpe proposed was a tedious technique called "arc mapping." They were looking for every spot where a break in the electrical line created sparks. But Walker knew that arcing was also something that could be caused by a fire. He couldn't look at an arced wire and tell the difference, but he was sure that Sharpe could, especially in the context of the fire damage to the wall or ceiling around it.

Instead of ribbons, Walker supposed they could also use string and trail it from arc to arc, which would give them the fire equivalent of bullet trajectory. On the other hand, if they used string and Guyette was right, that the wiring everywhere burst into flames at once, all they'd end up with would be a tangled knot that told them nothing.

So ribbons it was.

Sharpe said, "We'll also photograph and collect any physical evidence we come across as we go."

"My heart is racing with excitement already," Walker said.

"Mine too," Sharpe said, but he actually meant it.

It was going to be a long, dull morning.

CHAPTER NINE

They were only a thrilling hour into their arc mapping, and Walker was yawning as he tied a ribbon on some burned wiring in a family room wall socket, when Sharpe found something in the ashes on the floor.

"What is this?" Sharpe brought over a U-shaped piece of coiled metal and held it up to Walker to examine.

Walker recognized it immediately. "It's a Mr. Coffee."

"A coffee maker?"

"The heating element for one. But, yeah, a coffee maker."

Sharpe stared at him in total astonishment, which amused Walker. "How do you know that?"

"Because I've replaced ours twice."

"Why would you do that instead of just buying a new coffee maker?"

"They sell the part on Amazon for less than half as much as a new machine and it's not hard to install."

"I had no idea you were so cheap."

"It's not that, though I don't mind saving money," Walker said. "The coffee maker was a wedding gift from Carly's grandfather, who is dead now."

"So, he won't know if you toss it and buy a new one."

"But Carly will. She's very sentimental. To her, that's not Mr. Coffee on our counter. That's her Grandpa Joe making us a cup of joe."

"That's why I will never see a shrink."

"Because they're sentimental?"

"Because they are as crazy as the rest of us," Sharpe said, and examined the coil. "What's this doing in the family room?"

Walker wasn't sure if it was a rhetorical question, but he answered anyway. "It was probably fire-hosed over here from the kitchen."

"Where it would've been on the counter before the fire," Sharpe said.

Most of the kitchen counters were burned and their stone countertops had fallen and broken apart. But Walker could see the various electrical outlets, one of which already had a ribbon around the wiring and was along what had been the tiled backsplash above a countertop. He pointed to it.

"It was probably near that outlet."

Sharpe walked over to the kitchen and looked down at the fallen countertop, the charred cabinets, and then at the ribbon around the melted wiring. "Why was there a coffee maker in the kitchen?"

What an incredibly stupid question, Walker thought, but he had learned over the last year to play along, that it was often part of Sharpe's process to think out loud, particularly when he wanted to educate him.

"Because that's where people all over the world make coffee at home," Walker said, trying hard not to sound patronizing. "It's a common kitchen appliance."

"A countertop appliance. Like a toaster or blender."

"Yes, that's right," Walker said. "Are things different on your planet?"

Sharpe ignored the smart-ass remark. "I can understand why the stove, oven, dishwasher, and refrigerator would be installed before anybody moved in, because those are major, essential appliances. But that's not true of a toaster, blender, or coffee maker."

He has a point, Walker thought. But what difference did it make if there was a coffee maker in the kitchen?

"Maybe it was a housewarming gift from the builder."

"We'll ask Bell," Sharpe said.

"Or perhaps it was left behind by someone working on the house," Walker said.

"Why would a worker bring a coffee maker with him?"

"We hired a guy to repaint our house. He brought his own coffee maker with him each day and plugged it into one of our outdoor electrical outlets," Walker said. "The painter liked to drink coffee while he painted. He also liked to pee in our bushes, but that's another story. Anyway, his Mr. Coffee was covered with paint spatter and held together with duct tape. It wouldn't surprise me if it explodes someday."

"It wouldn't surprise me if yours does, too," Sharpe said. "I wouldn't let you change a lightbulb in my office."

"Your office is a fire trap, filled with papers and actual explosives. This was a brand-new kitchen," Walker said. "I don't get how a coffee maker could start a house fire that was as fast and hot as this one. It might burn the room, but an entire unfurnished house? I don't see it."

"Neither do I," Sharpe said.

"That's a first."

"What is?"

"You agreeing with me about what might or might not have caused a fire."

"It was inevitable," Sharpe said. "You've had an exceptional teacher."

Walker's phone rang. He took it out of his pocket and checked the caller ID.

"It's Nan Baker," Walker said.

"Put her on the speaker," Sharpe said as he continued prowling around the kitchen.

"Good morning, Nan," Walker said, holding his phone like a microphone. "You're on speaker with me and Sharpe. We're at the scene of another house fire."

"I'm at the morgue, so you're on speaker with Emilia Lopez, too. I've also conferenced in Eve Ronin and Duncan Pavone so we don't have to make a bunch of calls to share the same information."

Duncan said, "You're the epitome of efficiency, Nan."

"That is true," she said. "We'll start with the autopsy results, since Emilia just finished with it and it's still fresh in her mind."

"I have nothing unexpected to report," Emilia said. "It's definitely suicide and the evidence shows it happened precisely the way Sharpe figured it did."

Duncan said, "Take a bow, Sharpe."

As it happened, Sharpe was bent over, examining some wiring at the ribbon-wrapped floor-level electrical outlet in the kitchen.

"He is," Walker said.

"No surprise," Duncan said.

"I'm crouching," Sharpe said, "not bowing."

Emilia continued: "There were very low levels of carbon monoxide saturation in the victim's blood, no trace of hydrogen cyanide in his tissues, no soot in his nose, mouth, or respiratory tract, and no internal edema or damage to the larynx from inhaling hot gases. So he was alive when the fire started, but it wasn't the smoke or flames that killed him. It was the self-inflicted gunshot wound to the head. His body unquestionably burned postmortem."

Nan said, "We recovered the bullet, which went through his head and into the wall. The gun was badly burned, but we were still able to retrieve the serial number and learn that it was registered to Patrick Lopresti."

Eve spoke for the first time. "Do we know for certain that he's the dead man?"

"I confirmed it with dental records and fingerprints," Emilia said.

Eve said, "You were able to get fingerprints from a guy who'd doused himself with gasoline and set himself on fire?"

"There were a couple of fingertips with just enough epidermis left on them for me to work with."

Walker asked, "Were there any traces of the virus still in his body?"

"I doubt it, but I can't be absolutely sure."

"Why not?" he said.

"I can't run the tests. Right before we called you, FBI Special Agent Donna Leyland and a bunch of Feds came in and snatched the body and confiscated all of my organ, tissue, and fluid samples. They also took all of my notes."

Eve said, "They didn't waste any time starting the cover-up."

Duncan said, "Were the Feds in biohazard suits?"

"No," Emilia said.

"At least that's reassuring," he said.

"But we were wearing them," Emilia said. "Nan and I weren't taking any chances."

"We did," Duncan said. "We wore nothing at the crime scene. We'll let you know tomorrow if our skin starts melting off."

"Thanks," she said. "We'd appreciate that."

Nan said, "The results of our examination of the physical evidence collected from the house and the victim are consistent with Emilia's conclusions about cause of death and also support Sharpe's assessment of how the fire started and spread. So, I won't bore you with the details."

Emilia said, "Are you implying that I did?"

"Well, when you start by confirming it was suicide, it's like giving away the ending of a mystery novel on page one," Nan said. "It kills the suspense. But I have a twist."

Walker said, "What's that?"

"We managed to recover the SIM card from the melted burner phone that we retrieved from Lopresti's car," she said. "All the calls for the last three months were to and from a single number." Nan read off the number. "Does that mean anything to you?"

Eve answered right away. "That's Justine Bryce's phone number."

Duncan said, "They were definitely having an affair."

"Just like Walker and I figured they were."

"Glory hog," Duncan said.

"You told Sharpe he could take a bow for what he deduced," Eve complained. "Why can't we?"

"Because he's modest and self-effacing," Duncan said. "You're not. You have a TV series celebrating you. That's more than enough."

Walker said, "I don't have one."

Emilia said, "What about that show with Chuck Norris?"

Here we go again, Walker thought. "That has nothing to do with me."

"So you're just a superfan, a Chuck Norris Trekkie."

"I'm not a Trekkie," he said.

"Do you sleep in Chuck Norris pajamas?"

Nan said, "Chuck sleeps in the nude."

Eve said, "How would you know how Chuck sleeps?"

"Can you imagine Chuck in pajamas?"

"It's better than imagining him naked."

Walker said, "This has been lots of fun, ladies, but we've got to go. We have another pressing case to investigate. Thanks for the call."

He disconnected and Sharpe, who'd been silent for so long that Walker assumed he'd stopped listening, now turned and grinned at him.

"If you can't take the teasing, don't wear the hat. Or change your name. Otherwise, you're asking for it."

Walker didn't bother responding. "What were you looking for while I had that conference call?"

"Some sign of the melted coffee maker and a coffeepot. I don't see any."

"It's probably somewhere else in the house or in the mud down the street, washed away by the firefighters."

Walker looked outside as he spoke, as if following the path of the hose water, and blinked hard, not sure at first that what he was seeing was real.

At the end of the cul-de-sac, flames were licking out from the first-floor windows of a finished house, the one that Bell told him a family was supposed to move into tomorrow.

"Holy shit," Walker said.

Sharpe followed his gaze, then ran outside. Walker ran after him, stumbling over something on the floor, and when he got back to his feet, he saw Sharpe jump into a tanker truck parked across the street.

Walker yelled, "No!"

He ran outside just as Sharpe activated the tanker's front and rear water sprayers and sped toward the burning house, construction workers leaping out of his path.

Walker watched in sheer disbelief as Sharpe, a man he'd thought of as sensible and risk-averse, plowed the water-spraying truck through the home's living room window. An instant later, a huge ball of flame burst out of the gaping opening like a dragon's fiery belch.

Walker hurried to their Tahoe, grabbed a gas mask for himself and another one for Sharpe, took a pickax in case he needed to free his partner from rubble, then ran down the street. The house was in flames, and if it wasn't fully engulfed in fire, it soon would be.

When Walker reached the huge hole in the blazing living room, he saw Sharpe at the back of the tanker, getting doused with water from the rear sprayers as he unfurled a hose from a reel mounted on the bumper.

Smoke and wisps of fire swirled around Sharpe, who turned around with the hose nozzle in his hands, saw Walker, and barked, "Don't just stand there, open the water valve for me."

Walker put on his gas mask and rushed in, the intense heat immediately wrapping around him like a blanket. He stopped to put a gas mask on Sharpe's face, earning a scowl for his efforts, went to the valve, crouched in front of it, and twisted it open as fast as he could.

Water instantly surged through the hose, making it thick and heavy, and Sharpe began dousing the walls and ceiling around them.

Walker picked up the hose line, freeing it up and allowing Sharpe to move closer to the flames. The tanker's rear sprayers soaked them both and kept them from burning despite the new demand on the water supply.

Walker yelled, "What the hell do you think you're doing?"

"Saving our evidence from burning."

"You're not a firefighter."

"The whole house will be fully consumed if we wait for the fire-fighters to get here," Sharpe said. "We have to slow it down or the entire place will collapse."

"On us." Walker could understand jumping into the flames to fight a fire if there were lives at stake, but not to save an empty house. "There's always going to be evidence, no matter how much destruction there is. You taught me that. We need to get out of here before we both burn to death."

"We won't," Sharpe said. "I vented the fire down here by driving through the front of the house, and all this water should significantly reduce the temperature. We'll be fine until the firefighters get here."

Sharpe did seem to Walker to be making progress fighting the flames around them. But the fire was still raging upstairs. Walker could hear it crackling and could feel the heat radiating from above.

"If the second floor doesn't bury us first," he said.

"Relax," Sharpe said. "The tanker truck will break the fall of the blazing rubble and give us some cover."

"Oh good," Walker said. "I feel much better now."

"You should. You're not sitting at a desk. Isn't action what you've been craving?"

Walker was stunned that Sharpe knew how he'd felt the last few months, because he thought he'd kept it to himself.

"It's the chase I miss. This isn't a chase. It's stupidity. You're risking your life for an empty house."

"What are you doing here?"

"I'm trying to save you."

"Do I look like I need saving?"

"Yes. You've already lost your eyebrows."

It was true. They were gone, burned to stubble.

"They needed a trim anyway," Sharpe said.

That's when two fire trucks charged up to the house, and moments later, the firefighters swarmed in with their hoses, clearly astonished to see Sharpe in the midst of the flames.

A firefighter said, "We'll take over from here."

"If you insist." Sharpe handed him the truck's hose and walked out with Walker, both of them completely soaked and covered with soot.

Walker touched his face, streaking it with soot, and was relieved to find his eyebrows were still there. He wouldn't have to come up with a ridiculous story for Carly to explain it.

Captain Guyette stood out front, shaking his head in astonishment. "Nice work, Shar-Pei."

"Thank you, Captain."

"I always knew you secretly wished you were a fireman," Guyette said. "That's why you're so surly with us. You're projecting."

"Are you married to a shrink, too?"

"No, why?"

"Never mind. Please try not to take down any walls or pull up the floor," Sharpe said. "Keep as much debris as you can in the house and not all over the neighborhood or what I did will be for nothing."

"How can you still think it's arson after this?" Guyette said. "I'll bet you my left nut that this house was powered up today for a new homeowner and you just saw what that caused. This second fire proves it's bad wiring."

"Mr. Coffee would disagree," Sharpe said and walked past him, his soaked shoes making a moist squish.

Guyette called out after him. "You really are insane."

Walker walked along with Sharpe. "We're never telling Carly about this."

CHAPTER TEN

Bell, his sales staff, and a crowd of construction workers stood in the street, watching the fire.

As Sharpe and Walker approached him, Bell said, "This is a disaster. I can't believe this is happening."

"It's definitely peculiar," Sharpe said.

"*Peculiar?* It's a nightmare," Bell said. "Did you drive one of our tanker trucks into the house?"

"Yes, I did," Sharpe said. "I really appreciated that it had an automatic transmission instead of a stick. Otherwise, I might have crashed it."

"You *did* crash it."

Walker said, "It's why the house is still standing."

"How is the truck?" Bell asked.

"Fine, it just has some character now," Sharpe said. "Do you give new residents a housewarming gift when they move in?"

Bell stared at him, baffled, but he answered the question. "They have the choice of a gourmet espresso machine or a basket of artisan bath soaps, salts, and essential oils."

"What did you give these two homeowners?" Sharpe gestured to the two burned houses on either side of them.

"Nothing yet. Why?"

Walker said, "You'll have to step up to something a lot nicer than any of that to make up for this, like a pizza oven in the backyard."

"Oh God," Bell said. "Do you still believe it's the wiring?"

Sharpe said, "It's too soon for us to say. Ask us in a couple of hours."

They headed back to their truck and leaned against it. Their adrenaline highs were fading and Walker began to feel the sting of minor burns, the itch of his wet clothes, and the smell of soot in their nostrils. He'd have to wash his nose out with saline.

Walker glanced at Sharpe. His eyebrows were gone, and his skin was red, but it didn't look like he needed to go to the ER for the burns.

"How's your face feel?"

"No worse than it does after a day on the golf course."

"Have you ever reached the eighteenth hole without eyebrows?"

"Not that I've noticed, but I don't preen in front of the mirror," Sharpe said. "Would an outdoor pizza oven get you to move here?"

"Only if it came with a personal chef. Otherwise, who wants to go outside to cook a frozen pizza?"

"Good point."

◆ ◆ ◆

It took only an hour for the firefighters to put out the blaze, time that Sharpe and Walker spent outside watching them and letting the sun dry their clothes.

While the house was still steaming and dripping, Sharpe and Walker went back inside to survey the scene, working their way carefully around the tanker truck.

Sharpe picked up the pickax Walker left there and let his gaze drift over the walls, ceiling, and floor. Then something caught his attention. He used his pickax to gesture to it.

"Mr. Coffee has been here, too."

Walker looked where Sharpe was pointing and there it was, another heating coil in the ashes.

Sharpe went straight to a scorched portion of the wall near an electrical outlet, studied the surface for a moment, then swung at it with his pickax, tearing away the soaked and blackened drywall until he exposed the studs.

And something more.

Walker saw another coffee-maker heating element, absorbed in a plastic globule that still retained some of the distinct shape of a water bottle, wedged between two studs and wired to the outlet. He also saw the blades of what might have been a tiny fan, perhaps the kind in a laptop computer.

"What is that?" he asked, gesturing to the wall.

"The remnants of a time bomb," Sharpe said. "We need to go through this house and see if we can find evidence of more of those in the walls."

Walker had a better idea. "You get started. I'll be right back."

Before Sharpe could object, Walker marched outside, passing Captain Guyette, who was supervising his team as they packed up to return to the station.

"I hope you aren't too attached to your left nut," Walker said as he passed. He went to a fire engine and helped himself to a Pulaski, a fire-fighting tool with a head that was half-axe and half-hoe, then marched up the street to the completed, unoccupied house they'd visited yester-day. It was still unlocked and smelled clean and new, though he reeked of smoke and left sooty, muddy footprints on the shiny hardwood floors as he went into the living room.

Bell wouldn't like that, but Walker wasn't worried. The salesman wouldn't notice the footprints. It would be the least of the damage.

Walker faced the same wall and outlet that Sharpe opened up in the burned house, then swung the hoe edge of the Pulaski into the drywall, again and again, tearing it away until he exposed the framing.

Tucked into the space between two studs was a water bottle, filled with some kind of fluid, with the Mr. Coffee heating element affixed to it with electrical tape. The heating element was wired to the electri-cal outlet and was packed into the space, like something about to be shipped, with Styrofoam and wood chips. A tiny motherboard fan was in that same space between the studs and was also wired to the outlet.

This house was wired to blow, too.

Walker took a step back, looked around the room, found another electrical outlet, and hacked away at the wall. He kept doing that at every outlet and light switch he saw until he found another one of the hidden devices.

Encouraged and enraged by his discovery, Walker kept at it, destroying walls throughout the first floor, the effort making him sweat so much that his uniform was soaked again. He found and exposed four more devices before deciding to try his luck upstairs for a while.

He started with an outlet right above the floor in the main bedroom and ripped up the wall without finding another bomb. But at the base of the outlet, he noticed a wire that didn't seem to belong and that disappeared under the carpeted floor.

Walker used his Pulaski to pull up the carpet and then to destroy the plywood under that, exposing the floor joists and tracing the wire to another time bomb wedged between two wood beams in the middle of the room. There was even more Styrofoam and wood chips stuffed into channels created by the parallel joists.

He took out his phone, shot a picture of the device and stuff around it, and sent it to Sharpe, along with a note telling him where he was.

Sharpe showed up a few minutes later, just as Walker was swinging his Pulaski at another wall, tearing it open.

Sharpe said, "I hope the rule 'you break it, you buy it' doesn't apply to homes."

Walker gestured to the bomb in the bedroom floor. "I've found six of these in the house so far, but I have a feeling there are a lot more."

"I'm sure of it. But unlike the ones in the house that burned, these are intact."

Walker set down his tool and led Sharpe to the floor bomb. "I know this is an explosive. But how does it work?"

Sharpe bent down and examined the device without touching it or disturbing the surrounding stuffing.

"It's simple and ingenious. The heating element is wired to the electrical system. As soon as the home is powered up, it begins heating the juice bottle filled with an accelerant. Looks like gasoline to me. The bottle quickly melts, spreading the gasoline into the highly combustible foam and wood shavings packed around it. The melted bottle ignites into flames, detonating the vapors from the gasoline, which ignite the soaked kindling."

"How long would that process take?"

"Less than two minutes, especially with that fan," Sharpe said. "It creates ventilation that feeds the fire and draws the flames down the channel between the two joists. I'm guessing the floor joists are stuffed, wall to wall, with more of that kindling."

"That explains how the fire spread so fast and hot inside the walls and floors."

"The fire is so intense that every part of the device," Sharpe said, "except for that heating element and the wires, burns away."

"Even those pieces would probably go unnoticed in all the rubble from the fire, especially after the firefighters washed everything away."

"I noticed it," Sharpe said, scratching the skin where his left eyebrow used to be.

"But you ordinarily wouldn't be among the first responders on the scene. The firefighters would be. Captain Guyette would have called it a case of faulty wiring and we might never have known about it."

"Except this guy didn't rig just one house," Sharpe said. "He rigged three that we know of. Not only would we have started investigating after two houses went up in flames, but the builder would have, too, doing what you've done here . . . only far less crudely and destructively."

"You drove a tanker truck through the front of a house and you're talking to me about crude destruction?"

"The home was on fire and in imminent danger of being totally consumed and reduced to ash," Sharpe said. "This one wasn't. There was no rush."

Walker shrugged. "I'm relentless in my pursuit of justice."

"It doesn't matter." Sharpe got to his feet. "We've only just begun tearing things up."

"Want me to take down another wall? I love demo."

Sharpe shook his head. "We need to get Nan Baker and her people out here to methodically and precisely take down the rest of the drywall, pull up these floors, and recover the devices for analysis. And then they have to carefully take apart every completed, unoccupied home to search for more of these time bombs. It could take days."

Long, boring days better spent with Walker doing what he did best.

"While you're doing that," Walker said, "tell me about who I will be out there looking for."

Sharpe gestured to the bomb. "It's all right here. It's like a confession. We're looking for someone who has experience as a firefighter or arson investigator and who is familiar with construction and electricity."

"That could be any of the guys working on this site."

"Or who were fighting the fire," Sharpe said.

"The devices had to be installed after the houses were wired, the drywall was put up, and the plywood was laid on the floors," Walker said. "In other words, in the window of time before the walls were painted and the hardwood or carpet were put down. That means the arsonist was able to keep a close eye on progress here and had easy access to the site to remove drywall and flooring, insert his devices, and put everything back without worrying about being caught."

"Whoever it is will be someone with a lot of patience," Sharpe said. "These improvised explosive devices are triggered only when the houses are powered up for the first time. He had no way of knowing if that would be days, weeks, or months after the IEDs were installed."

"Someone was playing a very long game," Walker said. "That takes a lot of hate, not patience."

"Patience and hatred aren't mutually exclusive," Sharpe said. "Revenge is a dish best served cold."

"Obviously not this time," Walker said. "I'll start by asking Bell for a list of the developer's enemies and any disgruntled ex-employees."

"I'm optimistic that this device isn't done ratting out its maker. We'll get DNA, fingerprints, or key information from the various components of the IED that will point us to the arsonist. And often there's a signature element to how bombs like this are designed and built."

"A technique that might fit the MO of a known arsonist?"

"Or match the details of some other arson investigator's unsolved cases," Sharpe said, "since I don't have any."

"There's more of that famous humility of yours that Duncan Pavone talked about."

"It's not a boast. I simply and dispassionately stated a relevant fact, a record that is the envy of arson investigators everywhere."

Walker leaned on his Pulaski like it was a gentleman's cane. "I'm curious, what are you going to do with Captain Guyette's left ball?"

"Use it as a paperweight," Sharpe said, taking out his phone.

"His balls are that big?"

"They'd have to be for him to dare challenge me, a renowned arson expert, on the cause of a fire."

Sharpe called Nan Baker, and Walker went out to begin his manhunt.

CHAPTER ELEVEN

The Twin Lakes sales office was in the garage of one of the model homes. Three individual offices were arrayed around an open area with a model of the development on a large table in the center of the room. There were tiny flags in the lots that were still available for sale.

Walker sat in one of the offices and across from Ed Bell, who he'd informed about the bombs they'd found in the empty homes and then asked if he knew of anybody who held a grudge against Twin Lakes.

Bell's relief that faulty wiring wasn't to blame for the fires seemed to outweigh any other reaction he might have had to the news. He reached into a desk drawer, pulled out a thick file, and rose from his seat to drop it on the desk between them.

"I told you this morning that it was arson and that you should look at these radical environmentalists," Bell said, falling back into his seat, which creaked under his weight.

"Do you have something against clean air and water?" Walker leaned forward and pulled the file in front of him. His whole body itched and his dried uniform felt like it was made of cardboard.

"I'm all for that," Bell said, "but I think we can survive without the Santa Susana tarplant, Braunton's milk-vetch, and the western spadefoot."

"What are they?"

"Two weeds and a toad that smells like peanuts that have been spotted on this land. Because of that, the California Crusade Against

Manmade Extinction opposed this development for years, but we stuck it out and defeated them."

"Have you heard from them since?"

"Yeah, about two hours ago, when that house went up in flames."

"Before the fires."

Bell nodded at the file in front of Walker. "That is full of the posters they've littered our community with, calling our homeowners Nature Nazis. They also vandalize our signs, pop our balloons, and steal our flags. Now they are burning our houses. And for what?"

"Maybe the tarplant holds the cure for cancer, the milk-vetch could end lactose intolerance, and the toad's blood could increase male fertility."

Bell grunted in derision. "This isn't the only patch of land on earth, or even in Southern California, where those things exist."

"But if everyone has your attitude, they won't exist for long."

"Are you defending what the Crusade has done?"

"No, but I can see their point," Walker said. "Who else besides these guys have you pissed off? Maybe a disgruntled employee or dissatisfied homeowner?"

Bell thought about the question for a moment. "We fired a construction supervisor six months ago. Our night security guard caught him stealing lumber and other supplies."

"Was he arrested?"

Bell shook his head, and Walker wondered how much glue or Velcro held his celebrity toupee in place.

"He'd worked for us for nine years and had been going through some personal issues, so we terminated him on the spot and left it at that. But instead of thanking us for our compassion, he called us a bunch of heartless assholes and promised we'd be sorry for it."

"What's his name?"

"Larry Bogert."

Bell got up, went to his file cabinet, took out another file, and dropped it on the desk in front of Walker. "Here's his personnel file."

"Six months ago," Walker said. "Would that have roughly been when construction began on the phase two homes that are finished today?"

"Yes, it is."

"I'd like to talk to the guard who caught Bogert. Maybe he saw some other unusual activity at the time."

"Warren Pendle. He doesn't work here anymore."

"Was there a problem?"

"Not with us. Maybe with Big Valley Security, the people he actually worked for." The salesman wrote something on a notepad, tore off the page, and passed it to Walker. "You can reach them here. They might know where he is. Warren was a nice guy and took his job very seriously. We'd have been happy if he'd stayed, but turnover is high on the night shift."

Not surprising, Walker thought. It was dull work at low pay and probably very lonely. "What about pissed-off homeowners? You must have some."

"One. Mateo Salcedo sued us for a ground-subsistence issue that wasn't our fault."

"What was the ground-subsistence issue?"

"His backyard collapsed into Devil's Canyon," Bell said. "He got a geologist to say it was shoddy grading that caused it and threatened all kinds of negative publicity if we didn't settle. But we discovered he'd hired an unlicensed contractor to build his pool and that guy didn't pull any permits for the job. The pool leaked and undermined the hillside. He lost the case, his savings to his lawyers, and his house to us."

"Where is he now?"

"I have no idea. Our lawyer might be able to tell you more." The salesman dug a card out of his desk drawer and passed it along. Walker was accumulating a lot of paper. Bell seemed to notice. He went to his closet and came out with a canvas bag with the Twin Lakes logo on it. "Take this to hold all that stuff. There are some balloons, ballpoint pens, and a notepad in there, too. We give them to our hot leads."

"I'm not interested in buying," Walker said, taking the bag anyway.

"But you're looking. After you mentioned the pizza oven, a designer feature we have in the backyard of model home number two, I came back and checked our visitor sign-in sheets. You've been here before."

Walker grinned and held up his hands in surrender. "You caught me. My wife likes to visit model homes. Have you ever thought about being a detective?"

"Never, but it's part of being a good salesman. To close a sale this big, you have to know your customer."

They talked a bit more about what the crime scene unit needed to do in the remaining unoccupied houses. Walker was amazed that Bell was fine with that, and with giving the LASD written permission to enter the properties and do whatever deconstruction was necessary without any liability for any damage.

Walker thanked him, promised to keep in touch as the investigation progressed, and walked outside with his bag of files and goodies.

Things had changed while Walker was in the office. Two CSU trucks were there now, and an army of forensic investigators in white Tyvek jumpsuits were already crawling all over the two burned homes, the house Walker had begun to demolish, and others on the street. A half dozen uniformed sheriff's deputies were busy securing the large scene, which now encompassed two streets and about a dozen homes, with crime scene tape and traffic cones.

He'd expected all that, but not to see Eve Ronin, who casually leaned against her plain-wrap Charger in front of the sales office, her arms crossed under her chest.

"What are you doing here?" he asked.

"The deputies for this are being deployed out of Lost Hills station, my home base, so I came by to see if you needed any other assistance."

"Perfect timing. I was about to call an Uber. I've got some suspects I need to talk with but my pickup truck is at HQ in Monterey Park and Sharpe needs to keep our vehicle for the tools and supplies it contains."

"You want me to be your driver?"

Walker shrugged. "You can ask questions, too, if you like."

"Wow. I'll have a chance to be a real detective. How can I miss that?"

They got into her car and she drove them out of the development and down to the 118 freeway, where she stopped on Topanga facing the southbound road ahead and two on-ramps, one heading east, another heading west.

"No offense," she said, "but you smell like a pile of ashes in a men's locker room."

"Want me to open a window?"

"That'd be nice," she said. "Where to?"

Good question, Walker thought, and considered his options as he lowered his window. "What have you heard about the search for Justine Bryce?"

"It's still ongoing. At least that's what Dash Nolan told me when I called him this morning for an update."

"I have some research I need to do on the arson suspects before I'm ready to talk to them," Walker said. "Since we're so close to Triax, how would you feel about visiting Colin Oxley, the lab supervisor who called Patrick Lopresti and Justine Bryce about the virus leak?"

"I know who Oxley is," she said. "Do you think he's holding something back?"

"Oxley was the last person who spoke to her," Walker said. "That's the point I was underscoring. He may not know what he knows, especially given his emotional state yesterday. The poor guy."

"I happened to ask Dash Nolan about how Oxley was doing and he said they'd given him the week off."

"Do you have his home address?"

Eve grinned. "As a matter of fact, I do."

She told him. It was out in La Cañada Flintridge, along the foothills of the Verdugo Mountains, north of Pasadena. The community also happened to be in LASD jurisdiction, so they wouldn't be stepping on any bureaucratic toes.

Walker said, "We'll be heading in that direction to get my truck."

"Perfect." She drove onto the eastbound 118 on-ramp. "Since we're passing by Oxley's neighborhood anyway, it would be heartless of us if we didn't check on him after the ordeal he's been through."

"We're not working the case, we're just being thoughtful," Walker said. "Because we care about people."

"Deeply," she said. "Think that explanation will save our careers if the FBI, Homeland Security, or CDC find out what we're doing?"

"That depends on whether we find Justine Bryce before they do."

Colin Oxley's ramshackle clapboard house was on Chevy Chase Drive, set far back from the street under the shadow of several overgrown oak and eucalyptus trees. The driveway was crumbling and the grass was dead.

It was the worst-kept house in what otherwise was an upscale neighborhood of huge, immaculately landscaped new or remodeled homes on unusually large half-acre lots.

Eve parked on the street and they walked up the driveway to the house, which wasn't much bigger than Walker's and, he guessed, was probably about the same age. But it was in far worse condition. Oxley clearly wasn't spending any money on upkeep other than occasional weed abatement.

Walker knocked on the door. After a moment, Oxley answered, wearing a loose-fitting kimono, like Luke Skywalker might have worn, only without any lightsabers.

"Detectives, what are you doing here? Have you found her?"

"I'm afraid not," Eve said. "We just came to check on how you are doing. We are worried about you."

Walker added, "We can't imagine what you must be going through."

Oxley lowered his head. "I won't lie to you. It's been hell."

He stepped aside to let them in. It was like entering a comic book store. The shelves were filled with comic books, spaceship models, and *Star Wars* action figures. Framed posters for the *Star Wars* movies and years of San Diego SciCon conventions were on the wall. A full, adult-size *Star Wars* Mandalorian outfit, essentially a futuristic suit of armor with a cape, was displayed on a mannequin in a glass case. The helmet covered the entire head because the Mandalorians weren't allowed to ever show their faces. Walker had gleaned that much of the show's lore from a single episode, which he'd watched because the actor who'd starred as the Stetson-wearing US marshal on *Justified* was in that one, basically playing the same role again, but on a desert planet. The Mandalorian and the space marshal teamed up to kill a giant worm, which was the instant they lost Walker as a viewer.

Eve peered into the glass case. "Is that a real Mandalorian costume?"

"It's not a *costume*, it's Mandalorian *armor*, forged from beskar," Oxley said. "It's able to withstand a slash from a lightsaber." He pointed to burn slashes across the chest and on the shoulder plating.

"Beskar," Walker said. "I've always wondered what they call the fake chrome on car dashboards."

Oxley got testy. "That's authentic Mandalorian craftsmanship, tested in actual battle on Nevarro, Corvus, Sorgan, Tatooine, and Mandalore. I bought it from Lucasfilm at a charity auction to benefit crippled children. There's the certificate of authenticity." He pointed proudly to a slip of paper that was framed at the base of the display. "It's signed by Jon Favreau and Dave Filoni."

Walker had no idea who they were but could tell from Oxley's expression that he was supposed to be awed by that, or at least impressed.

Eve said, "My brother absolutely loves Mando. Can I take a picture of the suit?"

"Of course," Oxley said, then deepened his voice a few octaves to add: "This is the way."

Oxley grinned. Eve smiled politely, then took photos of the suit from various angles.

Walker browsed the action figures and spotted a few Baby Yodas mixed in among them. "You and Justine obviously shared a deep love."

Oxley blushed, then stammered, "I-I liked her. I mean, we were close coworkers. Why do you think we were in love? Did she say something to someone about us?"

"No, I meant a love for *Star Wars*," Walker said. "She had a huge bag of those Baby Yodas in her house."

"A *bag* of them?" His blush deepened.

"You know, one of those Hefty trash bags, full of ones like that," Walker said, nodding to the Baby Yoda on the shelf. "I thought she might've given that one to you, that maybe she gave them out to people who shared the same passion."

"We weren't sharing any passion," Oxley said, an edge in his voice.

"You weren't close?"

"We were friendly coworkers, and I liked her, but I really didn't know much about her. I mean, I know she thought Baby Yoda was adorable, but who doesn't?"

Eve said, "You also knew that she was single and lived alone."

"It was obvious," Oxley said. "Most people have pictures of their significant other in their cubicles, or you hear them talking about them at the water cooler. Not her."

"You told us that she was very responsible and you had faith that she would never risk infecting anyone," Eve said. "What gave you that impression?"

"She was very active in charity groups, raising money for kids, animal shelters, rainforest protection. She was always passing the hat, trying to get us to contribute to her causes." Oxley knocked a knuckle on the glass case. "That's how I found out about the auction for this armor. A person like that wouldn't infect humanity with a plague."

"Forgive me," Walker said, "but that begs the question, Why was she working on something with the potential to kill millions of people?"

"You have it backwards," Oxley said. "She was working to create a cure if a weaponized variation of that virus is ever used against us by our enemies. Or if it naturally comes here, which is possible."

Walker didn't believe the military was interested in a cure. They were probably trying to develop their own bioweapon first from the same virus. But he kept that opinion to himself.

"It is?" Walker asked.

"There have been a handful of outbreaks of the virus over the last sixty years in Angola, Uganda, Mozambique, and most recently, last year in China."

"Of course," Walker said. "It's always China. First SARS. Then COVID. Next the zombie ant fungus."

Oxley said, "The entire population of a rural village was infected, and hundreds of people died. The Chinese couldn't admit that but they also had to credibly explain the deaths and keep the virus from spreading. So their emergency containment method became the official, tragic story: a whole village was incinerated in a fast-moving, out-of-control wildfire."

Eve said, "Like the one in Paradise, California."

"Exactly."

"Was that an outbreak, too?"

"No. How could you think that?" Oxley said. "The United States government doesn't massacre their citizens to cover up mistakes."

I guess we'll see, Walker thought. "How did the virus get to China from Africa?"

"In the suitcase of a virologist who was sent to Africa several years ago to obtain a sample and bring it back to China for study."

"Was the lab in the village?"

"It was a hundred miles away," Oxley said. "But there's a prominent Chinese virologist who was born there. He went back for his sister's wedding two days before the outbreak . . . and hasn't been seen since."

And then, Walker thought, some idiot brought a sample of the virus back to Thousand Oaks in their suitcase . . . and history was repeating itself.

"Justine knows the story, too," Oxley added. "I'm sure she doesn't want Los Angeles, and everybody in it, incinerated because of her."

Eve said, "What do you think she's done?"

"Like Obi-Wan Kenobi, I'm certain that Justine has sacrificed herself for the greater good . . . and is now one with the Force." He started to tear up.

Eve patted him gently on the back. "Thank you for your help, Colin. We appreciate it."

He sniffled and wiped his nose on his sleeve. "But I didn't give you any."

"Actually, you did," Walker said. "We'll be in touch. May the Force be with you."

They walked out. As they went down the root-cracked driveway, careful not to trip on the slabs, Walker said, "Is your brother really a *Mandalorian* fan?"

"He watches all those *Star Wars* shows, but that one is his favorite," she said. "I'm sure he'd love to wear that suit while he cleans pools."

"Is that his job?"

"Yeah, he goes all over the valley," Eve said. "Did you see the way Oxley blushed when you suggested that Justine loved him?"

"I did."

"He was embarrassed. I think he might have had a crush on her."

"I don't know," Walker said. "Did you see the way he blushed when I mentioned the Baby Yodas in the trash bag?"

"I did."

"That was anger," Walker said. "Did you hear the edge in his voice when he said, 'We weren't sharing any passion'? What was that about?"

They reached Eve's car. "I don't know. What did you mean when you said he'd helped us find her?"

"I think he's right," Walker said. "She's not in Los Angeles."

"That doesn't help us find her."

"It does," he said. "It reminded me that we know something important that the FBI and all those other agencies don't—that Lopresti and Bryce were having an affair. We also have something they don't—his burner."

He gave her a grin.

"What am I missing?" she asked.

"We can get the GPS data from his burner for the last ninety days and compare it with her data over the same period. The overlap will tell us all the places where they hooked up. If one of those love nests is someplace remote, that's where she is."

They didn't have her phone, but the records he was looking for weren't stored on the actual devices. They were in the cloud.

Now Eve grinned. "I can get Duncan on that. He's the warrant whisperer."

"But we aren't supposed to be on this case. Is he going to be okay with aiding and abetting our insubordination?"

"We don't work for the Feds," Eve said. "Nobody in our chain of command told us to lay off."

"That's true," Walker said. "I like the way you think."

They got into her car and headed south on the 210 freeway toward LASD headquarters, where Walker wanted to not only get his truck but also take a quick shower and change into the fresh set of clothes he had in his locker. It was a loose-fitting polo shirt, a blazer to hide his gun, and jeans. It was the uniform he was supposed to wear on duty, but he wasn't on an arson investigation now.

On the way, Walker gave Eve the list of the information that he hoped Duncan could get for them.

"We're going to need cell tower information from the service provider and, if Lopresti and Bryce ever used Google Maps, we'll also need to serve Google with a warrant for geolocation data."

"You're hoping one of them used Google Maps for directions to their love nest and typed in the address."

"It doesn't matter whether they did that or not," Walker said. "If they ever opened the Google Maps app and the 'location services setting' on their phones was set to 'active,' which is the default, then they've been constantly tracked by Google since then without their knowledge."

"That scares me as a private citizen but thrills me as a cop," Eve said. "What's the difference between cell tower data and Google's?"

"Cell tower data will get you within two miles of the location," Walker said. "Google data will get you within two feet."

"How do you know all this?"

"Years of manhunting before I rode a desk."

"You aren't riding a desk," Eve said.

"Not today. But I have been for the last year. This is what I do best. It's great to be back in the saddle again."

"Giddyup," Eve said.

CHAPTER TWELVE

Eve called Duncan, put him on the speaker, and filled him in as they continued south on the 210 freeway until it petered out onto surface streets in Pasadena that were lined with grand, but formerly condemned, Victorian homes. For decades, the neighborhood had been slated for destruction to make way for a freeway connection to Long Beach that was never built. Walker knew Sharpe lived in one of those houses that'd been spared from demolition, though he hadn't been invited over for a visit yet.

Duncan said, "I can get you the cell tower information pretty quick, but I'll have to get a judge to sign off on a warrant for Google Maps, then fax it to their legal department."

"Fax?" Walker said. "Are you joking?"

"Google may be one of the biggest tech companies on earth, but their legal department is still in a cave, communicating with each other by drawing on the walls."

"How long will it take?"

"An hour on the cell tower data, two or more on Google," Duncan said. "They take long lunches at Google, and I've got to find a museum that has a fax machine on display."

Eve took surface streets to LASD headquarters. She stayed in the car while Walker ran in, quickly showered, and changed his clothes. He assumed she was avoiding a nasty reception from the other deputies.

He came out carrying a plastic bag and walked up to the driver's side window of her car, which she rolled down.

"Any news?" he asked.

"Duncan got cell tower info from both of their phones. There are two overlapping tower pings. One that's obviously her place and another in Ojai."

"That's where she is," Walker said.

"Duncan got a judge to sign off on the Google warrant and he immediately faxed it to them," Eve said. "Now he's waiting for a reply."

"He doesn't mind doing all that grunt work?"

"At his age, Duncan doesn't look at it that way," she said. "He likes it. He figures he's a lot less likely to get shot while sitting at his desk."

"Let's start driving towards Ojai," Walker said. "I'll follow you. That way we'll be in the right place when Duncan calls with an address."

He reached into his plastic bag and handed her a bag of potato chips, a granola bar, and a Diet Coke that he'd bought from the vending machines.

"It's the best meal I could find in the coffee room," Walker said.

"This is the life," she said in the same low, serious tone of voice that Oxley had used to say, *This is the way*.

Maybe, Walker thought, that made them Mandalorians of a sort, too.

Ojai was a farming community an hour or so north of Los Angeles that had a hippie vibe that attracted celebrities desperate for privacy and fresh organic produce. It was also popular with nature lovers for the hiking, horseback riding, and when there was water, rafting on the river. But what Walker remembered most vividly from his visit there with Carly was that it was a haven for women with excessively hairy underarms. His observation hadn't amused Carly so he decided not to share it with Eve.

He was forty minutes into the drive, and passing through Thousand Oaks, when he got a call from Sharpe.

"How's it going out in Twin Lakes?" Walker asked.

"CSU found two more devices in the house you started demolishing and another one in the finished house next door, but they just got started there."

"What have you learned from the devices so far?"

"The arsonist likes Sparkling Ice strawberry-kiwi water. Those are the bottles he used in every device."

"They sell that everywhere," Walker said.

"Nan is hoping he drank the water from the bottles and left some DNA behind."

"I think it's less of a hope and more of a pipe dream," Walker said. "Have you spotted his signature?"

"I haven't had a chance to examine the devices in detail yet," Sharpe said. "I have to wait for CSU to finish processing them for fingerprints, DNA, that kind of thing. I'm just documenting their locations and supervising their removal. How's your investigation going?"

Walker told him what he'd learned from Bell about possible suspects but that he still needed to do some background checking on them before his interviews.

"In the meantime, I caught a ride with Eve Ronin to HQ to get my truck. On the way, we stopped and did a welfare check on Colin Oxley. He's bereft."

"I'm sure he is. I'm also sure you're not at your desk doing those background checks on arson suspects. You're on the road with Ronin, trying to chase down Justine Bryce, even though it's a federal case now."

"There's no ticking clock on our arson case," Walker said. "The damage has already been done and future fires at Twin Lakes have been averted. But Bryce could be dead in a few hours."

"You can't stop that from happening unless you've come up with a vaccine."

"Dead or alive, she could spread a plague that could be the end of humanity."

Sharpe sighed. "Now you're saving humanity."

"Okay, let me put it another way. A day away from the Twin Lakes arson case won't kill me and my family but a day away from the Bryce case could."

"Well, when you put it like that, it makes more sense and doesn't sound like you think you're one of the Super Friends."

"You mean the Avengers."

"I mean the Super Friends," Sharpe said. "Superman, Wonder Woman, Aquaman, Batman and Robin, the extraterrestrial Wonder Twins, and their blue monkey Gleek."

"You made up that last superhero," Walker said.

"I did not and I will tell you this, Gleek is a lot more useful to have around than that archer Hawkeye. Gleek has a super-stretchy tail that can do all kinds of things. Hawkeye just has a bow and some arrows. Big deal."

Walker's phone beeped, signaling another call coming in. He checked the caller ID.

"I've got Ronin calling me," Walker told Sharpe. "I've got to take it. I'll stay in touch."

"Don't get infected."

"Don't worry," Walker said. "I'll leave the risky stuff to Gleek."

He punched a button and answered Eve's call.

She said, "Duncan got the address in Ojai from Google. It's a house in an orchard of avocados and pixie tangerines."

"She's definitely there," Walker said.

"How do you know?"

"Years of experience as a US marshal hunting fugitives. Trust me on this."

"Duncan said we should forward the information we have to the FBI and let the big boys handle it—Homeland Security, the CDC,

SHIELD, the Salvation Army, 4-H, and whomever else has been brought in."

"What did you say?"

"I said we would, once we know if Justine Bryce is really there," Eve said. "We don't want to waste their valuable time and resources if we're wrong."

"That's actually a reasonable argument."

"That's what Duncan said, too, like it was shocking to hear anything reasonable coming from me."

"We wouldn't want to piss off 4-H," Walker said.

"No, we wouldn't."

She hung up and they drove in, Walker following her farther north on the freeway for another twenty minutes, then east onto Highway 33, past acres of rusted oil pumps bobbing in the weeds.

The highway narrowed into a two-lane rural back road as it snaked through the hills into the Ojai Valley. They drove along the edge of town, past orchards and farms and a dry, rocky riverbed, before turning onto a dusty private road.

They followed the road past rows of fruit trees to a sprawling country-Victorian main house with a wraparound porch on a rise that overlooked the whole orchard. Ceiling fans spun slowly on the porch, which was lined with rocking chairs. All that was missing, Walker thought, was an ice-cold pitcher of mint juleps or lemonade to make it a perfect picture.

Eve parked in a crushed-gravel patch beside the house and Walker pulled his truck beside her car. They got out simultaneously and the first thing he noticed was how quiet it was, and that the air had a pleasing fruity, floral scent that was real, not something out of a can. The aroma was missing that metallic chemical after-smell with notes of disinfectant.

An elderly woman with a wide-brimmed straw hat was tending to an exquisite rose garden in front of the house and she turned to greet them with a warm, welcoming smile. But neither Walker nor Eve got too close to her in case she'd been exposed to Justine Bryce.

"Can I help you?" she asked.

Walker flashed his badge. "I'm Andrew Walker and this is Eve Ronin. We're detectives from the Los Angeles County Sheriff's Department."

"Cilla Gentry," she said, taking off her gloves. "I like your hat."

"Thank you," he said.

"You're a long way from home."

"We're trying to find Justine Bryce," he said. "Is she here?"

"Yes, she is, but I can't believe she's done anything wrong."

Eve glanced at Walker, then said, "She hasn't. This is a welfare check. Some of her coworkers are concerned about her and she's not answering her cell."

"Justine goes out of town for a couple of days and her friends call the police? That's ridiculous. They must be real tight-asses." Cilla wagged a finger at them. "You go back and tell them Justine is on vacation and is just fine."

"Have you seen her?"

"Justine called me on her way here and asked me not to disturb her. She and her boyfriend are having a romantic getaway, *incommunicado*, if you catch my drift." Cilla gave them a sly smile and, in case that was too subtle, added a wink. "I stocked the refrigerator before she got here with all kinds of goodies, including a few bottles of wine. There's also a pack of ribbed condoms in the nightstand."

That's hospitality, Walker thought. "So, you haven't actually talked to her face-to-face."

"I saw her car come in yesterday afternoon and they haven't left the cabin since. Probably haven't left the bed, either," Cilla said with a wistful sigh. "I wish I was that young and still had that kind of energy."

But tomorrow Cilla would be alive, and Justine probably wouldn't be, since they didn't meet in person.

The same thing must have occurred to Eve, who took a few steps toward Cilla now that she knew the old woman wasn't infected. "What's Justine's relation to you, Ms. Gentry? Is she family or a friend?"

"She's a friend, but I treat her like family. She's staying in the cabin."

"Is it an Airbnb or other sort of rental?"

Cilla shook her head. "This a working avocado and tangerine orchard, not a resort. Her late uncle Roy worked here for thirty years . . . and that cabin, which he built himself, was where he lived. When Justine was a child, she used to visit often to chase the chickens, pick tangerines, and have adventures. After Roy died, I gave the cabin to her. He would have wanted that."

"That was nice of you," Eve said. "Can you tell us how to get to the cabin? We need to make sure she's okay."

"You don't believe me? You think I'm holding her hostage or something?"

"Of course not," Eve said. "It's just standard procedure in these situations."

"Just continue straight down this dirt road. At the fork, make a left. On your way out, help yourself to some tangerines."

"Thank you," Eve said.

Walker added, "Is there a phone in the cabin?"

"No, and she's not answering her mobile, either. So I suppose you can't warn them to put on their clothes before you get there. You might want to honk as you drive up, though."

"We'll do that," Eve said, and they walked back to their cars, conferring for a moment before they got inside.

Walker said, "I think Justine and Patrick were supposed to come here for a sex-fest, but when she got the bad news, she decided to come here anyway . . . to die."

Eve nodded. "It makes perfect sense. It's remote and it's full of good memories. She won't feel like she's dying alone."

"At least we know she's still alive and on her feet."

"How do we know that?"

"Because she hasn't burned the place down yet," he said. "She'll wait until the last minute, but she'll do it. She's not going to risk Cilla discovering her body and getting infected."

"Let's go in your truck," Eve said. "It doesn't scream police and we don't want her dropping a match before we can talk to her."

They got into his truck and he drove down the road, through the orchard, and toward a cabin that was a miniature version of the main house, down to the porch and dormers. There was even a flower garden in the otherwise dry dirt. A Lexus was parked beside the cabin.

When they were about twenty-five yards from the cabin, Walker pulled the truck over and they got out, walking the rest of the way.

As they got closer, Walker could see the doors of the Lexus were sealed with duct tape. A skull and crossbones was drawn in lipstick on the windows and a few words were written underneath.

STAY OUT OR YOU WILL DIE.

CHAPTER THIRTEEN

Walker and Eve stopped walking about fifteen yards from the front of the cabin. The drapes were closed, but Walker had the feeling they were being watched.

"Justine," Walker shouted. "We're Detectives Andrew Walker and Eve Ronin with the Los Angeles County Sheriff's Department. We're worried about you. Can you open a door or window a crack so we can talk?"

The front door opened a tiny bit. "You have good reason to be worried," Justine shouted back. "I'm dangerous. Stay away and upwind."

Her voice was strong, but riddled with anxiety.

When Walker spoke again, it was loudly, but it wasn't a shout, and he tried to sound calm. "How are you feeling?"

"I can't stop sobbing and vomiting, but I don't think that's the virus. I do that when I'm terrified, heartbroken, and furious . . . and I'm all three. But I haven't started hemorrhaging blood from everywhere yet, if that's what you're asking."

Eve looked at Walker, then said, "You don't need to go through this alone, Justine."

"Actually, I do. The alternative is letting the military stick me in a tube and take me back to a quarantined lab, where they'll closely and coldly observe every agonizing, humiliating, and dehumanizing aspect of my death for all the data they can get . . . and then dissect my body for more. I'll be immortalized in tissue and DNA samples."

"Are you planning to do what Patrick did?" Eve asked.

"What did he do?"

Eve glanced nervously at Walker and whispered, "What do I say?"

Walker turned to the cabin and answered for her. "He set his car and house on fire, then shot himself in the head."

Eve swatted his arm.

Walker glared at her and said in a low voice, "What? It's true."

"That was so insensitive."

"What would you have said?"

"That he took his own life."

"That makes suicide sound gentle, even appealing, given what she's facing," Walker said. "I wanted to jolt her into reality."

"You might have jolted her into putting a gun in her mouth."

Justine stepped halfway out the door. "I don't have a gun. I have a rope."

Walker and Eve scrambled a few steps farther back, though he figured they had to be a safe distance away or she wouldn't have revealed herself.

She wore a loosely cinched bathrobe over a tank top and pajama bottoms, her long brown hair tied into a bun, revealing a slender neck.

Eve said, "You heard all that?"

"Voices carry out here."

"I'm sorry."

"I've also got propane tanks," Justine said. "I'll light a candle, open the tanks up, then hang myself. The explosion will obliterate the cabin and me, so you might want to move a few steps further back."

Walker said, "You're doing that now?"

"No, but soon," she said, "while I still can."

"I'm an arson investigator, Justine, and I have to tell you, that plan needs some work."

Eve swatted him again. "You're going to help her burn herself up?"

"Why not?" Walker said, more for Justine's benefit than to answer Eve's question. "She wants to be sure nobody else gets infected and I want her to succeed. It's a noble thing she's doing."

Justine said, "What Patrick did wasn't just about sparing his family and everyone else from this weaponized virus. He was punishing himself."

Eve said, "For what?"

"Me. Us. He felt deep guilt about our affair . . . but he couldn't quit me. I couldn't give him up, either. We could have died here together, in each other's arms, but he didn't want his infidelity to be the final impression he left with his family. I hope they never know about us. But the last thing he said to me was 'I love you.'"

"That was right after you got the devastating call from Colin Oxley," Eve said.

"I wish it had been anybody else," Justine said. "Getting the news from Colin, of all people, only made it worse, if that's even possible."

"Because you knew how heartbroken he'd be," Walker said. "I can tell you that he is. He treasures that Baby Yoda you gave him and always will."

Eve gave him a look, but he ignored her. Sometimes lies revealed interesting things.

"I didn't give it to him," Justine said sharply. "Did he tell you that?"

"Colin said you shared a passion."

"He wanted to but . . . yuck." Justine cringed and for a moment, Walker thought she might vomit. "I made the mistake of telling him I thought Baby Yoda was cute and then he inundated me with the damn toys. I told him to stop, but he claimed it wasn't him who sent them, and he kept doing it."

"Why did you save them all in a trash bag?"

"I was going to drop them off at Children's Hospital, where they could do some good," she said. "Right after I filed a complaint with human resources at Triax and showed them what he'd sent me."

Eve said, "The way to a woman's heart is not through her Yoda."

Justine laughed, surprising Walker and Eve. It also gave Walker some hope, encouraging him to ask a stupid question.

"How do you know that you're infected?"

"There was a leak," she said. "And this virus is aggressively contagious."

"But it's been almost twenty-four hours and you're not showing any symptoms."

"It's not unprecedented. A few victims didn't show symptoms for several days. They were outliers and so am I. I'll probably start turning inside out tonight or certainly by tomorrow. It won't be pretty."

"Before you do anything you can't undo," Walker said, "let us call someone to get a sample of your blood for testing."

"It's pointless," she said. "By the time the results come back, we'll already know if I'm infected. It will be painfully and disgustingly obvious."

"Then what do you have to lose by doing it?"

"The right to die how I want," Justine said. "You'll try to stop me from ending my life and the virus my way."

"I won't, and I won't let anyone else do it, either. You have my word."

Eve said, "The same goes for me. On top of that, while we are waiting for the results, Walker will help you fine-tune your plan to blow up the cabin so it will work."

Justine looked hopefully at Walker. "You'd really do that for me?"

"Sure. Just don't tell anyone."

"Who am I going to tell? I'll be dead."

He shrugged. "There are Ouija boards."

Justine laughed, long and hard, and so did Walker and Eve, easing the tension.

When the laughter died down, Justine was still smiling. "Thank you, Walker. I never thought I'd laugh again."

"I'm banking on you surviving," he said, "and the three of us sharing a secret."

Eve went back to the truck and made calls to Triax and the FBI while Walker discussed the fine points of her suicide plan for blowing up the house.

Thirty minutes later, a helicopter landed in a clearing near the cabin and a man wearing a bright-yellow biohazard suit and carrying a metal case went into the cabin. While he did that, two other men in biohazard suits emerged from the helicopter. One carried some kind of power-sprayer, the fluid in a tank on his back, and the other carried a metal box and long tool with a pincer at the end.

The first man came out of the cabin a few minutes later, carrying his metal case, and his colleague with the sprayer washed him down with some kind of foaming chemical. The soaked man peeled off his biohazard suit and stood there naked and unashamed as he was sprayed down again.

The third man opened his box, took out a Tyvek jumpsuit for the now disinfected naked man to put on, then used the pincer tool to pick up the discarded biohazard suit and place it into the box, which he closed and latched shut.

The first man, now in the jumpsuit, picked up the disinfected metal case, his colleague picked up the box, and the three of them went back into the helicopter and flew away.

"That was quite a show," Eve said.

Walker called out to the house. "How'd it go?"

Justine stepped halfway out of her cabin again. "He took blood, saliva, and urine samples from me."

Walker said, "No stool sample?"

Justine laughed. "I'm not a dog and I don't have worms."

"There you go," he said. "It could be worse."

Eve said, "I have to be honest with you. The Feds and all their friends are coming. They are probably going to treat you like a criminal."

"Because I'm a threat, and a resource."

"We made you a promise, Justine, and we are going to keep it," Eve said. "You let us know if you start feeling sick . . . and we'll keep them back until the house blows up."

It wasn't a promise Walker was sure they could keep, but he added: "You may hear me exaggerating some aspects of the situation to the Feds to keep them from bothering you. Just play along."

"What is there to exaggerate? Are you going to tell them I have a nuclear bomb, too, and that my shaky finger is on the trigger?"

"That's not a bad idea," he said. "I'll think about it. On a different subject, how are the tangerines here?"

"Like candy," she said.

◆ ◆ ◆

The first law enforcement agency representative to arrive was a captain from the Ventura County Sheriff's Department, who was furious that they'd come into his county without notifying him beforehand. He was still railing at Walker and Eve when the FBI arrived in a fleet of vehicles, along with a Triax biohazard team and Dash Nolan.

The FBI agent in charge of the operation was Donna Leyland. She was the agent who'd called Walker and Eve after they'd left Justine's house. Leyland didn't have to introduce herself for Walker to know it was her. Her attitude said it all.

Leyland was dressed in a power pantsuit Hillary Clinton would love and marched right over to them, pushing the VCSD captain aside so she could start her own tirade. The captain slunk away, wanting no part of it.

Walker started peeling a tangerine. It was his third. Justine was right—they *were* like candy.

"I told you both to stay out of this," Leyland said, "and yet here you are."

"You're welcome," Walker said, concentrating on his peeling. His hands were sticky with juice.

"I don't like your attitude."

"How was your search going? How close were you to finding Bryce here?" Walker asked. She just stared at him. "The fact is, you'd still be chasing your ponytail if it wasn't for us." Walker paused for a second to admire his perfectly peeled tangerine. "So, if you aren't going to thank us for doing your job for you, shut up and go back to your car."

Leyland got so close to him, he thought she might take a bite out of his fruit. "You are under the mistaken impression that you're in charge here, Walker. You're not. I am."

Walker smiled and popped a piece of tangerine in his mouth. Eve stepped between them, which wasn't easy, given how close they were.

"You're here because I invited you," Eve said, nose to nose with Leyland. "The only people Justine will talk to are me and Walker. And if any of you cross this line . . ." Eve stepped away from Leyland and used her foot to make a line in the dirt between all of them and the cabin, which was about twenty yards away. "It's over."

"Over?" Leyland said. "What is *that* supposed to mean?"

Walker said, "Justine has got that entire cabin rigged to blow with fertilizer explosives. You try to move in and there won't be anything left here but a crater."

"She's bluffing," Leyland said.

"A fertilizer bomb took down the entire federal building in Oklahoma City. You don't think it will destroy that little shack?" He ate another piece of fruit and offered the rest to Eve, who took it.

Leyland said, "What are her demands?"

Eve ate some tangerine before replying. "The right to die the way she wants, when she wants."

"She doesn't have that right. She signed it away when she took the job at Triax."

Walker said, "She gave Triax power of attorney over her life?"

"Bryce should have read the fine print in her employment contract," Leyland said. "In the event of an infection, she agreed to abide by the directives of those in charge. That's me." She poked herself with her thumb, in case there was any doubt.

"You keep repeating that like it's a magic spell," Walker said. "It isn't."

"There are bigger issues at play here than one person's life," Leyland said. "She's in possession of classified information."

Eve said, "She didn't take a file. She was infected with a virus."

"And it belongs to us."

"You mean her death does, and the data it could provide."

"Whatever," Leyland said.

Walker said, "Nobody is doing anything until we get the test results back from Triax."

"It's not your decision to make."

"You're right." Walker gestured to the cabin. "It's hers. Now back off. You're irritating me and I can smell the taco you had for lunch. My advice, lay off the onions."

Leyland glowered at him. "There are going to be serious repercussions for this."

"Not for us," Eve said. "We aren't the ones who failed. You are, Donna."

As Leyland marched back to her car, Eve caught her holding a hand up to her mouth, checking her breath.

Eve turned to Walker. "Chasing her ponytail?"

"Was that sexist?"

"At least you didn't call her sweetie, honey, or little lady."

"I didn't want you to shoot me," Walker said, then strolled toward the cabin, stepped over Eve's line, and stopped at what he hoped was a safe distance from the cabin to avoid germs. "How are you doing, Justine?"

She opened the door a crack but didn't show her face. "All of my sphincters are holding, my skin isn't bubbling, and I haven't seen any of my internal organs yet, so I'm good. I heard most of that conversation with the FBI agent. She's a bitch."

"Agent Leyland is just doing her job, same as us."

"You're doing more than that," she said. "I'm tempted to end this right now just to spite her."

"Please don't," Walker said. "It would really ruin our day."

"*Your* day? What about mine?" Justine said with amusement, not malice. He could hear the smile in her voice and it made him happy.

"Don't worry, I'll give you a few seconds of advance warning so you don't get any of me on your nice hat."

"I appreciate it," Walker said, and then turned his back to the house to face Eve as she approached. He whispered, "She's teasing me. That's a good sign that she's in no hurry to kill herself."

"Yes, it is," Eve whispered back. "You've established a rapport. You remind me a bit of Duncan."

"Do I have a gut? Have I stained my shirt with tangerine juice?"

"It's the way you both use humor and honesty to gain trust. But yes, you've got tangerine juice all over you."

Walker looked past her and saw Dash Nolan finishing a call and excitedly approaching Leyland, who turned and waved them over to join the conversation. Walker and Eve did.

Nolan spoke in a rush. "It's unbelievable. All of Justine's tests are negative. She's not infected. It makes no sense. Maybe she's got some kind of natural immunity."

"Or there was never a leak," Eve said. "You need to do a forensic deep dive on that lab."

"The lab has been incinerated," Nolan said. "There's nothing left to investigate."

"The computerized security alert system still exists, doesn't it? Maybe there's a bug, one that cost Patrick Lopresti his life."

Nolan bristled at that. "Even if there was, we didn't tell him to kill himself. We told him to come back. His death is on him."

"It certainly is," Walker said. "You don't think maybe you were even a little bit at fault?"

"It's over now and nobody else has been hurt, that's what matters," Nolan said, then looked at Leyland. "What's the next step?"

Walker answered for her. "You go in, Dash, and tell Justine the good news."

Nolan clearly didn't like that idea. "Why don't you simply tell her she can come out?"

"She might think it's a trap."

"How could we possibly trap her?"

"She steps out into the open, a sniper shoots her with a tranquilizer dart, and your biohazard team puts her in a jar to bring her back to the lab."

Leyland chortled. "That's ridiculous."

Eve said, "So what are those snipers doing in the trees? Duck hunting?" She pointed to the hillside. Walker hadn't seen any snipers and still couldn't. "What I'm wondering is if they'll fire tranquilizers or live rounds."

Leyland looked her in the eyes. "They are prepared for both. It depends on what I tell them."

"You're going to tell them to stand down," Eve said. "Because Justine isn't infected and Dash is going in to tell her."

"Okay, fine," Nolan said, raising his hands in surrender. "I'll go suit up."

Walker said, "You are already suited up, Dash. If the tests really are negative, you have nothing to fear. That's the whole point of you walking in there. Don't you have faith in your scientists and your equipment?"

"They aren't mine," he said. "I handle security."

"Either you believe what you've been told or you don't."

Nolan hesitated a moment, then nodded.

"That a boy." Walker put his arm around Nolan's shoulders and led him toward the cabin.

CHAPTER FOURTEEN

Walker and Nolan walked slowly, side by side, across twenty yards of dirt.

"Is Dash a nickname or short for something?"

"Dashiell," Nolan said.

"Like Dashiell Hammett?"

"My parents owned a mystery bookstore in Colorado. My sister's name is Agatha."

"You poor kids."

"Tell me about it."

Walker stopped at the duct-taped Lexus covered with lipstick warnings and raised his voice. "Justine, you better set the table with the good dishes. You're having company."

Justine replied from behind the closed door. "Should I light the candles?"

"Nope. It's just Dash and me. Take a peek."

She opened the door a crack and they could see the bewildered expression on her face. "You aren't wearing biohazard suits."

"That should give you a hint about what we're coming to tell you."

"Are you sure you want to do this?"

Walker glanced at Nolan, who looked uneasy.

"The tests all came back negative," Nolan said. "You aren't infected."

She opened the door but also took a step back into the house, out of sight of any snipers . . . or at least that's what Walker assumed she was doing.

"Then come on in and close the door behind you," she said. "I have ice-cold fresh-pressed tangerine juice."

They stepped inside and closed the door behind them. The walls were white shiplap, which Carly would have loved, because it was just like one of the modern country renovations that wholesome Texas couple did on *Fixer Upper*, an HGTV show she adored.

Justine was still wary, clutching her bathrobe tightly closed around her. "You're a fool, Walker. Why did you come in here with him?"

"To make you feel better."

"How is having your death on my conscience, in the few hours I have left, going to do that?"

"If you were infected, do you think they'd let us just walk in here?"

"Sure, so you two could walk me outside, into the open, for capture and study."

Nolan said, "That makes no sense, Dr. Bryce. We'd both be infected, too."

Justine shrugged off the objection. "Acceptable losses as far as the government and Triax are concerned . . . and a bonus. They'll have two more victims they can study."

That hadn't occurred to Walker. He took a seat at the dining room table. "I really should have thought this through."

Nolan shook his head. "Come on, Dr. Bryce. Do you honestly believe that they are so cold, calculating, and inhuman that they'd lie about the test?"

"You tell me, Dash. You're the Triax hatchet man. We were working with a genetically altered strain that no human being has been infected with before. Analyzing our sickness and death would provide a treasure trove of data. What do you think they'd be willing to do for that?"

"Okay, then what's your plan? We sit here together, drinking juice and playing cards for a few hours, waiting to see if you start to molt?"

Walker said, "And people say that *I'm* insensitive."

Justine said, "I want you to walk outside without me or Walker and go back to the others. If they don't run for their lives, and if you don't get shot, I'll know it's all true . . . and that this nightmare is over."

Walker glanced at her. "Why do you want me to stay?"

"Because if we *are* infected, and if you're in here, you can decide if you want to die fast and painlessly with me," she said, then tilted her head toward the front door. "Or slow and under a microscope with them."

"I think we're all going to be fine. Go on out, Dash, and prove it to her."

Nolan walked out the door. Walker and Justine peeked through the edges of the window drapes and watched him. He got all the way back to the others without anybody moving away. And nobody shot him.

Justine gave Walker a hug and kissed him tenderly on the cheek. "Thank you for saving my life."

"I didn't. That was always your choice."

"I nearly made the wrong one." She took his hand in hers and they walked out together, and were met first by Eve. "Thank you both for everything you've done. Can I ask you for one more favor?"

Eve said, "We haven't done any favors for you yet."

"You were willing to risk your careers to give me the right to die."

"It didn't come to that," Eve said, "so it doesn't count."

"Is there a way to keep Patrick's family from finding out about our affair? I don't want to add to their suffering."

"We'll do our best, but we can't make any promises."

Justine nodded, then joined Nolan and the Triax biohazard team, who were getting out of their suits. She seemed to know them all and there were lots of hugs all around.

Leyland approached Walker and Eve. "This isn't over for you."

"Yes, it is," Eve said. "This entire operation was off the books. You can't come after us without every single detail of it coming out, and I assure you, it will."

Walker said, "If you've seen Eve's TV series, you know she's not bluffing. She'll tell this all to the press and, if that wasn't bad enough, it will also become a *Ronin* episode. You'll be played by a talking duck."

Leyland glowered at them and marched off past Nolan, who was talking happily, and animatedly, to someone on his phone.

Walker turned to Eve. "She's right. It's not over for us."

"You believe the Feds will try to penalize us anyway?"

"Don't be coy," he said. "You know what I'm talking about."

"I have a legitimate homicide case to investigate now."

Walker nodded. "What are you waiting for?"

Eve marched over to Nolan, who was pocketing his phone. Walker followed so he could eavesdrop.

She said, "I suppose the news about Justine being found alive and that she's uninfected is all over Triax by now."

"Are you kidding?" Nolan said. "They're cheering so loud in Thousand Oaks, it's astonishing that we can't hear them."

"Did somebody think to call Colin Oxley?"

"Of course! I just did," Nolan said. "The poor guy took this harder than any of us. I can't imagine how relieved he must be now. I asked if he wanted to talk with Justine, but he could barely speak himself. He was too choked up."

"I'm sure he was," Eve said. Nolan went back to his happy team and Eve turned to Walker. "Think Oxley will run?"

"It might be fun if he tried, but I'd like to get home tonight for dinner and put my son to bed. I'm reading him *The Cat in the Hat*. That cat is very mischievous. Who knows what he will do next?"

"Does that mean you aren't coming with me to La Cañada?"

"Hell no, I'm coming," he said. "We still have a few more hours left until dinner and I want to see how this cat's story ends."

◆ ◆ ◆

Walker had lost track of how many times he'd crisscrossed the San Fernando Valley that day and he'd still have to do it at least once more to get home. But all the hours he'd spent on the freeway were a small trade-off for the excitement he'd experienced at his destinations.

He'd fought a house fire in Chatsworth in the morning, then found a fugitive in an Ojai tangerine orchard in the afternoon and rescued her from an explosive suicide.

He wished every day could be like that.

And the day wasn't even over yet, though now he was just an interested observer, following Eve Ronin out to La Cañada Flintridge. It was her case now, which reminded him that he needed to bring Sharpe up to speed.

Walker called Sharpe, who was still at Twin Lakes, and told him about Ojai.

"Good work," Sharpe said. "You've made a big enemy at the FBI."

"You, of all people, are criticizing me for that?"

"It was a compliment," Sharpe said. "Making enemies at the FBI means you're doing your job well. Keep this up, and soon you'll have enemies everywhere."

"Just like you."

"Something to aspire to."

"How are things going out there?"

Sharpe sighed wearily. "We've done exploratory demolition in the remaining completed homes and haven't found any more improvised incendiary devices near power outlets."

"Have you spotted any signature work in the bombs?"

"The devices are meticulously constructed using common products and are identical, right down to the precise measurement and application of the electrical tape he used to attach the coffee-maker heating elements to the juice bottles. Even the packing of wood chips, paper, and Styrofoam around the devices was done with care. It was as if he was going to be graded on it."

Walker said, "So we aren't looking for a deranged, drooling maniac who gets a hard-on from fire."

"You can be deranged without drooling or running around with an erection," Sharpe said. "Take yourself, for example."

"Did you mean that as a compliment, too?"

"Absolutely."

Walker promised to keep him informed, then called Carly to let her know that he'd be late again.

"Are you arresting some bad guys?" she asked.

"Eve Ronin is. I'm her backup. Want me to get you an autograph?"

"That's so last century," Carly said. "Get a selfie with her. Which case is this?"

"The arson from yesterday. You were right. It's all about adultery, guilt, and broken hearts."

"Sex is complicated."

"Not with us," he said.

"Yes, it is. You just don't think about all the emotional, psychological, and physical issues at play in our bed."

"Because there aren't any."

"I just had a baby and am working through my new sense of self, as a mother and sexual being, and dealing with the changes in my body."

"You are?" Walker said. "I haven't noticed any of that."

"Some detective you are."

"Commit a crime and I'll notice right away." His phone beeped and he looked at the caller ID. "It's Ronin. I've got to take this. I love you."

"Likewise."

"*Likewise?* That's kind of lukewarm."

"Because now I'm pissed at you."

His phone beeped again. "You are?"

"God, you're clueless." Carly hung up and, still bewildered by their conversation, he took Eve's call.

"I'm here," Walker said.

"I know, I can see you in my rearview mirror. I've got Duncan on the line with us. You're not going to believe what he's found out about Colin Oxley."

Duncan said, "He's an active member of the Southern California chapter of the incels."

"What's an incel?"

"Involuntarily celibate," Duncan said. "They're socially awkward men who're desperate to have sex, but no women will sleep with them despite their good looks, fancy educations, big salaries, and winning personalities."

"They have a club?"

"Not officially, but they get together on social media to vent their anger at the unfairness of it all and discuss ways to achieve their political and cultural agenda."

"What's on the agenda besides getting laid?"

"They believe they are entitled to sex and that feminism has wrongly empowered women to choose their lovers," Duncan said. "As a result, 80 percent of the country's sexual wealth, meaning all the hot women, is hoarded by the top 20 percent of men, who are rich, smooth talking, and very powerful. The incels want to spread that wealth . . . by violent revolution if necessary. That's why the LASD considers them a domestic terrorist group and Oxley's name was in our database."

"Oh boy."

Eve said, "It was bad enough that Justine rejected Oxley, but then she chose Patrick."

Duncan said, "A married man who already got his slice of sex pie and is gorging himself with another one."

"Sex pie?" Walker said.

"I'm hungry and it clouds my thinking," Duncan said. "What Justine and Patrick did was intolerable for an incel like Oxley. They could be the poster couple for the whole incel movement."

"Rage and revenge," Walker said. "Two strong motives for murder."

Eve said, "It's even better if you can get the people you hate to kill themselves for you."

Duncan said, "I'll send backup to meet you two at Oxley's place. He may not go down without a fight."

"That's true," Eve said. "He could come at us with a lightsaber."

"Even if it's a real one," Walker said, "it wouldn't worry me. There's an old saying. Maybe you know it."

"Don't bring a lightsaber to a gunfight?"

"That's the one," Walker said.

It was dark when they parked at the curb in front of Colin Oxley's property, where an LASD patrol car was already waiting.

Walker and Eve got out of their cars to confer with the deputies, who regarded her with open hostility. She gave Walker a nod and stayed put by her Charger while he went up to talk to them.

"What's the play?" one of the deputies asked.

"A routine arrest of a homicide suspect," Walker said. "I don't think he wants a gunfight but he might try to jackrabbit on us."

"We have another unit out back in case he tries to make a break for it."

"Stay here," Walker said. "We'll shout if we need you."

Walker turned and joined Eve, who said, "I wouldn't count on them backing us up."

"You don't think they're fans of yours?"

"Nope."

"Good." He took out his phone. "They won't try to horn in when I take a selfie with you."

"I don't do selfies, but I'll make an exception for you."

"It's for my wife." He got beside her, held up the phone, and took the picture with the deputies in the background. "I've got a question I forgot to ask you in Ojai."

"Shoot."

Walker pocketed his phone. "When did you spot those snipers?"

"I didn't."

"Nice bluff," he said.

"I've got a question I forgot to ask you, too." Eve started walking down the driveway and he fell into step beside her.

"Shoot."

"Why did you go in the cabin with Dash?"

"It felt like the right thing to do. At least until I got inside, and then it felt like the biggest mistake of my life."

"Thinking about becoming a mail carrier now?"

"And miss this? Hell no."

There was only a single light on inside the house, behind a half-open living room window.

Outside the house, Walker could see dots of blue light along the roofline, indicating the locations of several small security cameras mounted in the eaves. The blue lights were intended to let intruders, and now detectives, know that they were being watched.

Walker and Eve weren't dissuaded. They stepped onto the path that led to the front door. Oxley's voice boomed out from the speaker in one of the mounted cameras.

"Go away. I don't want to talk with you."

Walker stopped, midway between the driveway and the house, and looked up at the nearest blue dot. It was near the front door.

"We don't care."

Eve gave him a glare that reminded him that this was her show, not his. He shrugged his apology, and then she faced the dot.

"We know what you did, Colin," she said. "You lied about the leak. It was all a trick to get Justine and Patrick to kill themselves."

"I can't have her, but a *married* man can? He already has a woman," Oxley said. "It's so unfair. It's a crime."

"So is murder."

"Somebody had to punish them for their unforgivable offenses against me, man, and nature," Oxley said. "You certainly weren't going to do it."

"We'll make up for it by punishing you instead," Eve said.

"Who is going to punish *you*? How many men have you refused to mate?"

Walker turned to Eve. "And he wonders why he can't get laid."

Oxley said, "The world is out of balance and I can't live in it anymore."

All the lights inside the house went on.

Walker tackled Eve to the ground at the same instant that an explosion obliterated the house.

CHAPTER FIFTEEN

Walker rolled off Eve, bits of wood, glass, and stucco on his back, his Stetson lying in the weeds several feet away.

It felt like he'd broken out in a flash sweat. His ears were ringing, his back stung, and he was coughing on the dust that was everywhere.

He looked at Eve, who was face down beside him. "Are you okay?"

At least Walker thought he'd said that. He could barely hear himself speak. The ringing in his ears drowned out almost everything.

Eve sat up, nodded, and said something, but he couldn't hear it. But she was conscious, he didn't see any blood on her, and she wasn't writhing in agony, so he figured she was fine.

She spoke again, louder this time, but it still sounded like a whisper to him. "I thought we'd avoided our exploding house for the day."

"Me too," Walker said, the ringing in his ears slowly ebbing as the dust settled on them and the rubble everywhere.

He looked back at the house. It was still standing, but the living room was ablaze. One of the nearby eucalyptus trees was also on fire, shooting off embers like a sparkler. If firefighters didn't arrive soon, Walker knew that the tree alone could ignite the whole neighborhood.

Eve said, "How did you know the house was going to blow?"

"I didn't, not consciously anyway. The lights went on and then my reflexes took over. I'm as surprised by what I did as you are."

Walker stood up, staggered over to the weeds, and recovered his Stetson. The high center of the hat was perforated with holes from the shards of glass and wood that had passed through it.

He swept a hand through his hair, didn't feel anything sharp, and then wiped the sweat off the back of his neck.

"You're bleeding," Eve said behind him. He looked at his hand. The palm was red. It wasn't sweat on his neck. It was blood. "Take off your shirt."

While he did that, Eve shouted to the two deputies, who were getting to their feet from behind their patrol car. The deputies seemed dazed.

"Don't just stand there," she said. "Call this in. We need firefighters and paramedics."

Walker turned to her. "Paramedics? Is it that bad?"

"Look at your shirt."

He did. The front was fine, but the back was covered with tiny tears and bloodstains.

Walker balled up the shirt and tossed it on the ground. "My wife is going to kill me."

Sharpe and Duncan arrived at Oxley's house in separate cars an hour later, just as the firefighters were mopping up and the paramedics were leaving.

Walker and Eve sat on the tailgate of his pickup truck, sharing one of the four Domino's pizzas that had just been delivered.

Walker had a bandage on the back of his neck and was shirtless, letting his back dry in the warm evening breeze. His back was slick with the disinfectant cream applied by the paramedics to the tiny wounds from the glass and wood slivers they'd plucked out of his skin with tweezers. The paramedics wanted Walker to go to the ER, but he'd refused, put his hat on his head, and called Domino's instead.

Now Sharpe gave Walker a once-over, his gaze settling on the Stetson, dotted with punctures. "I see that you survived, but I'm not so sure about your hat."

Duncan faced Eve. "Are you okay?"

"Yes, thanks to Walker."

"This is a big moment." Duncan helped himself to a slice of pizza. "It's your first major case that didn't end with you in the ER."

Walker looked at her. "Is that true?"

"Sadly, yes." She turned back to Duncan. "We have to stick around. CSU won't be here for another hour or so because they know Sharpe will want to do his thing."

"By that, you mean my job," Sharpe said, then glanced at the house. "I've got this strange sense of déjà vu."

Walker said, "We do see a lot of burned houses in our line of work."

"But I don't think we've ever seen so many in one day."

Eve dabbed her mouth with a napkin. She'd been starving, too. "This is also the second house fire in twenty-four hours where a guy killed himself inside. The medical examiner is on her way, too."

Duncan spoke with his mouth full. "You sure Oxley is in there?"

Eve nodded. "The firefighters found his body inside and we had the house covered outside, front and back. Nobody came out before the blast."

"Just to be sure," Duncan said, "I'll get a warrant going for the security camera footage as soon as I finish eating."

"At least you have your priorities in order," Sharpe said.

"I need a full stomach and a clear head to be at my most charming and persuasive."

Sharpe turned to Walker. "How did you know the house was going to explode?"

"Eve asked me the same question," Walker said. "I saw the lights go on inside the house and I tackled her. Now that I've had some time to think about it, I suppose the lights subconsciously reminded me of those Twin Lakes homes that burst into flames as soon as they got power."

Sharpe grinned. "Of course it did."

"Why are you giving me that stupid grin?"

"Because you're beginning to absorb your experiences in the field, but most of all—"

Duncan leaned over to Eve. "Here it comes . . ."

"—you're internalizing the invaluable knowledge I've shared with you."

"And there it is," Duncan declared. "That legendary Sharpe humility again."

Sharpe ignored Duncan's comment and added: "My training has even sharpened your observational skills."

Walker shook his head, which made his neck sting under the bandage. "My wife would strongly disagree with that."

"It's an entirely different kind of observation than she's talking about."

"How do you know that?"

Duncan answered for Sharpe. "Women are all the same and so are their complaints about men."

Eve said, "That's a sexist generalization."

"The point is," Sharpe said, continuing to address himself to Walker, "the fundamentals of arson investigation are becoming instinctive to you."

"I don't think so."

"You just proved it. The lights going on an instant before the blast is probably related to how it was triggered."

"You think so?"

"Let's go find out," Sharpe said.

Duncan said, "I'll stay out here, guard the pizzas, and start working on that warrant."

The three of them went to Sharpe's Tahoe for the necessary equipment.

Walker put on a disposable Tyvek jumpsuit, which he didn't mind staining with antiseptic cream, blood, and soot. Besides, he couldn't keep walking around like Tarzan of the Arson Squad.

Eve got her own hard hat, gloves, goggles, and mask and also hefted Walker's evidence bag for him. He didn't argue with her about carrying the bag and accepted her thoughtfulness with an appreciative nod.

In a way, Walker was glad the house had exploded, or he'd have felt foolish tackling Eve for nothing. And she wouldn't have appreciated it much, either.

They joined Sharpe, who stood with his kit on the front path, roughly in the same spot where they'd been when the house exploded.

Eve said, "The fire chief says it looks bad, but the house is still structurally sound. It won't collapse on us."

"We don't know that," Sharpe said. "They're firefighters, not structural engineers. There's an 80 percent chance they're totally wrong."

On that troubling note, Eve and Walker both put on their hard hats and cinched the straps tight under their chins.

Sharpe looked at Walker. "Tell me what you saw when you arrived."

"One light was on in the living room, behind a half-open window. The rest of the lights were off, unless you count the little blue lights from the surveillance cameras."

Sharpe looked at the windows that had been blown out by the force of the blast, his gaze resting on a wall that had disintegrated, revealing the decimated kitchen. Only the dented appliances, obliterated cabinets, and twisted piping left behind indicated what the space had once been.

"The explosion clearly happened in the kitchen, where there is the most damage," Sharpe said. "Based on the apparent force of the blast, the level of destruction, the dispersal pattern of the debris, and the lack of soot on the glass shards, I'm guessing it was natural gas that ignited."

If a fire preceded the explosion, there would have been soot on the glass shards. That meant the fire came after the blast, and that bothered Walker, given how much flame damage he could see in the house.

"The fireball should have flamed out with the blast," Walker said. "But parts of the house are deeply burned. There must have been another accelerant involved."

"That's right." Sharpe gave him that big grin again. "You need to get blown off your feet more often. It's knocked some sense into your head."

"You really know how to flatter a guy."

Sharpe walked on to survey the debris. Eve turned to Walker.

"I'm lost," she said. "What are you talking about?"

"A gas explosion creates a wave of heat and pressure that radiates out in a circle from the source," Walker said. "If that force is in a contained space, like a house, it shatters everything in its path, the pulverized debris flying outward and ruining expensive cowboy hats."

"I get that," she said, her eyes straying from Walker as she noticed Sharpe wander off. "But what did you mean when you mentioned a secondary accelerant?"

"The flames should have died when the gas burned off, which was seconds after the blast," Walker said. "But half the place nearly burned down."

"I still don't get it."

"The blast moved at high speed through the house, and the flames did, too, riding the pressure wave. The passing flames might ignite curtains or papers, but not walls and furniture," Walker said. "For example, holding a match against a couch or a block of wood won't set it on fire. You need more sustained and intense heat to do that. It's why a campfire needs kindling to get the wood burning."

"Unless you've poured lighter fluid on the wood, or soaked the couch in gasoline," Eve said. "And the fireball ignites those vapors, too."

"Now you've got it," Walker said.

A few yards out from the house, Sharpe crouched in the weeds beside a crumpled stove that had obviously been blown through the kitchen wall. The appliance now resembled a huge crumpled beer can discarded by a slovenly giant.

Eve went over to Sharpe. "What's so interesting about the oven?"

"The force of the gas igniting around the stove propelled it through the wall," Sharpe said. "But that didn't happen with any of the other appliances."

"What does that tell you?" she said.

Sharpe wiggled the end of a half-inch-wide corrugated steel line that dangled from the rear of the stove. "That the gas line was disconnected."

"How do you know it wasn't severed when the stove was blown out of the kitchen?"

It was a reasonable question, one Walker might have asked himself a few months ago, but he thought by now Eve would know to just accept Sharpe's conclusions.

Sharpe gave her a withering look and she held up her hands in surrender.

"Never mind. Forget I asked."

"Look at the line," he said. "No tears. No crimping. No shredding. It's undamaged, which means it wasn't tethering the stove to the wall when the blast occurred."

Sharpe went back to the house and they followed him, putting on their masks before going in. They went inside through the kitchen's backyard doorway. The door itself was gone, presumably obliterated in the blast and strewn over the yard.

They moved carefully through the destruction in the kitchen and on into the adjoining living room, where the walls were charred, and the shelves of books, models, and *Star Wars* action figures were now piles of ash and melted plastic. The worst damage was to the captain's chair, the one that had faced the now-melted flat-screen TV, and to the blackened corpse that was sitting in it, heat-curled into the pugilistic stance. The distinctively shaped high-density-plastic gasoline can beside the chair left no question what the additional accelerant was.

Walker wandered over to the shattered remains of the Mandalorian display case, crumbled into a pile of debris that included the twisted frames from all the convention posters that had been hanging on the wall.

Sharpe went across the room to examine a deformed thermostat.

And Eve, the one homicide detective in the room, leaned over the charred body in the chair. "Looks to me like Oxley followed Lopresti's example. There's a gun in his hand and a gunshot wound in his head."

"Maybe," Sharpe said, still scrutinizing the thermostat. "Maybe not. Did you hear a gunshot?"

"Hard to say," she said. "If it happened the instant before the explosion."

Walker said, "We didn't hear a gunshot."

She turned to him. "How can you be sure?"

"Because that's not Oxley."

Now Sharpe turned to look at Walker, too.

Eve said, "You can tell that just by glancing at the burnt corpse from across the room?"

Walker gestured to the debris of the display case, a pile of ashes, broken glass, and bits of metal. "The Mandalorian suit is gone."

Eve walked over to him and inspected the debris without touching it. "Are you sure it didn't burn or melt?"

"There should be a lot of melted or obliterated plastic here from the so-called beskar armor plating. There isn't," Walker said. "Oxley treasured that suit. He couldn't incinerate it, and he thought nobody would notice that it was gone. But it is. And so is he."

Sharpe said, "I agree."

Eve whipped around to face him. "How can you say that? You never met the man or saw his Mandalorian suit."

"But I know about fire." Sharpe pointed to the thermostat. "That's one of those electronic thermostats. There's also a melted smart bulb in the lamp over there. This is a smart home."

"What does that prove?"

"I think he used his phone app to turn on the lights downstairs, maybe even the pilot light on the water heater, igniting the leaking gas in the kitchen and the gasoline vapors from the drenched couch,"

Sharpe said. "Colin Oxley wasn't in the house when you got here tonight. He was talking to you through the security app on his phone."

Walker was sure he was right. And it seemed to him that Eve thought so now, too.

She looked from Sharpe to the body in the chair. "So who is that?"

"He's your problem, not ours," Sharpe said. "You're the homicide detective here. We're just arson investigators."

The case wasn't closed after all, Walker thought. And that meant Eve still had a chance to end up in the ER before it was over.

CHAPTER SIXTEEN

Portable lights were set up around the perimeter of Oxley's property so that Sharpe, Nan Baker, and the CSU technicians could collect evidence inside the house and also from the wide debris field outside.

While they did that, Emilia Lopez documented the position of the body, briefly examined it, and then had it bagged by her assistants and taken to their van for transport to the morgue.

A crowd of two dozen neighbors and reporters on the street strained to see any activity, but their view was blocked by the trees, a couple of which were blackened by flames. The spectators were prevented from getting any closer by several stone-faced deputies and a line of yellow crime scene tape strung around the entire property. Several local news choppers circled overhead, getting "breaking news" footage for the 11:00 p.m. telecasts.

Walker should have been diagramming the debris field or bagging the evidence Sharpe collected, but his partner took pity on him because of his injuries and told him to sit.

So he did. Walker sat on the tailgate of his truck with Eve, waiting for some leads they could pursue.

Duncan stood a few yards away, talking on his phone, working his own angles on the case.

Emilia Lopez approached Walker and Eve on her way to her van. "I'm done here. All I can tell you is that it appears the victim died from a gunshot wound to the head, but I won't know for sure until I do the

Lee Goldberg

autopsy. The body has sustained a lot of damage from the explosion and the fire."

"Can you establish his identity?" Eve asked.

"Nan found Oxley's wallet, containing all of his ID, in the kitchen rubble," Emilia said. "Remarkably, it was only singed around the edges."

Walker wasn't swayed by that, or that Oxley's car was in the garage. "You could find the pope's ID in the kitchen, but that wouldn't mean the corpse is him."

Eve said, "Can you perform some more of your magic and lift his prints?"

"I don't know yet. We might have to rely on dental records, though he probably hasn't sat in a dentist's chair in decades. His teeth are a mess. I'm sure he smells better now than he did alive."

"Oxley's teeth were perfect," Eve said. "And he didn't smell bad."

Walker looked past Emilia and spotted Special Agent Leyland marching over to them. "I can't say the same for her."

"I'm going before she tries to take this body away from me, too." Emilia turned and made a beeline for her van.

Walker smiled cheerfully at Leyland. "It's so good to see you again today. You bring so much joy into our lives. Every time you show up, birds chirp, squirrels break into song, and flowers spontaneously bloom."

"What the fuck are you doing here?"

"See?" Walker said to Eve. "Pure joy."

"I'm investigating a homicide," Eve said. "Come for some lessons?"

"Who was killed?" Leyland asked.

"Patrick Lopresti."

"That was a suicide."

"Yes and no," Eve said. "He was having an extramarital affair with Justine Bryce, the object of Colin Oxley's unrequited affections. Oxley didn't take the rejection well."

"He's a member of the involuntarily celibate marching band," Walker said.

"Justine rejected Oxley for a married man," Eve said. "So he concocted the fake lab leak to get them to kill themselves."

Leyland put her hands on her hips. "That's vital information you withheld from us."

"They were leads we only recently developed."

"In the hour or so after the Ojai incident," Leyland said. "You honestly expect me to believe that horseshit?"

"We work fast."

"I'm taking over this investigation."

Walker glanced at Eve. "She never stops saying that."

Eve wasn't intimidated. "This is a homicide arising from a love triangle. That's not a federal case."

"It became one when we discovered that the leak alert was the result of a computer hack and that a vial of the virus is missing," Leyland said. "All the evidence leads directly to Oxley."

Walker shared a look with Eve. This was bad.

"Where are the smart-ass remarks now, Seinfeld?" Leyland said. "If you'd shared with us what you knew, we would have apprehended Oxley before he did this to himself. The only good thing to come out of this is that the vial was incinerated."

Walker grimaced, wishing he didn't have to tell Leyland the rest of the story.

"That's not Oxley in the body bag and I'm sure you won't find the vial in the house."

Leyland grimaced, too, and Walker could see her fighting to control her temper. The internal battle was all over her face. Or maybe she just had brutal acid reflux.

When she finally spoke, her voice was tight, controlled. "If you're right, then there's a killer on the run with enough doomsday virus to infect a stadium full of people. Thanks to you two. You are out of this. Do you understand me?"

"We don't work for you," Eve said, defiant.

"Your commanding officers have already promised me they'll put you on leashes and keep you in your backyards."

Of course they did, Walker thought. They didn't want to have anything to do with hunting down a "doomsday virus."

But Leyland wasn't done lecturing them. "You should be thankful that you still have your badges, at least for the time being. Because if Oxley causes any more death and destruction, it's on you two fuckups."

She marched away. Duncan watched her go, then joined Walker and Eve.

"Captain Dubois just called," he said. Then for Walker's benefit, he added: "That's our commanding officer at Lost Hills. He said the Feds are taking over. But he congratulated us on our fine work."

"That's nice," Eve said. "I must be growing on him."

"Before he called, I got a judge to give me a warrant over the phone for Oxley's camera footage and I notified the security company's law enforcement rep."

Walker was impressed. "You really are the warrant whisperer."

"But it was all for nothing."

"Because we're off the case?" Eve said.

"Because there's nothing to see. This morning Oxley wiped all the footage for the last thirty days." Duncan glanced at Leyland, who was in a huddle with a bunch of other Feds, who wore windbreakers emblazoned on the back with "FBI" in big yellow letters. "Should I tell the Feds what I know and save them the trouble of going after the video?"

"If you want to score some brownie points."

"Only if it comes with actual brownies."

"I don't think so," Eve said.

"Then screw them," Duncan said.

Sharpe walked down the front path to the three of them. He was covered with soot from his evidence-collecting.

"I just got a call from the LT, who felt, for some odd reason, that he had to remind us that we are arson investigators and not homicide detectives or federal agents," Sharpe said. Walker gestured to the huddled Feds. "Oh, I see. They have the nicest windbreakers in law enforcement."

"They sure do," Duncan said. "They almost look tailored."

"Anyway, I told the LT no problem, our job is already done here. The evidence is conclusive and overwhelming: the explosion was arson. Case closed."

"Oxley is still out there," Walker said.

"I hope the FBI catches him soon," Sharpe said. "But now we can focus all of our energy and attention on finding the arsonist who burned down two homes, planted a bunch of incendiary devices in two others, and is still at large."

Eve smiled at Walker. "You should be thrilled. At least you have someone to chase. You'll be too busy to be bitter and frustrated about this. But not me."

Duncan could see the disappointment on her face and said, "Hey, look at the bright side. Now there's a lot less work for us to do and Taylor's Steakhouse is still open for dinner."

"You already ate an entire pizza," she said.

"But Taylor's is legendary and I rarely get out here. I don't want to waste the opportunity."

Eve held her hand out to Walker. "Thank you for protecting me, Walker. I owe you one."

They shook hands. "No, you don't. It was nothing. Pure reflex."

"Until today, I believed there were only three people in this department that I could trust with my life," Eve said. "Now I know there's four."

Sharpe said, "What about me? You don't trust me?"

"I'm not even sure I like you."

"You don't," Duncan said. "Nobody does."

Duncan winked at Sharpe and left with Eve, both of them getting into their separate cars and driving off, presumably to a late steak dinner.

Sharpe watched her go. "I don't get why every deputy in the department wants to kill her. She's no more irritating than you are."

"It must be sexism."

"Must be," Sharpe said. "What are you going to tell your wife about all of your cuts?"

"I tripped and fell into a rosebush?"

"Yeah," Sharpe said. "That'll fly."

Walker drove to Reseda, crossing the valley yet again that day, his back stinging, a faint ringing still in his ears. He hoped that Carly would be asleep when he got home, but he also knew there was no way he'd be able to hide his injuries from her.

The house was quiet and dark when he arrived. He moved quietly down the hall, stopping to peek into Cody's room, and saw him sleeping peacefully in his crib, curled around Sharpie.

He crept into the main bedroom, where Carly was lightly snoring under the sheets, his side of the bed remarkably undisturbed. It amazed him. When he slept alone, he messed up the entire bed. How did she manage not to do that? It was a mystery he'd yet to solve.

As quietly as he could, he slipped into the bathroom and closed the door. He set his Stetson on his sink, took off his Tyvek suit, and temporarily stuffed it into a drawer until he could sneak it out to the trash. He didn't want her seeing the blood.

Walker started the shower and stepped under the spray, wincing as the water hit his raw back. But he didn't want to get into bed with Neosporin all over him. He put shampoo in his hair, lathered up, and was rinsing away any debris that might be there when he sensed he wasn't alone.

"Oh my God," Carly said.

He wiped the water and soap out of his eyes and saw his wife standing outside the shower in a tank top and panties, staring at him and holding his perforated Stetson in her hands.

Damn. I should have left that in the truck.

"It's nothing," he said. "A few little nicks. No worse than a morning shave."

"How can you say that? There are cuts all over your back and a big bandage on your neck. What happened to you?"

He turned off the water and stood there, naked and wet, in front of her.

"The thing is, if I tell you, it's going to sound much worse than it was, because there's no way to say it that doesn't exaggerate the situation."

Carly tossed his hat on the sink, took a bath towel off a nearby rack, and held it out to him. "Tell me."

He took the towel from her and dried off. "We went to arrest a guy and his house exploded."

"Holy shit."

"See, that's the reaction I was afraid of, just because I said 'explosion,' which is a loaded word. It was really no big deal."

She stuck a finger in one of the holes of his hat and held it out to him. "You could have been killed."

He wrapped the towel around his waist and stepped out of the shower. "I could get killed crossing the street or slipping in this shower. I've been through much worse."

That day, in fact, but he wasn't going to tell her about running into a burning house to rescue Sharpe.

"Don't be an idiot." She dropped the hat and pulled him into a hug.

"You're supposed to tell me how heroic and noble I am."

"Where do you get that crap?"

"Spenser."

She took her head off his damp chest so she could look at him, but she didn't let go and neither did he. "Who is Spenser?"

"He's a Boston private eye whose girlfriend is a psychiatrist. She's always telling him that kind of stuff and that she accepts the risks that come from his gallant pursuits."

"That's ridiculous. He told you that?"

"They're characters in some books and an old TV show."

"You expect me to behave like a TV character? Life doesn't work that way."

"Eve Ronin is a TV show and what happened today could become an episode."

"Her life and the show are two different things," Carly said. "We're living in the real world. There's no guarantee you're coming back in the next episode."

They were still hugging. She didn't seem to want to let go. He kissed her on the forehead.

"I'm always going to come back."

"You can't make that promise," she said. "Nobody can."

"So, it wouldn't change things if I was an accountant instead of a cop."

"Accountants don't walk into exploding houses."

"It exploded before we walked in."

She slapped his butt and pulled away. "Don't be a smart-ass."

He took off his towel, put it back on the rack to dry, and walked naked into the bedroom. "What I'm saying is, there is no escaping risk. Maybe I take on a bit more than most people, though a lot less since I left the Marshals Service, and sometimes I get some cuts and bruises on the job. But this is what I do. It's who I am."

He got into bed.

Carly got into bed, too, and rolled on her side to face him.

"That's okay with me," she said. "Because what you're fighting for is an ideal, a set of righteous values that are bigger than the both of us, and yet essential to who we are, the love we share, and the child we brought into this world."

He looked at her. "You're bullshitting me, aren't you?"

"Isn't that what you wanted to hear? Isn't that making you hot?"

"Actually, it's making me nauseous."

"Good. Because no actual human being talks that way," Carly said. "You came home bloody and cut up. What kind of wife would I be if I wasn't concerned about it?"

"You're not mad because I got hurt?"

"I'm relieved that it's minor stuff and not a broken bone or a bullet wound. I know there are risks to being a cop. What worries me is how much you enjoy them."

She kissed him and rolled over, turning her back to him. He lay there in the dark, not sure if things had gone well for him with her or not.

CHAPTER SEVENTEEN

Early the next morning, Walker woke up in bed alone and in pain, feeling as if he'd been in a fistfight. His entire body ached and his back stung. But he also kind of liked it. It meant he'd been *doing* something—not sitting, not looking at ashes. It was the kind of pain that felt good. It was *action* pain.

He brushed his teeth and got dressed in a loose-fitting polo shirt and jeans. He'd have to get a fresh uniform at the office to replace the one that got shredded.

Walker put his Stetson on his head. The holes gave it character. He was ready for work, his Glock and badge already locked in the gun safe in his truck.

He went into the kitchen to find Cody squirming joyfully in his high chair, wearing his cereal on his hands, arms, and face and getting only some of it in his mouth. But he was having a grand time. He seemed to like the feel of the food more than eating it.

Carly was dressed for work, drinking a cup of coffee and reading the morning news on her iPad at the kitchen table within arm's reach of Cody's high chair.

Walker went to the Mr. Coffee, which reminded him of the day ahead, investigating the Twin Lakes arsons.

"How are you feeling this morning?" she asked.

"Terrific." Walker poured himself a cup of coffee and grabbed a raisin bagel from a bag on the counter.

"You're such a liar. You are sore all over."

"It feels great." He'd replied without thinking and instantly regretted it.

She gave him a smile. "Now *that's* an honest answer. Revealing, too."

He brought the coffee cup and bagel to the kitchen table and sat across from Carly. "I like doing what I'm good at again, except I'm afraid that it's a problem for you."

"What makes you think that?"

He took a bite out of the bagel. He liked them untoasted and without anything on them. "You said so last night."

"That's not what I said. I don't mind you enjoying what you're good at. That's healthy."

"I'm confused."

Carly set down her iPad, grabbed a napkin from a stack in the middle of the table, and wiped the baby food off Cody's face and hands. "What's unhealthy is running into a fire because you're bored and crave the excitement."

He felt a jolt of panic.

Do I talk in my sleep?

"What happened last night was a freak occurrence. Don't worry. In my job we usually arrive long after the fires have been put out. We just sift through the ashes, looking for clues."

She took some food out of Cody's hair, too, which made him giggle. "And that's dull and the bad guys have been too easy to catch. I get it, you're bored. But boring is safe."

It's unsettling how well she knows me, he thought. *That's the problem with marrying a shrink.*

Eager to change the subject, he said, "I got that selfie with Eve Ronin that you wanted."

"Let me see."

He took out his phone, found the picture, and passed the device over to her.

"She's a brave woman," Carly said. "I admire what she's accomplished with all the obstacles in her way."

"Me too. But I'm in the minority in our department."

Carly slid the phone back to him. "That's obvious from those deputies giving you the finger in the background."

Walker picked up the phone and zoomed in on the deputies in the background. Sure enough, they were flipping him off. "That's what happens when you put some corrupt deputies in prison."

"And shoot a few others, not that I blame her. But please try not to do that."

"I will do my best." Walker put the phone in his pocket and got up. "I should be home for dinner tonight unless something totally unexpected happens today. What's your day look like?"

"Clinical depression. Paranoia. Serial infidelity. Crippling anxiety. Paralyzing insecurity. Sex addiction . . . and that's all before lunch."

He kissed her and then the baby, who grabbed Walker's nose in his tiny fist. Walker freed himself. "I hope you're talking about your patients and not you."

"I am," she said. "But it could be me if you keep leaving me alone at night."

"Uh-oh. I don't want that." He gently pinched Cody's nose and went to work.

Walker was stuck in rush-hour traffic on the freeway in Studio City, facing another forty-five minutes of commuting hell before he got to work, when he got a call from Eve Ronin.

"I didn't expect to hear from you so soon," he said.

"I thought you'd like to know that Lopez identified the dead man at Oxley's house from his dental records. He's a drug addict who has been living on the streets in Pasadena. He's been arrested a couple of times for selling blow jobs to support his meth addiction."

"How did she get his dental records?"

"He's in the missing person database," Eve said. "His family up in Portland hasn't seen him in years but figured he was probably somewhere in California, if he wasn't dead."

"So they submitted his dental records to the police just in case his body ever showed up."

"It was prescient and pragmatic," she said, "but also very sad."

"You keep using big words like that, I am going to have to buy a dictionary."

"It wouldn't have been difficult for Oxley to lure him into his car or back to his house with the promise of drugs or money in exchange for sex."

"But I wonder how Oxley got away without his car while lugging that Mandalorian suit. Uber? Lyft? A friend?"

"Oxley had a second vehicle registered with the DMV. An old Ford Econoline van. It wasn't at the house. There's an APB out for it, but I'm sure he's changed the plates by now."

"He didn't buy as much time for himself by faking his death as he probably thought he would," Walker said. His truck had moved about a foot closer to headquarters since Eve's call. "So maybe the FBI won't be too far behind him."

"I wonder what he intends to do with that vial."

"A bargaining chip, maybe? Hey, don't let Leyland catch you snooping around the edges of her case or you could get in trouble."

"Trouble doesn't scare me," she said. "What does is knowing that the doomsday virus is in the sweaty hands of a homicidal incel."

She ended the call and Walker edged forward another few inches and wondered, for perhaps the hundredth time, if he should install a siren in his truck.

◆ ◆ ◆

Sharpe's office had a window overlooking the parking lot and another window into the squad room, where Walker's space was one of a dozen tiny cubicles. But none of the detectives ever got to enjoy any of Sharpe's sunlight, even though the blinds were always open on his squad room window. The stacks of papers, binders, and files piled high on Sharpe's couch completely blocked the glass and the inside of the office from view. It was like entering a storage unit, only without the roll-up door.

The path to Sharpe's desk was indirect and required Walker to duck under coatracks covered with jackets, coats, and hats and weave around file cabinets and piles of books and papers topped with bits and pieces of incendiary devices he'd collected over the years.

Walker found Sharpe sitting at his desk, facing an apple fritter, a cup of McDonald's coffee, and one of the unexploded bombs from Twin Lakes. Sharpe poked the device with a Bic pen.

"Don't set that thing off," Walker said. "There's so much flammable and explosive material in this office that there will only be a crater left where this building stands."

"Thanks for the warning. I was about to plug this thing into the wall and see what happens."

Walker removed half a stack of technical manuals and phone books, dumped them on the floor, and sat on the remaining stack like it was a stool.

"Did we get any DNA or fingerprints off the components in that thing?"

Sharpe took a bite out of his morning fritter and shook his head. "But it still has a story to tell."

"It better have car chases and some sex or I might doze off. I slept terribly last night. I woke up every time I rolled on my back."

"Whoever made these devices wasn't in a rush when he placed them in the homes, and he'd visited them before to take measurements," Sharpe said. "That's all obvious from his work. This was designed to fit perfectly in a particular space. The kindling around the devices was carefully mixed and packed. That takes access and time."

"Which means he wasn't worried about getting caught . . . he felt safe on the property." Walker reached across the desk and tore himself a piece of Sharpe's fritter, an action that only a few months ago might have got him shot.

"He obviously came at night when he wouldn't be seen," Sharpe said, "but he'd have to be careful not to be spotted by the security guard."

Walker chewed the fritter and thought about the Twin Lakes development for a moment.

"That's not so hard. The site is unfenced, except for the gate on the main street into the development. It's also a lot of property for one guard, no matter how diligent he is, to cover and watch in pitch darkness."

Sharpe tore off a piece of fritter instead of taking a bite out of it, since they were apparently sharing the pastry now.

"Not only that, but whoever it was also knew when the drywall was going up so he could remove it to place and hide his explosives. That means he also had eyes on the property during the day, too, so he'd know when to come back."

Walker graciously left the last bit of fritter for Sharpe. "That could be anybody with a pair of good binoculars who doesn't mind hiking into the hills surrounding the property and finding the right lookout spot."

Sharpe gobbled the last piece before Walker could change his mind. "Do any of these requirements narrow down our list of suspects?"

"Actually, it fits them all."

Walker walked out and came back a moment later with the files that Bell had given him.

He briefed Sharpe about the California Crusade Against Manmade Extinction's failed battle to stop the Twin Lakes project and their continuing harassment.

He also told him about Larry Bogert, the construction worker fired for stealing supplies at night, and about Mateo Salcedo, the homeowner the developer sued into bankruptcy for trying to blame them for geological issues he'd actually caused himself by having his pool built by an unlicensed contractor.

When Walker was done, Sharpe said, "The environmental activists should be at the top of our list."

"Because of their ideology?"

"Because Haley Frost, the leader of CAME, is a known arsonist," Sharpe said. "Her group has a long history of torching equipment, trailers, and construction supplies at developments."

"Have you ever arrested her?"

"Twice."

"Okay, she's at the top of the list, but I think Larry Bogert, the construction foreman, looks good for it, too," Walker said. "He's got motive, means, and opportunity."

"That's true."

"But before we confront Bogert, I'd like to talk to the security guard who caught him." Walker checked his notes, which were scrawled on one of the files, for the guy's name. "Warren Pendle, but he's working someplace else now. I'll call his old employer and see if he knows where."

"What can the guard tell us?"

"I don't know," Walker said. "He might not know, either. But if we ask the right questions, we might learn something we can use against Bogert. Maybe he saw Bogert doing more at night than just stealing stuff."

Sharpe finished his coffee and tossed the empty cup somewhere into the dark regions of his office. "What about Salcedo, the aggrieved homeowner?"

"The lawyer for Twin Lakes thinks he fled to Mexico to avoid his creditors."

"Nice alibi," Sharpe said. "But Salcedo could have hired someone to burn the houses for him."

"Problem is, Salcedo left here broke . . . and if he did come into some money and hire an arsonist, these bombs were planted months ago. That arsonist is probably long gone, too."

"Unless Salcedo hired someone currently working on the construction crew, and arsonists like to see their work. That's mostly why they do it."

That opened the door to a lot more suspects. If the arsonist was a current worker at the site, Walker had an idea how to zero in on him.

"If Bogert didn't do it, I'll encourage him to convince us of his innocence by fingering someone he knows who is still on the construction crew—someone who could be bought."

"You're ruthless," Sharpe said.

Walker nodded. "It's one of my best qualities."

CHAPTER EIGHTEEN

Walker parked the Tahoe in the parking lot of the massive Lowe's Home Improvement store at the corner of Roscoe and Topanga Canyon Boulevards in West Hills, a few miles south of Twin Lakes.

He looked over at Sharpe. "The leader of California Crusade Against Manmade Extinction works at Lowe's? I thought we were going to a shack out in the boonies, or maybe an abandoned warehouse somewhere."

"Environmental activism doesn't pay and it's a great place to work if you're an arsonist who wants a discount on supplies."

"Is that how you caught Haley Frost before?"

"Everything she used came from Home Depot, which is where she worked back then."

They got out of the Tahoe and went into the Lowe's. As Walker passed the cash registers, he noticed a glass-doored refrigerator in the checkout line. It was filled with bottles of Sparkling Ice strawberry-kiwi water. It was the same brand as the bottles in the bombs.

"Look at that," Walker said.

Sharpe said, "This could be a simple case."

"Most of them are," Walker said, but after the last two days of activity, he didn't mind a rest, unless he was given the opportunity to go after Colin Oxley. But he was holding out hope that he could still jump into that game.

Sharpe approached a male cashier and asked where they could find Haley Frost. The cashier pointed them to the garden department, which was outside, at the far end of the store.

The two detectives crossed the store and walked out into the garden department's nursery. Sharpe immediately spotted Frost holding a hose and watering trays of flowers. The young woman wore a weather-beaten straw hat with a wide brim, but her face was still deeply tanned from days spent outdoors. Her red, zippered Lowe's vest was too big, making her look like a child playing "hardware store."

Haley looked up as they approached and didn't seem upset to see the man who'd sent her to prison.

"I was wondering when you'd show up, Shar-Pei."

"Why is that?" he asked.

"I heard about the fires at Twin Lakes."

"You could've seen the smoke from here."

"Actually, I did. I smelled it, too. Because I was right here," Haley said. "You can check my time cards. I was working here when the fires happened."

"Your alibi is worthless."

"I have witnesses, too."

Sharpe waved that argument away. "The improvised incendiary devices were planted in the homes long ago and had a simple but ingenious time delay."

"Really? That's cool." Haley turned off the hose and set it aside. "Tell me more."

"My job isn't to instruct ecoterrorists. It's to catch them."

Haley laughed. "I love how the people who protect nature and wildlife are branded as terrorists, while the corporations that destroy nature and kill wildlife are the good guys who need protecting."

Walker said, "We won't tell you how the bombs were made but, coincidentally, most of the parts in them are sold right here."

"That's true of *any* bomb, even a nuclear one, if you happen to have some uranium at home. It proves nothing." Haley glanced at Sharpe and gestured to Walker. "Where did you find this rodeo clown?"

Walker could see from the sparkle in Sharpe's eyes that he liked the "rodeo clown" reference, but he still ignored her question.

"You have a strong motive and ever since your group failed to stop the development in court, you've been vandalizing the property and harassing the new residents."

"We've been *educating* the residents. And if you'd read any of the material that we distributed, you'd know it's ridiculous to accuse us of setting those fires."

"It wouldn't be the first time you've done it," Sharpe said. "You torched fifteen bulldozers at the Desert Oasis Estates project in Lancaster."

"That was different."

"Maybe I'm a rodeo clown," Walker said, "but I don't see the distinction."

"Twin Lakes is destroying one of the last refuges of the Santa Susana tarplant and Braunton's milk-vetch and one of the few remaining habitats of the western spadefoot," Haley said. "You know what would make that devastation complete? A wildfire. I want to protect the ecosystem. A house fire could easily spread to what little patch of land for that ecosystem is left. Have you seen that hillside? It's nothing but dry fuel. It's a miracle that the wildfire last year didn't wipe it all out already."

Sharpe and Walker knew that fire well. It was a miracle it didn't wipe them out, too.

Walker said, "Maybe burning down the houses, and scaring off the residents and potential buyers, was worth the risk of igniting the hillside if it put the developer out of business."

"We don't take risks with endangered species."

"Okay," Walker said. "How do you feel about strawberry-kiwi Sparkling Ice?"

Walker's question seemed to briefly confuse her, but after a moment, she took a shot at answering.

"The drink is loaded with sucralose, which was developed as an insecticide; potassium benzoate, an additive used as an anticorrosive agent in automotive coolant; and calcium disodium EDTA, an additive which is also used in skin creams and deodorant. It's a cocktail of ant poison, industrial chemicals, and artificial fruit flavors. If I wanted to kill myself with a drink, I'd rather guzzle Drano and get it over with."

"Got it," Walker said. "How do you feel about whiskey?"

"I love it," Haley said. "Is there a point to this?"

"You're helping me win an argument with my wife about what's healthier for our baby to drink."

She looked at him incredulously. "You give your baby whiskey?"

"Only a teaspoon when his teething is really bad."

She turned to Sharpe, who'd been watching her closely during her conversation with Walker. "You ought to arrest the rodeo clown, not me."

"I've thought about it," Sharpe said. "Have a good day, and try to stay out of trouble, Haley."

"You too, Shar-Pei." She picked up the hose and continued watering the plants. "Don't let the rodeo clown shave off your eyebrows again while you're napping."

The garden department had its own exit to the parking lot and Sharpe headed for it.

Walker kept pace beside him. "What do you think?"

"It's not her or her group."

"I agree," Walker said, "but I hate it when someone takes themselves off the suspect list by using logic and reason to convince me."

"Why?"

"It makes me feel dumb for not coming to the same conclusion myself before talking to them."

"It makes me feel good about myself and renews my faith in my fellow man."

"How?" Walker asked as they went out to the parking lot. Heat radiated off the asphalt and made his back sting.

"It reassures me that I have an open mind and can be swayed by a good argument."

"What's that have to do with your fellow man?"

"It means that someone who is capable of committing a particular crime, with a strong motive and maybe even a propensity to do so, made the choice not to do it."

"That's most of us." They reached the Tahoe and Walker unlocked the car.

"You just proved my point." Sharpe got inside the Tahoe.

Walker got in, too, and started the engine. "I did?"

"In our line of work, we see far too many people in the minority in that regard and it can color how you look at everyone."

"I'm not sure that's a bad thing," Walker said, leaning back slowly onto his hot vinyl seat and wincing when he felt the burn on his wounds. "A healthy cynicism will keep you alive in this job."

"But harm everything in your life outside of it, assuming you're a cop lucky enough to have one," Sharpe said. "And we both are."

Yes, we are. And Walker knew he had to work harder at keeping it that way.

◆ ◆ ◆

While they were still in the Lowe's parking lot, the AC running in their Tahoe, Walker called Ethan Dryer, the ex-cop owner of Big Valley Security, to ask about Warren Pendle, the security guard working at Twin Lakes when the homes that burned were being built.

Dryer praised Pendle as a good man who'd left to become a patrolman for the Freeway Service Patrol, which he explained was basically a tow-truck service run by the California Department of Transportation and the California Highway Patrol to help stranded motorists along the 118 freeway.

Walker thanked him for his help, then called the CHP and had the FSP dispatcher ask Pendle to meet the detectives at the Denny's in Porter Ranch, which was off the 118 freeway a few miles east of Twin Lakes.

Walker and Sharpe got there first, took a window booth, and ordered lunch, since they didn't know how long it would take Pendle to arrive.

They'd finished their burgers, and Walker was contemplating getting a chocolate shake for dessert, when Pendle arrived in a gleaming white tow truck, which he parked on the far end of the lot. On both sides of the truck was the FSP logo—a blue circle with a CHP logo on one half and the Caltrans logo on the other, with a yellow triangle in the middle, a tow truck in the center.

"I need sunglasses to look at that tow truck," Walker said. "It's so clean you could eat off the tires."

"Why would anyone want to eat off the tires?" Sharpe asked.

Pendle emerged from the truck wearing a crisp blue uniform, with the FSP logo on a big patch on the breast pocket and a pair of black leather shoes that actually gleamed. He had a neat, conservative haircut that Walker thought would make him fit in naturally as either a Mormon missionary or a Disneyland employee.

"Look at that uniform," Walker said as Pendle walked to the restaurant. "Perfectly pressed with spit-shined shoes. He'd make even the meanest drill sergeant proud."

"You think anybody who doesn't roll their uniform into a ball and toss it into their locker is paying too much attention to their clothes."

"He's a tow-truck driver," Walker said. "They get covered in grease and grime. A uniform that clean is unnatural."

"I have a news bulletin for you," Sharpe said. "Some people actually wash their uniforms and take pride in how they present themselves to the public."

Pendle came in, scanned the dining room, and recognized Sharpe's uniform. Sharpe waved him over. Pendle came to their booth and practically stood at attention in front of it. Walker half expected him to salute.

"Sorry I'm late," Pendle said. "I was in the middle of helping a stranded motorist when I got the call."

"No problem," Sharpe said. "The job comes first."

They introduced themselves and Sharpe offered him a seat. "Can we buy you lunch?"

"Sure, thanks." He slid in beside Sharpe and the waitress came over to take his order. "I'll have a burger, fries, and a Coke, please." Once she was gone, he turned to Walker. "How can I help you?"

"We'd like to ask you about Larry Bogert."

Pendle leaned back in his seat and sighed. "I knew this would happen."

"What would?"

"That he'd go right back to burglary if they let him walk. What's he stolen this time?"

Sharpe said, "Nothing that we're aware of. We're arson investigators. His name came up as someone who might have a grievance with Twin Lakes."

"I saw those fires from the freeway," Pendle said. "I wondered what was going on. You think Bogert did that?"

"We don't know," Sharpe said. "We wanted to get some background from you before we talk to him."

Pendle grinned. "This is so exciting."

"What is?"

"Having the opportunity to brief two detectives on a case. He was my first big arrest. A citizen's arrest, of course. I'm not in your league."

"You've made other arrests?"

"No, he was the only one so far. But it wasn't petty theft and I'm sure it wasn't the first time he did it, either. I'd seen him around at night before, from a distance, but he'd already be gone, or driving away, when I got out there to investigate."

The waitress brought Pendle his Coke and a straw, then left again. He unwrapped the straw, put it in his drink, and took a sip.

Sharpe said, "Did you see anything suspicious at the construction sites after he left?"

"Nothing. But I don't know anything about construction, so I wouldn't notice sabotage and I wouldn't know if wood or other supplies were missing unless someone told me."

"Did you report the incidents?"

"There was nothing to report," Pendle said. "He was the foreman. Staying after nightfall wasn't a crime."

The waitress came with Pendle's burger and fries and set the plate down in front of him.

"Could I have some extra napkins, please?" he asked. She went to get them.

Walker said, "But you didn't leave it at that."

"Would you, sir?"

"Nope."

"I didn't think so," Pendle said. "You look like a man of action."

"I am," Walker said. "So, one man of action to another, what did you do?"

"Instead of walking the property all night like usual, I hid in one of the uncompleted houses, waiting to see if he'd show up. It took a few nights, but he did."

The waitress returned with a stack of napkins. Pendle tucked one into his collar, another between two shirt buttons, and spread a third on his lap before carefully picking up the burger and taking a bite. A man of action.

"What did you see him doing?" Walker asked.

Pendle answered him, and their questions that followed, between bites of his burger and an occasional french fry.

"He was inside another house for a while and I couldn't see what he was doing. But then he came into the house I was in, stole some boxed kitchen and bathroom fixtures, faucets, and that kind of thing, and took them out to his pickup truck."

"Did you see him doing anything else?"

"I was hiding upstairs. I watched him from the stairwell but I didn't see him at all times as he went through the house."

"Did you hear anything?"

"Maybe some hammering. I'm not sure. When he left the house, I slipped out after him. He was loading some wood into the flatbed when I came up behind him and informed him that he was under arrest."

"How'd he take that?"

"He laughed and tried to play the 'I'm the foreman' card, that he was simply moving the supplies to another house, and told me to fuck off," Pendle said. "I ordered him to turn around and put his hands behind his back so I could cuff him. He got in my face and said, 'Make me.'"

"Did you?"

"I tased him in the balls, cuffed him, and called my supervisor."

Walker smiled at Sharpe. "I like this kid."

Sharpe didn't respond to that. Instead, he turned to Pendle, who was grinning with pride. "What happened after you tased him?"

Walker answered for Pendle, "Bogert couldn't pee without crying for a week."

Pendle laughed. "Are you speaking from personal experience, sir?"

"Yeah, back in my US marshal days, I got zapped after a struggle with a perp, but that's another story," Walker said. "The good news is, it cured my infertility issues and now my son can shoot lightning bolts out of his eyes."

Sharpe sighed, unamused, and turned back to Pendle, who was regarding Walker with something akin to hero worship. "How did things go with your supervisor?"

"He showed up an hour later with Mr. Bell, the three of them chatted, and they let Bogert walk. They didn't even call the police. I couldn't believe it."

"But they fired him," Sharpe said. "And he can't use them for a reference to get more work."

"Boo-hoo," Pendle said, pushing his empty plate aside. There wasn't a crumb on it. "Forgive me for being crass, but he committed a crime. He should have gone to jail. That's the law. It wasn't right. That's one of the reasons I traded my badge for this one." He tapped the patch on his chest.

"That's a patch," Sharpe said. "Not a badge."

"It's considered a patch-badge," Pendle said. "It's a money-saving thing."

"Ah, I didn't know that."

"I realized after the arrest, and seeing the perp set free, that I was wasting my abilities standing watch over empty houses. My talents were needed on the streets."

"Or in this case," Sharpe said, "the freeway."

"I'm a people person, but I was all alone out there at Twin Lakes. Just me and the coyotes. The Freeway Service Patrol allows me to make a difference. We're the CHP, only we don't carry firearms and our primary role isn't law enforcement."

"It's towing vehicles," Sharpe said.

"It's much more than that," Pendle said. "My beat is the portion of the 118 in Los Angeles County, from the Rocky Peak exit to the west all the way to the interchange with 405 to the east. I work 6:00 a.m. to 10:00 a.m. and again from 2:00 p.m. to 7:00 p.m., making sure there are no vehicles obstructing rush hour traffic. I mostly help stranded motorists, giving them gas if they've got an empty tank, changing flat tires, jump-starting their batteries, that kind of thing. But I'm often the first officer on the scene of traffic accidents . . . and that can get real very fast."

"I can imagine," Walker said. "What do you do during your four hours off?"

"To be honest, I grab lunch, go to the bathroom, and then hit the road again."

"Are you saying that you work four hours a day without pay?"

Pendle nodded. "People get stranded or have accidents all day long, not just during rush hours. Someone has to be there for them."

"What about Triple A?"

Pendle snorted in derision. "They contract out to the nearest towing company. A motorist doesn't know what kind of guy is going to show up. It could be a murderer or rapist. Or some guy who shows you his ass crack every time he bends over. With me, you get a trained peace officer you can trust, vetted by the CHP and Caltrans." Pendle turned to face Sharpe. "Who would you rather have assist your wife or loved one to change a flat? Me or the ass-crack guy?"

Sharpe didn't answer, but Walker did.

"I see what you're saying, Warren. But the CHP knows you're still out there in their vehicle, helping people, and that they aren't paying you for the extra hours. They are screwing you."

"I don't see it that way," Pendle said. "I look at it as gaining necessary experience toward my next step up the ladder."

"Which is what?"

"Maybe working with you two someday," Pendle said, then glanced at his Apple Watch. "Uh-oh. I'd better hit the road. Thanks for the lunch."

"Our pleasure," Walker said.

Pendle slid out of the booth and stood up. "Please let me know if there's anything else I can do to help. I'd like to see Bogert go down for his crimes."

"Will do," Walker said, and watched Pendle leave the restaurant and go back to his shiny tow truck. "The Freeway Service Patrol is really taking advantage of that kid's dedication."

"If my wife has a flat, I'd rather ass-crack guy shows up to help her," Sharpe said. "Odds are he'd be a real mechanic rather than a wannabe cop with a patch-badge. Pendle gives me a stomach cramp."

"Yeah, I can see why his overenthusiasm irritates you. But it's interesting what he said about Bogert. As a construction foreman, Bogert had plenty of opportunity to plant those devices, day and night, without getting caught."

"But he was," Sharpe said. "By a young, low-paid, and woefully inexperienced security guard."

"Pendle was probably right to tase the guy in the nuts," Walker said. "It might've saved his life."

"You think Bogert would've killed him over some faucets and showerheads?"

"Not for that, but maybe for seeing him plant enough bombs to level the whole development and start another massive wildfire."

"Pendle *didn't* see that," Sharpe said.

"Bogert didn't know what Pendle saw until later."

"Better bring your Taser. Bogert will be expecting us," Sharpe said. "Although he's probably wearing a crotch cup nowadays."

"It won't do any good," Walker said. "If I shoot him in the crotch, it will be with my Glock."

CHAPTER NINETEEN

Without leaving the Denny's parking lot, Walker and Sharpe used the LASD computer in their Tahoe, their cell phones, and an iPad to track down Larry Bogert, who they quickly discovered had an active California state contractor's license and a construction company in his name.

They used the online databases of the Los Angeles County Building and Safety division, and those in similar departments in other county municipalities, to create a list of the building permits that he'd been granted, or had applied for, within Los Angeles County.

They learned that he was primarily doing work in the San Fernando Valley and that his most recent permits were for a home renovation on Styles Street in Woodland Hills, a few blocks west of the Topanga mall on Topanga Canyon Boulevard.

It was a fifteen-minute drive from the Denny's south to Styles Street, which was in a neighborhood that was an early-1970s housing tract. The remaining original homes, which were the majority of those on the block, all appeared to be variations on the same four floor plans and exteriors.

The house they were looking for was easy to spot. There were several dirt-caked pickup trucks parked in front of it. There was also an overflowing dumpster on the driveway that was filled with wood, a porta-potty situated in the side yard, various craftsmen cutting tiles and wood on lathes in the open garage, and a sign reading ANOTHER BOGERT HOMES TRANSFORMATION stuck in the dead front lawn.

Walker parked and got out with Sharpe. They walked up the driveway toward the backyard, where all the construction activity was taking place.

They both smelled the burned wood before they saw it, piled high in the dumpster. There were also scorch marks on the cinder-block wall that divided the property from the house next door.

They didn't need to be arson investigators to know there had been a fire here.

At the rear of the house, there were more signs of a blaze on the singed roof, which had been largely demolished to make room for a new addition that was being framed out below it and that stretched well beyond the house's original footprint.

Larry Bogert leaned over a set of blueprints spread out on a picnic table, where he was conferring with several construction workers. Walker recognized him from his driver's license photo.

Bogert was a big, burly man with thick brown hair on his head and chest, tufts of it spilling out of his dusty, sweat-soaked denim shirt, which was unbuttoned to his breastbone. The man looked to Walker like a grizzly bear who shopped at Old Navy.

Sharpe said, "Larry Bogert?"

Bogert looked up and groaned loudly with irritation when he saw Sharpe's uniform. "Ah, shit. Not again."

"Excuse me?" Sharpe said.

Bogert stepped away from the table and walked over to them.

"Look, Officer, we're doing a job, okay? We've got as much right to park on the street as anybody else. We aren't blocking the old biddy's driveway anymore or 'her view,' which is of the house directly across the street from her, so she's got nothing to complain about. But, if you ask me, you've got to wonder what is going on in her neighbor's house that she's so desperate to see. The old perv."

"We aren't here about the parking situation," Sharpe said.

"Or the old perv," Walker added.

"We're arson investigators," Sharpe said, and introduced them.

"You're a few weeks late, fellas," Bogert said, his tone softening a bit. "The fire department and the insurance company both signed off on this. Besides, the damaged rooms have been demolished and we're deep into rebuilding, as you can see."

Walker could see they were also deep into digging a new lap pool—a small Bobcat excavator at work within the obvious contours. He asked, "Was Mr. Coffee to blame for this fire, too?"

"Wrong appliance," Bogert said. "It was a Mr. Breadmaker. The homeowner bought it at a flea market, plugged it in, and left the house for the day. Must've been a short in it or something, because a few hours later, *whoosh*, the whole kitchen went up. They're lucky the entire house didn't burn down."

Walker and Sharpe shared a look. They were both thinking the same thing: another empty house up in flames because of a faulty appliance.

What a shocking coincidence.

Sharpe said, "I wonder if Mr. Breadmaker uses a similar heating element as the Mr. Coffee. In your experience, which one works better at igniting water bottles full of gasoline that are embedded in walls and insulated with wood chips and Styrofoam as kindling?"

Bogert seemed bewildered. "What are you talking about?"

"The bombs planted in the walls of several finished homes up in Twin Lakes," Sharpe said.

"You know," Walker added, "the housing tract that fired you for stealing supplies."

His comment definitely got the attention of the eavesdropping people that Bogert had been talking to at the picnic table. Bogert forced a smile.

"Oh God, not again. This is a big misunderstanding. You have me mistaken for *Lance* Bogert. He's another contractor. This happens all the time. Look, guys, this has to stop . . ."

Bogert led Walker and Sharpe to the side yard and then, with his back to his workers and his voice low, he snarled, "I've never been arrested for a goddamn thing, so you can't go around accusing me of theft in front of my employees. I will sue you into fucking oblivion."

Sharpe said, "There might not have been any charges filed, but we know what happened."

"You only know *their* side."

"You were caught red-handed, in the middle of the night, stealing construction materials."

"I wasn't *stealing* anything," Bogert said. "I was *borrowing*."

Walker turned to Sharpe. "Gee, I've never heard that before, have you?"

"No, never," Sharpe said, then looked at Bogert. "That changes everything."

"It's the truth," Bogert insisted. "My wife was diagnosed with breast cancer and my insurance didn't cover all her bills. I had to. I asked for a raise, or for them to cover the deductible, but they refused, saying it would set an expensive precedent that others would demand. At the same time, I had a side hustle renovating and flipping homes and the housing market took a dump. I was sitting on homes with expensive debt that I couldn't finish remodeling to unload. I had a serious cash-flow problem and was backed into a corner."

Walker filled in the rest. "You couldn't buy the supplies you needed to finish the flips, so you took whatever you needed from your day job."

"It was only temporary," Bogert said. "When I was flush again, which only would've been a few months, I would have replaced everything and nobody would have noticed."

"Because you were the foreman and could do some sleight of hand with the paperwork," Sharpe said.

"I worked for that company for fifteen years. They knew the pressure I was under. They could have shown some understanding and sympathy instead of firing me and making a horrible situation even worse."

"They showed you sympathy by not calling us to arrest you," Sharpe said. "You showed your appreciation by calling them heartless assholes and saying they'd be sorry."

"They are heartless and if they have any conscience, they will regret what they did."

Walker said, "You weren't just stealing supplies at night, Larry, you were planting your Mr. Coffee bombs. The guard saw you."

"No, he didn't," Bogert said. "That little shit is just licking your asses because it makes him feel like a real cop. If he'd seen me with bombs, he would have said something that night . . . and he didn't. Because it didn't happen. He's lucky I haven't gone after him for assault with a deadly weapon."

Walker chuckled. "Only because you'd have to admit your balls were zapped during the commission of a burglary."

The mere memory of that experience made Bogert contort a bit. "All of that is in my past. I'm doing fine now as a general contractor, thanks to strong word of mouth, which dredging up old shit could ruin. I have nothing to do with any fires at Twin Lakes. So, unless you're going to arrest me, we're done."

"We're just getting started, Larry," Walker said.

"My wife had a mastectomy and is cancer-free now," Bogert said. "Thanks for asking, you heartless pricks."

He walked away, returning to the men at the picnic table. Walker and Sharpe went back the way they came.

Sharpe stopped and peeked into the dumpster as they went by. "The similarities between what happened at this house and the ones at Twin Lakes are awfully close."

What Sharpe really wanted to do, Walker knew, was climb into the dumpster and search the debris for clues. But they'd need a warrant for that. Or they could wait until the dumpster was taken to the dump and go through the garbage there without a warrant. But this could be the second, third, or even fourth load of debris taken away from the site.

"I'm sure most of the damaged portion of the house has already been demolished and taken away. This dumpster isn't big enough for all of it," Walker said. "Certainly whatever damning evidence there was is long gone now. Bogert would have seen to that if he torched the place. But this wasn't arson."

"According to the clueless Los Angeles Fire Department, some inept insurance investigator, and a thieving contractor."

"But not according to you, which is the only opinion that counts."

"That's right," Sharpe said. "You really have learned a lot."

Walker looked at Bogert's sign in the front lawn, advertising his work to attract any neighbors who might be interested in a remodel.

The sign gave Walker a thought. "Bogert said that word of mouth is what's getting him his jobs."

"*Strong* word of mouth," Sharpe said.

"Let's see where that word is coming from."

CHAPTER TWENTY

Walker and Sharpe got back in the car and scanned through the list of building permits granted to Bogert. They found a cluster of jobs in Woodland Hills and West Hills, so Walker decided to drive past them and take a look.

The first home they visited was in Woodland Hills and still had one of Bogert's signs in their lawn. The home was part of a housing tract, and the first floor was identical to the single-story houses next door and across the street. But this one also had a second story, which Walker assumed was a new addition.

However, the most interesting thing to him was the old oak beside the house. A portion of the thick trunk was charred.

"Do you see that tree?" Walker asked.

"No, I missed that. Thank you for pointing it out to me. It's the last thing an experienced arson investigator would ever notice," Sharpe said without lifting his gaze from his iPad, where he was looking at a Google Earth street-view photo dated two years earlier. "What you can't see is that the house didn't have a second story before the fire."

I would never have guessed, Walker thought. But what he said was: "It looks like the homeowners found a way to turn a tragedy into a benefit."

The next house, this one in West Hills, had new windows and was freshly painted, but otherwise, Walker couldn't tell what work had been done on it. But there was a new ski boat on a new trailer in the driveway.

"There was a fire in the laundry room, caused by lint in a faulty dryer," Sharpe said, reading from his iPad. "The blaze and water damage spread to the kitchen."

"How do you know?"

"I ran the address through the Los Angeles County Fire Department incident report database."

The next house they went to, also in West Hills, had a new two-car garage. A search in the LACFD database showed that the previous single-car garage had burned down due to an electrical short in an old freezer.

"I'm sensing a pattern," Walker said.

It was one that continued for three more houses. The final home on their list was back in Woodland Hills. It appeared that the detached garage now had a new second-story guesthouse.

Sharpe checked it out on his iPad. "That was just a garage before. Now it's a rental property. It's going for $2,000 a month."

"Another short?" Walker asked.

"I don't know. This house is in LAFD jurisdiction. I can't get into their database."

Walker spotted an old man walking a dog, pulled up beside him, and rolled down his window.

"They sure fixed it up nice," Walker said, gesturing to the house. "Were you here for the fire?"

The old man nodded and came up to the window. "It was the most exciting thing to happen in the neighborhood in years."

"What was the most exciting thing before that?"

"When Sally Pamuk mowed her front lawn naked while singing 'I Am Woman.' That was in 1972."

"It was quite a fire if it could beat that."

The old man's poodle lifted his leg and peed on the Tahoe's front tire.

"It ruined the Silvermans' vacation," the old man said, pretending not to see what his dog was doing. "Joel and Hildy came back from

Reno to find their garage burned to the ground. All the old paint and rags they had in there just caught fire. Who knew that could happen?"

"You'd be surprised how often we see that. Have a good day."

"You too, Deputy."

Walker turned to Sharpe. "Okay, so every one of his remodeling jobs involves a residential fire. It may not be anything criminal, just the contractor equivalent of ambulance chasing. He's hitting up fire victims while the ashes are still smoking and offering them low-cost renos."

"No, it's a scam and he's not in it alone," Sharpe said. "I'll bet that it's the same insurance investigator every time, too, a freelancer with fire expertise."

"I didn't know there was such a thing as a freelance arson investigator."

"It's usually an ex-firefighter or a guy like me," Sharpe said. "I've been approached several times about going into the private sector. The money can be great. It's even better if you get a kickback from the contractor for telling the insurance company that the fire was an accident."

"What do the homeowners get out of it?"

"Free renovations or additions beyond what was damaged by the fire, like a new pool or a garage conversion, or perhaps a cash kickback instead, which they can use to reimburse their deductible or to buy nice toys, like a boat or new car."

Walker glanced at the Silvermans' new rental unit. "Everybody wins."

"Except the insurance company."

"Nobody cares about them. But I'd sure like to nail Bogert for it anyway . . . and use that as leverage to get him to confess to the Twin Lakes arsons."

Sharpe sighed. "It's going to take a lot of time and patience."

"Why is that?"

"Because there's no evidence. To prove that Bogert is running a big insurance scam, we'll have to wait for him to do it again," Sharpe said. "But the good news is, we know he will. It's the cornerstone of his business plan."

"I'm not waiting."

"What's the alternative?"

"We do a Danny Cole," Walker said, referring to the con man and thief who'd sparked the biggest wildfire in California history as part of an elaborate heist.

"What are you suggesting we do? Set a house on fire?"

"Close." Walker put the Tahoe in park, turned off the ignition, and got out.

Sharpe hurried after him as he crossed the street and headed for the Silvermans' house. "What are you doing?"

"Follow my lead."

"I think you've forgotten who is the experienced senior officer here and who is the struggling rookie."

"Not in this situation. Watch and learn."

Walker marched up to the front door and hammered his fist insistently on it. "Open up. Police."

The door was opened by a startled middle-aged guy wearing a cardigan sweater, slacks, and loafers, like he was preparing to host a reboot of *Mister Rogers' Neighborhood*.

"What is going on?" he said, looking past them to the Tahoe, with the LASD badge on the door and the words Arson Unit emblazoned on the side panel.

"I'm Andrew Walker and this is Walter Sharpe. We're arson investigators with the Los Angeles County Sheriff's Department. And you're right, Joel, we do."

"We do what?"

"Know everything. That's what you're thinking, isn't it?" It was obvious from the expression on the man's face that Walker was right, so he pressed his advantage. "We know all about Larry Bogert, the fire he suggested, and the insurance scam that got you that sweet rental unit. I bet the rent you're asking for will pay your whole mortgage, won't it?"

Joel Silverman started to speak, but Walker held up his hand. "Wait, don't answer that. Before you say another word, we need to read you your rights. I don't want this arrest thrown out on a technicality."

Walker pushed past him into the house and Sharpe followed, closing the door behind him.

The living room had popcorn ceilings and shag carpet and was wallpapered in a floral pattern that might have been stylish up until the early 1980s.

Walker shouted, "Hildy, come out here. You need to hear this, too."

A rotund woman came out of the kitchen wearing a housedress that clashed painfully with the wallpaper and she looked terrified, her eyes almost as big as her cheeks.

Walker said, "You two have the right to remain silent. Anything you say can and will be used against you in a court of law—"

Hildy Silverman interrupted him. "You're arresting us?"

Walker held up his hand to silence her and continued talking. "You have the right to an attorney. If you can't afford one, one will be provided to you free of charge. Do you understand your rights as I have explained them to you?"

Joel said, "But we didn't do anything wrong."

Walker pinned him with a stern look. "Answer the question, Joel."

"Yes, we understand our rights."

"Turn around, put your hands above your head, and face the wall." Walker put his hand on his holstered gun, as if he expected trouble, and glanced at Sharpe. "Frisk him."

Sharpe nodded and did as Walker asked.

Hildy said, "We aren't criminals."

"You conspired with Larry Bogert to commit an arson and defraud your insurance company," Walker said. "Those are multiple felonies that will put you in prison for ten to fifteen years."

"He's clean." Sharpe stepped back from Joel and took out his handcuffs. "Turn around, put your hands behind your back."

Joel did, but he looked like he was about to cry. "He told us it wasn't a crime, that even if it came out, we wouldn't be held responsible. It would all be on him."

Sharpe put on the cuffs. "And you bought that?"

Hildy said, "He burned the garage down, not us. We weren't even in town."

"Come on, Hildy." Walker gave her a withering look. "That's why you were gone, so you wouldn't be here when it happened. You gave him the key, knowing exactly what he was going to do." He turned to Sharpe and tossed him his handcuffs. "Frisk the lady and cuff her."

Hildy gasped and took a step back. "I'm not carrying a weapon, I promise you."

"I believe you," Sharpe said. "That's the first honest thing either one of you has said so far. Turn around, put your hands behind your back."

She did. Sharpe handcuffed her and she stood, her head lowered in what Walker assumed was shame, beside her husband, who looked imploringly at Walker.

"We've been paying homeowner's insurance for years . . . and for what? We got nothing out of it," Joel said. "We've paid for that garage three times over with our premiums. So, what harm did we really do?"

Walker snickered. "Try that defense out on the judge. He'll rupture his spleen with laughter."

Sharpe said, "Then you'll be guilty of manslaughter, too."

Walker and Sharpe laughed.

Hildy's head shot up and her shame quickly transformed into anger. "That's not funny. Not one bit. This is our lives you're joking about. If we go to prison, we'll lose everything. We'll probably die behind bars."

Joel was still in imploring mode. "Isn't there anything we can do? I see them make deals all the time on *Law & Order*."

Walker looked at Sharpe, who said, "They don't seem like bad people, Walker. Maybe we can give them a break."

Walker frowned, as if debating with himself, then said, "Larry told you it would all be on him, right?"

Joel nodded repeatedly. "Yes. Yes, he did. He was quite definitive about that."

"Okay, so maybe there's a way you can convince us that's true and possibly get a lesser sentence with no jail time in return for your cooperation."

Sharpe added, "But we can't make any promises. All we can do is put in a good word for you with the DA."

Joel glanced at Hildy for her consent, and Walker used that instant to shoot Sharpe a chastising glance, which they didn't see and Sharpe ignored.

Walker turned back to the Silvermans. "The DA takes our word as gospel, so assume right now that you're talking to God. Who recommended Larry to you?"

Hildy replied instantly. "The Costigans. Ted and Karen. They live a few blocks east. We can give you all of their contact information. They got a bid from Bogert for a kitchen remodel, which was beyond what they could afford."

Now that she'd given up their friends, Joel was ready to dig the grave for them. He said, "But then Larry told them there was a way they could afford it and also get Ted's dream home theater out of the deal, too, for nothing. Larry said, 'Just let me start a little fire in your kitchen and it'll all be free. The insurance company that's been taking your money for years will pay for it all . . . and I'll absorb the deductible.'"

Sharpe said, "Larry Bogert offered you the same deal?"

"How could we say no to that?" Hildy said. "We're retired. Turning our garage into a rental unit will create cash flow we could use to travel."

"Okay, here's the way out for you," Walker said, giving Sharpe a nod to uncuff the Silvermans while he explained how they could save themselves.

"You don't tell anybody, not even your lawyer, about this conversation," he continued. "In a few days, I'll call you with a couple's name. Let's say Mike and Carol Brady, for example. Then you'll get a call from Larry asking if you recommended him to the Bradys. You'll say yes, you did, that they're dear friends who are looking for the same great deal that you got."

Joel rubbed his wrists as if he'd been tightly shackled for hours. "You're setting him up."

"That's right, Joel. It's how we're going to prove that your story is true," Walker said. "You'll be helping yourselves by voluntarily helping us arrest him and his accomplices. And you'll remain free in the meantime."

Hildy shared a smile of relief with her husband. "I like that part."

"So do I," Joel said. "But what happens to us after you arrest Larry?"

"We'll tell the DA about your invaluable cooperation and recommend that you don't get any jail time," Walker said. "That's when you contact your lawyer, and he'll work out your deal with the DA."

Sharpe spoke up. "Or you can choose not to cooperate. You can call your lawyer right now, tell him about your arrest, and he can meet you down at the station after you've been booked. It's up to you."

Why is Sharpe giving them a way out? Walker wanted to slap his partner.

Joel looked at his wife. "Maybe we should call Mel."

Walker spoke up fast, before she could. "Go ahead, call Mel. But if you do, you can forget about getting any deals because Larry will hear about your arrest and disappear. That'll leave you and the Costigans and everyone else he's conned to pay for his crimes, while he enjoys his freedom, sipping martinis on his yacht in Morocco."

Hildy nodded. "He's right. Forget about Mel."

Joel wasn't convinced. "We need a lawyer's advice."

Hildy glowered at him. "You didn't think to get it when Larry offered us his deal."

"That was different."

"Yeah, because you knew Mel would tell us it's a crime," Hildy said. Walker was beginning to like her. It was always nice when a crook did his job for him.

Joel looked at his wife while gesturing to the detectives. "How can you say that in front of them?"

"They already know, Joel. That's why they're here. And once we're led out that door in handcuffs, the news of our arrest will be all over the neighborhood in thirty seconds. The Costigans will call whoever recommended Larry to them, and those people will call whoever recommended Larry to them, and so on and so on . . . and Larry will hear about it before we even get to the police station. He will be on the first flight tonight to Morocco."

Joel nodded glumly and turned to Walker. "We'll help you set him up."

CHAPTER
TWENTY-ONE

Sharpe was silent and stewing over something as Walker drove them back to headquarters. They were going to be stuck in traffic for at least an hour and Walker thought a lively conversation would make it go a lot faster.

"What are you sulking about?" Walker said. "We're going to take Bogert down."

"It's how we're doing it that bothers me. What we just did was highly irregular, maybe even illegal."

"Why?"

"Because it's coercion."

"We told them they could call their attorney and this was strictly voluntary."

"*I* told them," Sharpe said. "You wouldn't have."

"But you did and they decided to cooperate, didn't they? Besides, if we bring down Bogert and his massive insurance scam, and use that as leverage to get his confession on the Twin Lakes arsons, nobody will care how we did it. I say it's worth the risk. How about you?"

Sharpe sighed, signaling his reluctant consent, or his realization that they were too deep into the con now to stop. "Where are we going to find Mike and Carol Brady . . . and a sting house?"

"Leave that to me," Walker said.

"That frightens me. But I'll distract myself from the terror by putting together a file of all the houses Bogert remodeled that were burned first in supposedly accidental fires."

"Good idea."

"It's not an idea," Sharpe snapped, so angrily that it startled Walker. "It's called building a case. It's part of something else we call 'police work.' You ought to try it sometime."

Walker grinned. "Staging cons is more fun."

Sharpe wasn't amused. "It's also what put Danny Cole in prison."

"He's not in prison now."

"That reminds me," Sharpe said. "Why would Bogert have a yacht in Morocco?"

"Morocco doesn't have an extradition treaty with the United States."

"Why do you know that?"

"Back when I was a US marshal, two big-time embezzlers I was chasing fled there before I could catch them. Every Christmas for years, they'd send me a picture postcard of themselves sunbathing on their yacht in Tangier."

"Ouch," Sharpe said. Walker could see that his story had made his partner forget about being angry with him. Probably because, at least for the moment, Sharpe enjoyed imagining Walker's humiliation.

Never underestimate the power of a good story.

"I finally got them," Walker said. "Right before I left the Marshals Service to partner up with you."

"Did you kidnap them in Tangier, shove them into a crate, and ship them back with you to the US?"

"I thought about it."

"Oh, I'm sure you did."

"I kept tabs on the location of their yacht with an international maritime traffic app on my phone. The instant they sailed into Spanish territorial waters, I got pinged, and I notified the British government. The Brits sent a gunboat out of Gibraltar to nab them."

"Why did the British do that for you?"

"Because one of the people the fugitives embezzled from was a distant member of the royal family," Walker said. "The fugitives were extradited to the US and are currently doing time in Corcoran State Prison."

Sharpe thought about it a moment, then said, "Now, every Christmas, you send them a picture postcard of yourself sunbathing at a beach or poolside at some resort."

Walker grinned at Sharpe. "You're getting to know me well."

◆ ◆ ◆

They spent the rest of the day at their desks, doing the mountain of paperwork required for their investigations of the Lopresti fire in Calabasas, the arsons at Twin Lakes, and the explosion at Oxley's house in La Cañada Flintridge.

Sharpe also used the time to start compiling his list of Bogert's postfire remodels and to learn more about them.

Walker didn't talk to him about his planning for the Bogert sting because he didn't start on that until he was in his truck and on his way home for dinner.

He gave Eve Ronin a call from the freeway and began by filling her in on the latest developments in the Twin Lakes case that had led them to Larry Bogert and his insurance scam.

"That's all great and I'm happy for you," Eve said. "But why are you telling me?"

"Larry Bogert has met me and Sharpe, so we need a cop he doesn't know for this sting."

"You're asking me to be Carol Brady." It was a statement, not a question.

"You're the only person in the department I know well enough to ask and who I trust to pull off the con."

"I was part of a house-trap sting once before and I nearly got killed."

"You nearly get killed all the time," Walker said. "There's less risk for you doing this than there is walking into your station's locker room."

"That's true," Eve said. "Okay, I'm in. Let me know once you've lined up the house and cast Mike Brady."

"One more thing," Walker said. "Can you send me those photos you took of Oxley's Mandalorian costume?"

"Sure," she said. "But why?"

"It's the only lead we've got on him."

"We aren't chasing him."

"I know, but it's all we have," Walker said. "Maybe the case will boomerang back to us someday. And I don't ever give up."

It was an argument he knew Eve Ronin would understand.

"I'll message the photos to you now," she said.

Walker spent most of dinner telling Carly about the Twin Lakes case, but he left out the part about Sharpe driving a water truck into a burning house.

Afterward, as Carly was doing the dishes and Walker was helping Cody feed himself with a spoon instead of his hands, she said, "This contractor sounds fascinating, psychologically speaking."

"He's a crook," Walker said, watching Cody try to stick the spoon of baby food into his own nose.

"Or he's a decent man who was pushed into committing a crime out of desperation to provide for his family," Carly said. "And to get his wife the lifesaving medical care she needed."

"So we should give him a pass for torching the houses at Twin Lakes? It's pure luck that nobody was hurt or killed." Walker tried to gently redirect the spoon to Cody's mouth.

"Of course not."

Cody pushed the spoon away, which flung the food into Walker's face. The boy giggled with delight.

"And what about his current business plan of arson and insurance fraud?"

"That's the part that intrigues me, almost as much as his apparent fascination now with fire," she said. "Unless it's always been there and he's found a way to use it to his benefit."

"I'm glad you're intrigued and fascinated by him and an Eve Ronin fan."

Walker wiped the food off his face with his fingers and licked them, which Cody took as instructions to do the same thing. He stuck his fingers into the food on his tray and then shoved them into his mouth.

"What does one have to do with the other?"

Walker took a spoonful of the food from the Gerber jar and put it in his mouth, hoping the demonstration would inspire Cody the way his finger licking did.

"She's agreed to be a homeowner in our sting, once I find a house for it, one that's authentically lived in and needs some work."

Carly stopped washing dishes and turned to look at him over the kitchen counter. "You want to use *our* house?"

"Not just the house." Walker put the spoon in Cody's hand, then guided him into taking some food out of the jar, then waited to see what Cody would do.

"You want to play her husband, too?"

Cody used the spoon to fling the food in Walker's face again and laughed, kicking his chubby little legs with glee.

"I can't play the husband. Larry has met me," Walker said. "But how would you like the opportunity to observe a felon in action?"

Walker wiped the food off his face with his fingers and offered them to Cody, who licked them clean.

"That's how you feed the baby? With your fingers?" Carly marched out of the kitchen and sat down at the table again. "What are you thinking?"

"I was trying to teach by example and things went awry."

Carly took the spoon and fed Cody with it. "I was talking about your sting. You want me to play Eve's spouse, is that what you're saying?"

"I want you to be her sexy, lovable, intelligent baby-mother."

Carly set down the spoon on the baby's tray and faced Walker. "You want Cody in on this, too?"

"Larry will never suspect that he's walking into a trap if there's a woman and a baby involved and it's in a house that looks and smells so lived-in."

"You think our house *stinks?*"

"I think it smells like a family with a baby lives here. You can't fake that . . . or the baby puke stains on the carpet."

"You're going out tonight and buying air freshener and carpet cleaner."

"It's hardly noticeable," he said.

"You think we're three slobs who live in a stinking dump."

"I think we're two working parents with a baby and the way our house looks and smells is completely normal . . . and that you're straying from the subject."

"I know what I'm doing, thank you," Carly said. "It's intentional."

"Oh. Why?"

"Because I need a second to think."

She took her second, and they both noticed something remarkable. Cody was feeding himself with the spoon from the jar. While they were arguing, Cody had reached a milestone on his own.

"Great job, Cody," Walker said with a smile. "Good boy."

"He's not a puppy."

"I'm offering encouragement."

Carly kissed Cody on the cheek, untied his bib, picked him up out of the high chair, and carried him over to his playpen. On her way back to the table, she said, "How could you even think about endangering your wife and child?"

"I couldn't and I wouldn't. Larry will come here to offer you a quote on a renovation, that's it. There is no danger besides sticker shock."

She sat down across from him again. "He sets fires in houses."

"Empty ones. He doesn't even break into them, he uses a key provided by the owners. Nobody will be here when he comes to torch the place."

"Are you going to let him burn down our house, too?"

"Of course not," he said. "We'll nab him before that happens. The point is to catch him in the act, not to let him complete it."

"You're saying we won't be at risk and nor will our house."

"More than that." Walker reached across the table and took her hands in his. "Think of what you could learn from this experience. Not just about him, but about what I do . . . and why I do it."

"You see this as a bonding opportunity for us that will strengthen our marriage."

"Exactly."

She yanked her hands from his. "You are so full of shit. You're trying to play me just like you're playing Bogert. This is all about you wanting to make your case."

"Two cases," Walker said. "One with Larry and one with you."

She sat back in her chair, folded her arms under her chest, and all but dared him to go on. "Me?"

"You've only seen my work as measured by the time I've spent away from you and the injuries I sustain."

"That's not fair. I know what you do and that you're good at it. I've never questioned that."

"But you don't know how I do it, how it feels, or what it means to me," he said. "What better way is there for you to find out?"

Carly thought about that for a long moment, then unfolded her arms and sat forward again. "Go get the air freshener and carpet cleaner."

"You're straying from the subject again," he said, and she gave him a harsh look that reminded him that she was doing it on purpose. "Oh, yes. Right. I'll go get them."

He got the car keys and ran to Ralph's grocery store for air freshener, carpet cleaner, and, to seal the deal, some Oreo Cookies & Cream ice cream.

When he got home twenty minutes later, Carly had put Cody to bed and was waiting for him at the kitchen table with two bowls and two spoons already set out. He was amazed. She'd somehow predicted that he'd come back with ice cream.

"Okay, I'm in," she said. "You better open up the ice cream before I change my mind."

He did.

CHAPTER
TWENTY-TWO

It took two days for Walker and Sharpe to set everything up. First, they needed to get approvals from their lieutenant and from ADA Rebecca Burnside for the operation, though both had their reservations about the participation of a civilian, namely a deputy's wife. But Walker managed to convince them and they signed off on the sting.

Walker went out to Woodland Hills and personally briefed the Silvermans about Eve Beckett and Carly McKinnon, a lesbian couple with one child who lived in Reseda.

The cover story would be that the Silvermans knew the couple through Carly McKinnon's work as their son Lester's psychologist. McKinnon was Carly's maiden name and also the one that she used professionally, so that would check out, not that anybody expected Bogert to research the couple. But if he did, he'd discover that the house was in Carly's name, since she'd inherited it from her grandmother.

With the Silvermans prepped, Walker invited Eve over for dinner so she could get comfortable with the house, Carly, and the baby and to discuss the roles they'd be playing.

The dinner of take-out Chinese food went smoothly. Carly and Eve hit it off immediately and by dessert, they were behaving like old friends, much to Walker's relief and amazement.

At some point, Eve picked up Cody without any awkwardness at all and, when the conversation moved to the family room, carried him over to the couch, where she and Carly sat side by side. Cody seemed to be very comfortable in Eve's arms, so much so that he began to nod off.

"There's something Walker probably didn't tell you, Carly, but I will," Eve said, gently rocking Cody to sleep. "You don't have to go through with this. In fact, you can back out at any point."

"Thank you for that," Carly said. "But I'm actually excited about this. I can't wait to hear Bogert's pitch. I want to see what techniques and language he uses to manipulate us into doing something that's obviously illegal."

"Probably the same techniques and language Walker used to manipulate you into this."

Carly smiled at Walker, who sat in the armchair, watching the women interact as if he were a stage director overseeing a rehearsal, though he didn't dare offer any actual direction.

"That was an entirely different kind of manipulation," Carly said. "It was based on his intimate knowledge of me and his deft use of our existing conflicts. But Bogert doesn't know us at all."

Walker said, "He knows what it's like to be short on cash and desperate. And he knows you've been talking to the Silvermans, who didn't come right out and say how they got their great deal, only that you need to be flexible in your thinking."

"And our morality," Eve said.

"You obviously are," Walker said. "You're a lesbian couple with a baby."

Eve and Carly stared at him and he felt the temperature in the room instantly drop below freezing.

Eve said, "You're saying that's immoral?"

"I'm not, but I'm assuming that's what he believes," Walker said. "I looked into his background. He comes from Alabama, which is not a state known for their liberal attitudes on sexuality and marriage."

"What else do you know about his past?" Eve asked, apparently satisfied with his answer. He felt the room getting warmer again.

"Larry likes playing with fire. His family's barn mysteriously burned down when he was a teenager. His car caught on fire when he was in college in Texas, and so did the laundry room in his dormitory."

"I'm not surprised by any of that."

"Neither was Sharpe," Walker said.

Carly asked, "What about his family history?"

"His father lost the family farm over gambling debts and went into the construction business, which is where Larry learned his trade. But his father lost that business, too, for the same reason."

"What's his family life now?"

"Married, no children," Walker said. "His wife is a hairstylist who works out of a salon he built for her in their home in Valencia."

Carly said, "I wonder if it was Larry Bogert who burned down his family's barn . . . or if his father did it."

"Does it make a difference?" Walker asked.

"It might explain some things."

Eve said, "None of which will be relevant in court."

Carly replied, "Unless his lawyer hires a shrink to argue some sort of mental illness defense."

Walker said, "Don't volunteer for the job."

"I'm probably already on enough shaky ethical ground here as it is."

"Bogert isn't your patient."

"It doesn't matter," she said. "I'm sure it could be argued that helping to lure someone into committing a crime is a violation of my oath."

Eve said, "This isn't entrapment. He's going to encourage *us* to break the law, not the other way around."

"That's exactly what I've told myself," Carly said. "He's run this scam a dozen times already and he has to be stopped."

"You don't have to be the one who stops him."

"But he does." Carly motioned to Walker, then looked back at Eve. "And I'm sure you're glad to be part of it, too."

"It's what we do," she said.

"No, it's who both of you are."

"It's not who you are."

"I guess we'll find out." Carly smiled at Cody, asleep in Eve's arms. "You're very natural and relaxed with children."

"I've basically raised two of them already," Eve said. "I'm the oldest of three kids in a single-parent household where the parent was never around. So, mothering duty fell to me."

"You're good at it and Cody senses it, too, or he wouldn't feel safe enough to fall asleep in your arms. Bogert will be convinced that we're both mothers."

Walker asked, "And lovers?"

Carly wagged a finger at him. "Get that picture out of your head, you sicko."

"Is 'sicko' a psychological term?"

Carly looked at Eve. "But Andy raises a good point. Will you stiffen up if I take your hand or put my arm around you in front of Bogert to sell our affection?"

"Only if you reach for my Glock."

"You'll be carrying a gun?"

"Absolutely," Eve said.

"I thought you said that Bogert isn't dangerous."

"He's not," Eve said. "I carry my gun at all times for personal reasons. I've got it on me now, in a holster on my lower back."

"It must be hard living that way."

"It would be harder if I didn't, because I'd be dead. Speaking of which, I've got something in my car for Walker that I need to bring in."

Eve carefully passed Cody over to Carly, got up, and went outside. Once she was gone, Carly turned to Walker.

"Why does Eve call you Walker? Didn't you tell her it was okay to call you Andy?"

"It hasn't come up. Besides, everybody calls me Walker, except for you and our family."

"Does it make you feel more comfortable, maintaining that distance with your coworkers?"

"Are you psychoanalyzing me?"

"Always," she said.

"You're supposed to be pondering the unshakable ethical code I live by and how much you want me in bed."

"Is that what Spenser's girlfriend does?"

"Yes, and you should try it," Walker said, just as Eve returned carrying a very large gift-wrapped box in her hands.

She presented it to Walker. "This is for you."

"What's the special occasion?"

"Me being here, breathing," Eve said. "It's a gift for saving my life."

He tore open the wrapping paper to reveal a hatbox, which contained a new Stetson—a tan Shasta with beaver fur felt, a classic cattleman crown, and satin interior lining. It was identical to his own hat, minus the wear and tear, the sweat, and the recent barrage of shrapnel.

"Eve, this really wasn't necessary," he said. "I was just doing my job."

"Put it on," she said.

He did. It was a perfect fit. Like it had been made for him. "How did you know my size?"

"I'm a detective."

Walker was touched and he didn't know how to handle the feeling. It wasn't one that he'd had often in his life.

Carly had a big smile on her face. "That's so sweet of you, Eve."

"Yes," he said. "Thank you."

Eve bent down in front of Carly, gave Cody a little kiss on the cheek, and said, "See you soon."

She was nearly out the door when Walker said, "Eve?"

She stopped and looked over her shoulder at him.

He took off his hat and set it on his lap. "You can call me Andy if you want."

"Okay, sure," she said and went out the door.

Walker turned to see Carly still giving him that big smile.

"I guess that makes her family," Carly said.

"She'd better be," Walker said. "She's marrying my wife."

◆ ◆ ◆

Walker's house was wired with cameras and microphones the next morning by an LASD surveillance crew disguised as Spectrum cable workers, in case any neighbors were paying attention. And Walker knew from experience that they almost certainly were.

He gathered all of his clothes, toiletries, and photographs in the house, packed them up, and took the boxes to their small storage unit in Canoga Park.

Meanwhile, an LASD graphic artist, a position Walker didn't know existed until that day, took photos of Eve and Carly in front of a green screen, digitally replaced the backgrounds with different locales, and then printed out, framed, and hung the new pictures on the walls.

Eve brought over some of her clothes and toiletries, though it would be difficult for anyone to distinguish what was hers and what was Carly's, since they were roughly the same body type.

It was midafternoon when Carly made the call from her office to Larry Bogert and got his voice mail. She left a message saying that the Silvermans had enthusiastically recommended him to her for a remodeling project that she wanted to do.

The Silvermans reported that Bogert called them a half hour later and that they'd vouched for Carly and Eve, all according to the script. Within the hour, Bogert called back Carly, and after a short conversation, they agreed to meet the next morning at the house.

◆ ◆ ◆

At 7:30 a.m., Walker, Sharpe, Duncan, and Assistant District Attorney Rebecca Burnside were in the back of a fake AT&T van parked across the street from Walker's house. They stood in front of a bank of monitors that showed all of the surveillance camera feeds from inside and outside the house. They could see and hear everything. All Burnside had to do was hit a button on the console to start the recording.

Walker had worked with Burnside before. She was the ADA who oversaw the prosecution of most of the LASD's major crime cases. Every man in the department, including him, thought she was smoking hot.

But she put a lot of effort into undercutting her beauty so people would be able to focus on whatever she was saying and doing rather than gaping at her. She artfully used her makeup and clothes to hide or blunt her best features. It was a magic trick that worked best from a distance, like a few feet away from the jury box. It didn't work too well up close, and now she was in a very cramped space with three men.

Her beauty made all three men in the van awkward and unsure about what to do with their arms, legs, and gazes. So they stood still, their arms at their sides, focused on the screens, even though the only thing to see was Carly changing Cody's diaper while chatting with Eve about the evils of talcum powder.

Burnside turned down the volume on the talcum discussion and said to them, "They know not to lead Bogert on, right? To let him do the talking?"

Duncan said, "Eve is a law enforcement professional."

"But his wife isn't," Burnside said, nudging Walker with her elbow, which zapped him with static electricity. Or, perhaps, just static beauty.

"Carly is even more adamant about not entrapping Bogert than any of us are," he said. "He'll be hung on his own petard."

Sharpe said, "It's 'hoisted,' not 'hung.'"

"Same thing," Walker said.

Duncan scratched his cheek along the faint outline of a scar. "Does anybody actually know what a petard is?"

"Of course," Sharpe said. "It's a dangerous explosive device invented by the French in the sixteenth century to blow up locked doors and thick gates. It often also blew up whoever was using it."

"Huh," Duncan said. "I thought it was a necktie."

Walker said, "I thought it was genitalia."

Burnside gave him a look. "How could you be hoisted by your own genitalia?"

"I think we're about to find out." Walker knocked on one of the screens. "Bogert is here."

CHAPTER TWENTY-THREE

Bogert parked his pickup truck in the driveway beside Carly's BMW, which had been placed there as a prop to make a statement to him about their professional and economic status.

He got out of the truck carrying a clipboard in his hand and a tape measure clipped to his belt. His hair was combed and moussed. His clean denim shirt was buttoned up nearly to the collar, preventing his wild chest hair from bursting out into anyone's face.

Bogert gave the house a professional visual appraisal as he went slowly to the front door and rang the bell.

Carly answered, holding the baby. "I'm Carly McKinnon. I'd offer you a hand but I'm occupied."

"I can see. What a cutie he is."

"Thank you for coming to see us so soon."

"It's my pleasure. The Silvermans are good people and they said you're anxious to get a reno done quickly."

She stepped aside to let him in and Eve greeted him.

"I'm Carly's wife, Eve. We love what you did with Joel and Hildy's garage. It's amazing."

"It was a fun project," he said, his gaze shifting around the room, and sizing up the problems, while he breathed in the lived-in smell of the place. "Is that what you want to do here?"

"It would be the answer to so many problems," Carly said, setting Cody down in his playpen.

"Tell me about them."

Carly and Eve led him over to the kitchen table, where they all took seats and got right down to business, Eve taking the lead.

"We're working parents and day care for our son is becoming a real problem for us financially," she said. "You would not believe what it costs. It's like a spa day at the Four Seasons."

"I can imagine," he said.

"But there's a solution. My mom lives in Palm Springs in an active senior living facility that is so expensive, she barely has any money left after paying her rent."

Now Carly jumped in. "But if we could convert our garage into an apartment, she could live here rent-free and keep an eye on Cody. A win-win."

Bogert smiled. "Sounds like a great plan. What about your kitchen?"

"What about it?" Carly said.

"No offense, but it's pretty dated, and those appliances belong in the Smithsonian."

Eve said, "We know. A new kitchen is on our wish list."

"Our *endless* wish list," Carly said, putting a hand on Eve's. "But one thing at a time."

Bogert took out his pen, clicked it, and held it over the legal pad on his clipboard. "What else is on that list?"

"How many hours do you have?" Carly said.

Eve didn't wait for his answer. "We'd like to redo our bathroom, and Cody's room needs a makeover. Right now, it looks like an office with a crib in it. We'd like to paint the house, too, which you probably noticed is faded and peeling."

Eve watched Bogert take notes and, when it looked like he'd caught up, she gave him more.

"We also need to replace all the leaking windows, and we have to do something with that backyard besides harvest weeds, and—"

Carly interrupted her. "But we have to prioritize, and right now, the garage is the crucial project. It's also the most expensive."

Eve looked at Bogert hopefully. "But Joel and Hildy told us not to worry, that you could make it possible for less than we could imagine. Or are we kidding ourselves?"

Bogert laughed. "Do you mind if I look around and take some pictures and measurements?"

"I don't see the point," Carly said. "We can't afford to do anything else."

"Humor me," Bogert said.

"Yeah," Eve said to Carly. "Humor him."

Carly scowled playfully at Eve, then shifted her gaze to Bogert. "I bet you can guess who in this marriage spends the money and who creates the budget."

Bogert took his pen and clipboard and stood up. "I'm not taking sides. That's a no-win situation."

"Smart man," Eve said.

For the next half hour, Bogert went through the house, followed by Carly and Eve. He took measurements and pictures in every room. He asked them what they'd like to do, if money were no object, in the main bathroom, Cody's room, and the kitchen.

They told him.

When they were done inside the house, they finally went out to the garage, where he took more measurements and pictures. He asked them to describe, if they had no limitations, their dream mother-in-law suite.

They told him that, too. And when they were done and heading back into the house, Carly said, "You can tell from looking at the state of our house that we can't possibly afford to do everything we'd like to do in here, even with two paychecks."

"Especially with so much of it going to day care," Eve added. "Are we crazy to think we can afford the garage renovation?"

"Not at all," Bogert said. "The garage has good bones. Making this into a mother-in-law suite is not as big a job as you might think. Let me crunch the numbers, work up some sketches, and get back to you in a day or two."

Carly said, "Don't you want to know how much we have to spend?"

"Nope. No offense, Carly, but that's a classic mistake that dishonest contractors wish every homeowner would make."

"Why?"

"You're negotiating against yourself and are guaranteeing that you'll get a bid that devours your entire budget," he said. "Instead of possibly getting one that could be substantially below it."

"I don't think that's likely to happen this time."

Bogert smiled at Eve. "Is your wife always so optimistic?"

Eve put her arm around Carly's waist. "I'm the dreamer, she's the realist."

Carly kissed Eve on the cheek. "I prefer to think of myself as a pragmatist."

Bogert laughed again. "You two are great. I can tell it's going to be a lot of fun working with you."

They exchanged a few pleasantries, he gave them his card, and then Eve walked him out to his truck, staying outside as he drove off.

Burnside turned to the detectives in the van. "Carly and Eve were born to do undercover work."

Duncan nodded in agreement. "It's hard to believe they aren't actually a married couple."

But Sharpe didn't share their enthusiasm. "We don't have anything we can use. He didn't incriminate himself."

Burnside said, "We got exactly what we needed from this meeting."

"We did?"

"We're trying to build a case that will hold up in court," Burnside said. "They baited the hook and did it without giving the defense anything they can use against us to argue entrapment."

Eve knocked on the van's rear door. Walker opened it up, letting in some much-needed fresh air, but she remained on the street. It was cramped enough in the van already and smelled like it.

"How did we do?" she asked Burnside.

"You were totally convincing."

Duncan said, "You should be playing yourself on your TV series."

"I don't want to play a cop, Duncan. I want to be one."

"Well, you obviously learned a few things about acting from your mother," he said.

"Don't you ever say that in front of her or I will shoot you."

Walker assumed Eve's mother was an actress, which would certainly explain Eve's natural ability. But not Carly's. Her performance amazed him. He excused himself from the others, jumped out of the van, and went back to the house.

He found Carly in Cody's room, putting him in the crib for his morning nap.

"Is everyone happy in the van?" she asked.

"They're ecstatic. How about you?"

She grinned. "It may be the most exciting thing I've ever done. It's a natural high. My dopamine levels must be stratospheric. I can see how this work can become addictive. I'm getting a new understanding of you."

"I like that," he said. "What did you learn about Bogert?"

She waved him out of Cody's room and answered his question as they walked back to the kitchen.

"He's a fascinating individual. He uses tried-and-true psychiatric techniques, urging you to talk about your feelings, your needs, and your desires while he listens and literally takes notes."

"On how he can convince you that setting fire to part of your house and committing insurance fraud is a reasonable thing to do."

"He's saving that for our next session," Carly said. "Today, he was gathering information and assessing our weaknesses while, at the same time, giving us hope."

She opened the refrigerator and surprised him by taking out a cold can of Kona Big Wave beer. It wasn't even 10:00 a.m. Drinking this early wasn't like her at all.

"Interesting that you're calling it a session and not a meeting," he said. "Are you talking about it from his point of view or yours?"

"Perhaps both." She popped the tab, took a big sip, then leaned back against the counter. "It's very much like the early stages of analysis. He's making us believe that if we trust him and are open, a solution to our problems is possible . . . because it's already within us."

"And once you know that, it's hard to walk away."

"That's right." Carly offered him the can, but he shook his head.

"It's 10:00 a.m. and I'm still on duty."

"Oh, yes, right. Where was I?" Carly took another sip, then remembered what she'd wanted to say. "He's also a great listener with a keen understanding of human behavior. I wonder how he learned it . . . or if it's somehow innate. And then there's his use of fire to pull off his swindle. It's almost as if he's transformed his desire to burn things into something productive rather than . . ."

"Kinky? Crazy? Perverted?"

"I was going to say 'compulsive.' Now instead of being driven by his forbidden desire, he can feel that he's mastered it, transforming what was a source of shame into income."

"It'd be like making money out of jerking off."

Carly gave him a warning look and tipped her head upward, presumably to the hidden cameras, reminding him that someone could be watching or listening. But Walker wasn't embarrassed.

She said, "I don't see how that metaphor fits at all."

"I guess we'll find out soon."

"If your metaphor fits?"

"If your theories about him are true," he said.

Carly sipped some more beer. "How will we know that?"

"After his arrest," Walker said, "I'll ask him."

CHAPTER
TWENTY-FOUR

Walker and Sharpe went back to headquarters, where Walker tackled the remaining paperwork on their cases while Sharpe did a deep dive into Bogert's renovation history. Sharpe bounded out of his office two hours later and went straight to Walker's cubicle, which was decorated with photos of Carly and Cody. The desktop itself was perfectly clean, because Walker kept all of his files in Sharpe's office, where they went unnoticed amid all of his partner's other crap.

"I was right," Sharpe said.

"Just once, I'd like to hear you say you were wrong. That would really be news."

"The same freelance arson investigator worked each of Bogert's fire claims. I'll bet he also recommends him to the insurance companies to handle the renos and gets a kickback from Bogert on every job."

"Do you know the investigator?"

"Martin Graff. He worked for the San Bernardino County Sheriff's Department until his retirement five years ago. He had a reputation for discovering the causes of major wildfires without ever catching the arsonists. That's because the arsonist was him."

"You've got to be more understanding," Walker said. "It's awkward arresting yourself, and you can only do it once."

"I saved him the trouble," Sharpe said. "I led the multiagency task force that caught him."

"Why isn't he in jail?"

"The county preferred to quietly kick him out, with his full pension, rather than face the blowback if his string of arsons was revealed."

"*With* his pension?" Walker said. "You've got to be kidding me."

"I wish I was. It was cheaper than outing him as an arsonist. Eventually the courts would've overturned the convictions of everybody he'd ever arrested for arson, whether they were guilty or not. San Bernardino County would've ended up paying out tens of millions of dollars in settlements, not only to the people Graff jailed but to everybody who'd suffered any personal injuries or property damage in one of his wildfires."

From a cost-benefit analysis, Walker could see why the county made that decision. The problem was that justice never figured into their equations. "So, the politicians hushed up what Graff did, made him promise to be a good boy, and threw him out of the county."

"You got it."

"As part of the deal, I'll bet the county gives Graff an enthusiastic recommendation whenever an insurance company calls about him."

"They do."

It was sickening to Walker. "The politicians who signed off on that insane deal are going to have a lot to answer for after you arrest Graff. I'd like to arrest them, too."

"Good luck with that."

Walker's iPhone rang. He glanced at the caller ID. "It's Carly." He answered the phone.

"Larry Bogert just called," she said. "He has a bid for us and is coming by this evening at 6:00 p.m. to walk us through it."

"Damn, he moves fast," Walker said. They didn't have much time to assemble everyone and get the surveillance vehicle in place.

"He got us excited and wants to keep us in a high state of arousal."

"I wish you'd picked a different word."

Lee Goldberg

"Arousal isn't strictly sexual," she said.

"I am relieved to hear that."

"He knows we'll be more susceptible to suggestion if we are excited and rushed into making a decision," she said. "Car salesmen in particular excel at manipulating those human weaknesses."

"It's ironic, because we're using the same techniques against Larry to get him to incriminate himself," Walker said. "Or, to put it another way, he'll be hoisted on his own petard, which isn't a necktie or genitalia, in case you were wondering."

"I absolutely was not."

Walker let her go and told Sharpe the news, and they started making the arrangements.

CHAPTER TWENTY-FIVE

The surveillance van was re-sheathed as a mobile dog-grooming vehicle and was parked in a different spot on Walker's street by 5:15 with Burnside, Duncan, and Sharpe all in attendance again.

Until that afternoon, Walker didn't know that the LASD motor pool kept a wide array of various company and utility service-vehicle skins, made by a Hollywood prop house, for these kinds of surveillance operations.

Carly put Cody to bed at 5:45, and he was fast asleep when Bogert showed up promptly at 6:00 p.m.

He sat Carly and Eve down at the kitchen table, opened up his MacBook, and proudly showed them a 3D rendering of their garage conversion.

On the outside, the garage looked pretty much the same, except he'd replaced the roll-up door with a front door and picture window. Inside, he'd turned the two-car space into an industrial-style urban-chic apartment, the kind found in renovated factories and warehouses in downtown Los Angeles.

Bogert walked them through every design detail, explaining his choices.

"To save money, but also to create a trendy, stylish look, we'll clean, seal, and shine the existing concrete floors, use premade cabinetry and remaindered surplus stone for the kitchen and bathroom, and keep the ceiling beams and ducts exposed to give the space a cool industrial-loft feel."

Eve grinned excitedly at Carly. "Mom will love that. It's the exact opposite of the bland studio she's in now, which looks like the offspring of a drunken hookup between a horny hospital room and run-down motor home."

Bogert laughed. "You just described the studio apartments in every active senior living facility in America. They are soul-sucking spaces that destroy your will to live."

Carly said, "The design for the garage conversion is fantastic. It doesn't look like we're cutting corners at all. But even so, what is it going to cost?"

Bogert put his hand on hers. "I haven't shown you the best part yet. Your new kitchen."

"Wait, what?"

He pulled up another 3D rendering on the screen. It was an entirely new kitchen.

"We'll keep the same footprint, just replace the aged cabinets with new premade ones and surplus stone for the countertops," Bogert said. "For the new fixtures and appliances, we'll buy floor models or closeouts at steep discounts."

"That's very nice," Carly said, "But we can't afford—"

Bogert interrupted her, talking over her as he brought up yet another 3D rendering.

"And here's Cody's new room, a nursery today but a journey into deep space and his limitless imagination tomorrow."

Three walls and the ceiling were painted like outer space, while the remaining wall was devoted to a custom bunk bed designed to look like a starship docking above a space station.

"The desk in the space station below the starship bed is a play area now but can become his workspace when he grows up," Bogert explained. "The panels on the bed that give it the spaceship look can be unscrewed and easily removed when he finds it too childish, though I still have them on my bed."

Eve and Carly laughed.

◆ ◆ ◆

In the van, Duncan let out a low whistle. "Damn, he's good."

Walker agreed with him. "I'm ready to sign the contract and I'm sure Carly is, too."

Burnside said, "His design is very clever, but the way he's using it to seduce Eve and Carly is true brilliance."

"Think we can keep his plans when this is over?" Walker asked.

Burnside didn't answer, turning her attention back to the screen.

◆ ◆ ◆

"I love this all so much," Eve said.

Bogert smiled, pleased. "Why should your mom be the only one who gets a special space out of this renovation?"

Carly sighed. "These renovations are wonderful, and very inspired, but we have to be realistic about what we can afford."

Eve looked at her. "Do we?"

Bogert said, "You can afford it all."

"You don't know what we have to spend," Carly said, "and I'm sure it's nowhere near enough for all of this, even with the creative cost cutting you've incorporated into the design."

"What's your homeowner's insurance deductible in case of fire or earthquake?"

"Twenty thousand dollars."

"That's all this is going to cost," he said. "Not a penny more."

Eve seemed confused. "You're saying that you can convert the garage, give Cody a boy's dream bedroom, and renovate our kitchen for just twenty grand?"

Bogert lifted his right foot onto his left knee and pointed to the heel of his leather dress shoe.

"I used to have this horrible pain in my heel, so I went to a podiatrist, who said I had plantar fasciitis. But he said he could cure it with an insert in my shoe, you know, like those Dr. Scholl's things they sell at Walmart, but custom."

Carly looked at his foot and said, "What does this have to do with our remodel?"

"I'm getting to that. The podiatrist had me stick my feet into a box of wet clay to create an impression, and a few weeks later, I got a pair of custom insoles."

He took off his shoe, pulled out the insole, and showed it to them. It was a strip of vinyl with a tiny plastic heel. "What could that cost? Fifty bucks, tops?"

"Not even that," Eve said.

"I agree with you," Bogert said, putting the insole back in his shoe and his shoe back on his foot. "So, naturally I was shocked when I got my insurance statement and saw a charge of $717 per insert."

"That's outrageous."

"I thought so, too, Eve. I called my podiatrist and screamed at him, but he said, 'Relax, Larry, look closely at your statement. Yes, the cost per insole is $717, which the insurance company negotiated down to $500, which is what they paid me. But your cost is the $10 co-pay. That's the insurance game. We all play it.'"

Eve said, "My mom has COPD and has a prescription inhaler that costs $350 a month if you're uninsured, but her co-pay is only $8."

Bogert snapped his fingers. "That's what I'm talking about, Eve. My podiatrist made a huge profit on his insoles and my plantar fasciitis was cured for almost nothing. Everybody is happy. I am going to do the same thing for you."

Carly said, "We don't have plantar fasciitis."

Eve smiled at Bogert. "You'll have to excuse Carly. She's very literal."

He said, "The insurance game works the same way in construction, Carly, except I'm not as greedy as the doctors and pharmacists. I can give you what you want, and so much more than that, and I'll still make a profit."

"But why would the insurance company pay for our renovation?"

"Let's say you started the galactic nursery project on your own, went down to Home Depot for some paint, and began painting. Before you were done, though, you left everything in the room and went down to Palm Springs for the weekend to visit Grandma . . . and turned your AC off before you left to save money. Why cool an empty house, am I right?"

"Yes," Carly said, "but I don't see the point."

"Did you know that in the heat, the paint fumes in those rags could spontaneously combust? The fire department gets here fast, but you come home to find Cody's room burned . . . and some smoke and fire damage to the rest of your house. You file an insurance claim . . . and ask your friend Larry to do the repairs."

Eve gestured to the iPad. "You can do all of this for the insurance settlement on the fire and our deductible?"

"That's right, Eve."

Carly held up her hands. "Wait a second. Let's take a step back. Are you suggesting that we set fire to our house?"

"No, of course not," Bogert said. "You go to Home Depot, get all the supplies, start painting the nursery, and then give me a key to your house before you go to Palm Springs. I'll take care of the rest."

"How can you be sure you won't burn down the whole house?"

"Because I know what I'm doing and I'll phone in an anonymous tip to the fire department before the blaze spreads."

Carly and Eve shared a look, then Carly said, "Couldn't we get in a lot of trouble for this?"

"You will have nothing to do with it," he replied. "You'll be down in Palm Springs, having a great time with Grandma, when the fire happens. It will all be on me if anything happens, but there won't be any trouble."

"How do you know?"

"Because this is the construction game and I've played it many times before for other families."

Eve said, "Like the Silvermans."

"That job was a pleasure and look how happy they are with their new rental property. As it happens, a project just fell through and I have an opening in my schedule. If you go out of town this weekend, I can squeeze your project in right away before another one I have on the books. Otherwise, I won't be able to get to yours for six months."

Carly smiled at Eve, who smiled back at her. They'd reached a decision without saying a word, because they were a couple so in love that they knew each other's thoughts.

"We'll do it," Carly said to Bogert. "We'll go to Palm Springs tomorrow night."

Bogert stood up and grinned. "That's great news. All you need to do is get the paint. Make sure to talk to the sales associate about your project so they remember you if anybody ever asks, though I doubt anybody ever will."

Eve said, "Getting Carly *not* to disclose everything about our lives to the salespeople, and the cashier, and strangers in the aisle, would be a bigger problem."

Carly went to a cookie jar in the kitchen and fished out a key. "It's called being personable."

She tossed the key to Eve, who handed it to Bogert. "Here you go."

"I can't wait to get started. One last thing: Who is your insurer?" Bogert asked and Carly told him. "Perfect. We work with them and their fire investigator all the time."

They said their goodbyes and Bogert walked out.

◆　◆　◆

In the van, Burnside pressed the button on the video console that stopped the recording and said, "Okay. It's game on."

"It's game over," Sharpe said, watching Bogert get in his truck. "We have enough to arrest him right now, before he backs out of the driveway."

"I want more than just his arrest," she said. "I want him to give up everyone involved in the conspiracy and to testify against all the homeowners who participated in his scheme. And then I want him to confess to the Twin Lakes arsons. For all of that, I need the leverage of catching him in the act."

That made Walker nervous. "But if we don't time it just right, I mean down to the second, he could set my house on fire."

Duncan shrugged. "So what? You'll gain a rental unit, a new kitchen, and a rocket ship bed for your kid."

"Well, when you put it like that, a fire doesn't sound so bad," Walker said, and turned to Burnside. "Never mind. Take all the time you want."

Walker hoped that Burnside knew he was joking, but he couldn't tell from the expression on her face. She was watching the monitor that showed Bogert driving away.

Once he was gone, Burnside said, "Eve needs to stay here until Friday night, and Walker can't be around, in case Bogert drops by."

"Why would Bogert do that?"

"I don't know, but I don't want to take any chances," she said. "From the moment they leave the house on Friday, I want this property under 24/7 surveillance and a firefighting unit on standby."

"Firefighters are always on standby," Sharpe said. "That's what they do."

"I'm beginning to see why you are so beloved in the department."

Burnside left the van and walked back to her car, which was parked on the other side of the block. Walker's truck and Duncan's Buick were parked there, too. Sharpe had driven the van from headquarters and would drive it back, where it would be sheathed in a new skin with the logo of a different company or utility.

Duncan faced Walker. "Let's go tell Eve and Carly that they are having a sleepover."

Walker didn't like the idea of being away from Carly and Cody. He hadn't spent a night away from them since Cody was born. It made him uneasy. But he understood Burnside's logic and would make the sacrifice for his case. Besides, he was confident that his family would be safe with Eve. He knew that she wasn't afraid to use her gun if she had to . . . even up against someone wearing a badge.

The two men walked across the street and were met at the front door by Carly and Eve.

Eve said, "Carly and I have been talking. We need to go to the hardware store together tomorrow and get the paint. Bogert might come back, too, so I should stay here tonight and tomorrow, to play it safe."

"Sounds good to me," Duncan said and looked at Walker. "What do you think?"

"Great idea. I wish we'd thought of it ourselves."

Duncan said to Eve, "Do you need me to go get you clothes or anything from your house?"

"She can fit in my clothes," Carly said.

"And I've already got my badge, my Glock, and extra ammo," Eve said. "Everything a girl could need."

Carly looked at Walker. "Where are you going to stay?"

Before Walker could answer, Eve said, "Go to the Calabasas Hilton Garden Inn. Show the clerk your badge and ask for the Eve Ronin rate."

"You have a rate?" Walker said.

"I've had to stay there a lot."

Duncan added, "She knows what it's like to have your house torched."

"And your car," Eve said.

Carly said, "It sounds like we're going to have a lot to talk about tonight."

"Excuse us." Walker gently led Carly by the arm out onto the lawn, where they couldn't be overheard by the others. "Are you okay with all this?"

"It's been fascinating. Bogert is a complex man. He's a creative designer and a skilled salesman who clearly doesn't need to resort to arson to succeed—but it's the arson that's driving him."

"I think it's the greed."

"It's both," she said. "The money justifies the arson, which he wants to do anyway. It's also a reward, reaffirming the bad behavior. I could write a paper on this guy."

"I'm glad you're enjoying yourself."

"I'm also learning more about you as this goes on."

"Are you going to write a paper on me, too?"

She pulled him close. "It's not a paper. It's a long-term study."

"How long?"

"As long as we both shall live."

"That sounds vaguely familiar," he said.

She kissed him tenderly. "Go say good night to Cody and get out of here."

He did as he was told.

CHAPTER
TWENTY-SIX

The Calabasas Hilton Garden Inn actually did have a secret Eve Ronin rate for law enforcement. Walker even got Eve's preferred room on the second floor, facing the front parking lot.

"She must stay here a lot if she has a preferred room," Walker said to the clerk as he signed in.

The clerk, a young woman in a black dress shirt and slacks, leaned forward conspiratorially and whispered, "She stayed here after the killing in her kitchen. The cleanup and remodel took forever."

"It's not easy getting the blood out," he said.

"Then she stayed here again for months after her house was firebombed."

"I hate it when that happens."

"How long will you be staying?" she asked.

"I'm not sure yet," Walker said. "It depends if my house burns down this weekend or not."

She nodded, as if that made total sense to her. "Homeowner's insurance for detectives must be astronomical."

"It's not so bad," Walker said. "I get the Eve Ronin rate."

He went up to his room, ordered some Chinese food delivered by Grubhub, and spent the evening eating in bed and watching a *Law & Order* marathon for pointers. He was almost at the moment in every episode when the judge throws out the prosecution's key piece of evidence when his iPhone rang. He didn't recognize the number but muted the TV and answered it anyway.

"Detective Walker? This is Justine Bryce. I hope you don't mind me calling you."

"No, of course not." Walker sat up in bed. "How are you doing?"

"Crying a lot. Grieving. When I'm not beating my pillow in fury over what was done to Patrick and me by that psycho Colin. Do you want to know the worst part?"

"He's still out there," Walker said, wiping some rice off his chest.

"That's right."

"What has the FBI told you?"

"Absolutely nothing," she said. "Neither has Dash, which is how I know they aren't any closer to catching him."

Walker wondered if she knew that Oxley had a vial of the virus, but he didn't dare ask her. It could be top secret.

"I don't think you're in any more danger, if that's what you're worried about."

"I'm worried that he's going to get away with murdering Patrick. He needs to be caught," she said. "And I think you're the only one who can find him."

He thought she was right, but he couldn't say that, not because he was modest but because it could get him into a lot of trouble if she repeated it to the FBI.

"I'm off the case and the FBI is all over it," he said. "They have massive resources and they are very good at catching bad guys."

He didn't believe one word of that but hoped he sounded sincere and provided her with some comfort.

"But they didn't find me, did they," she said. "You did."

"The FBI didn't have all the information that I did and you weren't trying as hard not to be found as Oxley is."

"You're making my argument for me," Justine said. "It doesn't bother you that he's still out there?"

"Of course it does," he said.

"Good. Sleep well, Detective."

She hung up.

He couldn't concentrate on *Law & Order* after that, so he turned off the lights, got undressed, and tried to sleep.

But he couldn't, and not because his back itched, or because he kept finding chow mein noodles and rice on the sheets. Justine's words were bouncing around inside his skull, just the way she knew they would.

You're the only one who can find him.

The problem was, he had nothing to go on, except that Oxley had fled with his Mandalorian suit.

He picked up his phone and looked at the photos that Eve shot of the Mandalorian display during their first visit to Oxley's house.

Her photos were taken from multiple angles, showing all the key details, like the scorch marks Oxley bragged were left on the beskar plating by laser blasts and lightsabers. It was those battle markings, from episodes of the show, that made the suit unique and provided one of the few ways to tell one Mandalorian from another. The Mandalorians, Walker remembered, took a sacred vow to never remove their helmets and reveal their faces to anyone.

Walker wondered if that mythology was created as a cost-saving move by the producers. It meant they could put anybody with a heartbeat in that suit. Nobody would know or care. So their star, Pedro Pascal, rarely had to show up on set. All he had to provide was his voice, which he could do from anywhere, anytime. He could probably perform his part while taking a hot bath and sipping champagne.

In every photo Eve took of the suit, Walker could also see the framed SciCon posters on the wall behind the glass case, charting Oxley's attendance at the annual San Diego convention going back years.

Curious about the convention, Walker pulled up his web browser and went to the SciCon website. He discovered that SciCon drew tens of thousands of science fiction and fantasy fans, most of them in costumes, to the San Diego Convention Center for the four-day event, which featured movie premieres, celebrity panels, and a massive sales floor full of souvenirs, books, DVDs, and more costumes.

The next SciCon was a week away and would feature the premiere of a new *Star Wars* movie, with the full cast in attendance, but not Colin Oxley. He couldn't make it this year. He was on the run with a vial of plague.

Then Walker thought about the Mandalorian vow, and Pedro Pascal, and saw everything from a different perspective. He soon fell into a deep, restful sleep.

◆　◆　◆

The next morning, Eve and Carly, with Cody in a stroller, went to Home Depot in Van Nuys and pestered the helpful sales associate in the paint department about what kinds of paint, brushes, and rags to buy and told him so much about their boring lives that as soon as they left, he took his break in the parking lot and sucked his vape pen dry.

They went back to the house in Reseda and began painting Cody's room but didn't finish the job, piling the dirty rags, paint, and thinner in the center of the room to come back to later, knowing they never would. But it looked good.

Carly packed some suitcases and put Cody in a stroller, and they piled into the BMW and called Walker as they were leaving the house in the late afternoon, not for Palm Springs but for the Calabasas Hilton Garden Inn.

Eve escorted Carly and Cody to the room, then went down to wait for Walker in the lobby for a ride to Reseda Park, the staging area for the surveillance team.

Walker unfolded Cody's playpen while Carly spread a towel on the bed, laid Cody on it, and changed his diaper. As she did, something caught her eye.

"Is that rice on the pillow?"

"Yes," Walker said.

"Thank God. For a minute I was afraid it was lice."

"This is an upscale hotel," Walker said. "And I wash my hair nearly every week."

"You think you're funny." She put the dirty diaper in the bag and tossed it in the trash.

"I am funny." Walker pinched his finger in one of the playpen hinges and swore, which made her laugh.

"I stand corrected," she said, lifting Cody up and holding him. "I wish I could be there for the arrest."

"That wouldn't be appropriate."

"How is it any less appropriate than being part of the sting?"

"An arrest is different and it could be dangerous. You never know what someone might do when they're cornered."

"He might burn our house down."

Walker put on his hat and gave her and the baby each a kiss. "I'll try not to let that happen."

"He emailed me the reno plans," she said as Walker reached the door. "I really like the aesthetic and the thinking behind it."

"Are you saying I shouldn't try too hard?"

Carly shrugged. "I'm just saying don't put yourself needlessly at risk."

"I never do." He winked at her and went downstairs.

Walker spent the next couple of hours at his dark house, sitting on a stepladder in the hall closet, surrounded by brooms, mops, and umbrellas and under winter coats that never got used and reeked of mothballs. There was also a fire extinguisher in the closet for emergencies.

Sharpe and Burnside were in a catering company van parked across the street. Duncan and Eve were in separate cars along the block. Two LAPD patrol cars were on standby, two blocks away, ready to move in if needed. Walker wore earbuds so he could stay in contact with the surveillance unit on his phone.

Walker passed the hours on his phone, first watching some of *The Mandalorian* on pirate sites, then surfing the web to see how much a Mandalorian costume cost. He learned that he could get a nice one shipped to him overnight for only $200. It came with everything but the weapon, which was fine, since Walker had his own. His phone vibrated. A call was coming in. He answered it.

"Bogert just arrived," Sharpe said. "He came in a Cadillac instead of his truck and parked around the corner."

"How did you spot him?"

"Bogert parked right behind Duncan," Sharpe said. "He's walking down the street toward the house now."

"Got it."

He hit "BUY IT NOW" on his phone, then pocketed the device, careful not to hang up on Sharpe. A moment later, Walker heard Bogert slipping the key into the dead bolt and opening the front door, the hinges squeaking.

Bogert walked in, gently closed the door, and then stood a moment, likely letting his eyes adjust to the darkness.

"He's in the house," Sharpe said. Walker didn't need the commentary, but he kept quiet. "He's wearing leather work gloves."

When Bogert started moving, Walker could tell exactly where he was from the familiar creaks in the floorboards.

"He's walking down the hall," Sharpe said.

Walker could feel a shift in the air as Bogert passed the hall closet.

"He's in your son's room," Sharpe said in Walker's ear. "He's looking around. I don't think he's impressed by the paint job. Now he's approaching the pile of rags. He's picked up the can of paint thinner and is drenching the pile with more fluid. You better get going."

Walker took off his hat, picked up the fire extinguisher, and eased open the closet door, glad that he'd sprayed the hinges with WD-40 that afternoon so they wouldn't squeak.

"Bogert has tossed the can and is picking up one of the rags. He's got a disposable lighter in his other hand. What are you waiting for? He's going to light the rag."

"*That's* what I'm waiting for."

Walker burst in just as Bogert tossed the burning rag onto the pile, which instantly ignited into flames. He shoved the contractor aside and doused the fire with the extinguisher.

"You're under arrest," Walker said, dropping the extinguisher.

Bogert staggered back to a far corner, a trapped animal desperately looking for a way out. With Walker standing in the doorway, that left him only one possible exit.

The window.

"Don't," Walker said.

Bogert made a dash for it, protecting his head with his arms, and took a leap.

Walker tackled him in the air, just short of the glass, and slammed him face down onto the floor.

Bogert tried to scramble away, but Walker planted his knee in the man's back, pinning him down.

"A swan dive out the window was a really stupid idea. You'd have been diced and sliced." Walker took out his cuffs and wrenched Bogert's arms behind his back. "Which is okay with me, but those windows cost a fortune to replace."

"What do you care?"

He cuffed Bogert's wrists and stood up, hefting the man to his feet at the same time, then whispered into his ear, "It's my house."

Bogert's brow wrinkled with confusion. "I don't understand."

Walker clutched him by the arm and hauled him out the front door, where Eve stood on the lawn, holding up her badge, a smile on her face.

Bogert stared at her in shock.

Walker said, "Now do you get it?"

"Oh shit," Bogert said.

"It sure is, Larry, and you're in it deep."

Larry Bogert sat handcuffed in the Lost Hills station interrogation room facing Rebecca Burnside, who sat across the table from him with a blank yellow legal pad in front of her and a pen in her hand.

"Here are the facts, Mr. Bogert," she said. "We have you on video attempting to set a home on fire as part of a conspiracy to commit insurance fraud. We can tie you to at least a dozen other arson-related insurance frauds in Los Angeles County. You'll be celebrating your eightieth birthday in prison, assuming you're still alive. But there's a way you can shorten your sentence."

Bogert nodded. "You want me to testify against all the homeowners I worked for."

Walker said, "More than that, Larry."

"Like what?"

"We want Martin Graff," Sharpe said. "The arson investigator who declared those fires accidents, and we want any claims adjusters who got kickbacks from you."

"I can do that," Bogert said.

"We're not done, Larry," Walker said. "You also have to confess to planting the incendiary devices at Twin Lakes."

"I can't," he said.

"Why not?" Burnside said. "You're already going down for everything else."

"Because I didn't do it. Why would I?"

Sharpe said, "You hated them for not paying for your wife's cancer treatments and firing you once you were caught stealing."

"*Borrowing*, not stealing. But let's think this through."

"Let's," Walker said.

"If that dipshit guard hadn't caught me, and everything worked out, I would have still been a foreman there when the houses blew up.

I'd have been one of the first guys you two looked at for it. I'd have to be pretty goddamn dumb to do that."

Sharpe said, "You haven't exactly demonstrated stunning intelligence with this insurance scam."

"The only reason you got onto me was because you thought I was responsible for those fires at Twin Lakes, or I could've kept doing this scam until I retired. I'd say I'm pretty damn smart, just unlucky." Bogert looked at Burnside. "Like you said, you got me. If I did Twin Lakes, I'd use it to bargain my sentence down even further. But I didn't. So, let's get my lawyer in here and make a deal."

Walker believed him. He glanced at Sharpe and saw that he did, too. What felt like a huge win just a few moments ago now felt like failure.

Where did we go wrong?

But there was still more Walker wanted to know. "Tell me something, Larry. Why are you obsessed with fire?"

Bogert said, "It's not an obsession."

Sharpe said, "You've been burning things since you were a kid."

"It gives me power."

"Anybody can light a fire."

"Sure, to roast marshmallows or warm up a room," Bogert said. "But I use it to get things done . . . to change my life, to set things right, to make money."

"You don't feel any shame?" Sharpe asked.

Bogert looked him in the eye. "I feel pride."

"You must be very proud of yourself now," Sharpe said.

CHAPTER
TWENTY-SEVEN

A deal was struck with Bogert's lawyer to get him back on the street that night so none of his coconspirators would learn of his arrest. Burnside told Walker and Sharpe that it would take days, if not weeks, for her and her investigators to build the wider case, identify all of his coconspirators, and, if necessary, use Bogert to get them to incriminate themselves.

Burnside and the hierarchy of LASD saw this as a headline-making case that, once the arrests were made, would generate enormously positive attention for law enforcement. The department hired a commercial crime scene cleaning service to fix any smoke or fire damage done to Walker's house and to totally repaint Cody's room. They also agreed to put up his family at the Hilton Garden Inn until the work was done.

Walker and his family enjoyed their weekend at the hotel, spending hours at the pool and enjoying meals next door at the Commons, where Cody got his first moviegoing experience. It was a Disney cartoon that opened with a preview of the next *Star Wars* film, reminding Walker that Oxley was still out there somewhere, carrying around a weaponized virus in a tiny vial. The thought gave him a tickling anxiety that watching singing and dancing animals for two hours couldn't ease.

On Monday, Walker arrived at headquarters rested and energized, ready to tackle the Twin Lakes case again. He found Sharpe in his office looking exhausted, which was notable, considering the perpetual weariness already conveyed by the craggy, droopy folds of skin on his face that had earned him his nickname.

"It's Monday morning, so why do you look like it's late Friday night?" Walker cautiously removed one of the Twin Lakes explosives from the guest chair, set it gently on Sharpe's desk, and sat down.

"I've been working all weekend."

"On what?"

"For starters, checking Bogert's claim that he didn't do the Twin Lakes bombings. Arsonists like to see the fires they create. But he was at a jobsite in West LA when the fires happened. I've confirmed that. And since I don't believe he'd place the bombs without being nearby to see them go off, he's cleared."

Walker was convinced at the interrogation that Bogert didn't do Twin Lakes, and he'd thought that Sharpe was, too. But if Sharpe had to go prove it to himself for his own peace of mind, Walker was fine with that. At least Sharpe didn't try to drag him away from the Hilton pool to help him do it.

"That leaves us with that pissed-off homeowner who sued the developer, lost, and fled to Mexico," Walker said. "Or we have to come up with some new suspects."

"No, we don't," Sharpe said. "We've already met the arsonist, but the clues were pointing so clearly at Bogert that I ignored my gut."

Walker nodded. "It's Haley Frost, the ecoterrorist."

"It's Warren Pendle, the Freeway Service Patrol officer," Sharpe said. "That's who got my gut rumbling."

"Are you sure? You'd eaten a big, greasy lunch."

"It's a fact that the majority of wildland arsonists are either first responders or failed to become one," Sharpe said. "That's why I'm usually suspicious of any wannabe cops or firefighters circling an unexplained fire. Pendle is both."

"You're kidding. The man of action?"

Sharpe tapped the file in front of him. "I spent the weekend doing the digging that I should have done after we met him. The first thing I learned is that Pendle was a volunteer at Fire Station 75."

That was the same station that responded to the Hellmouth car fire and the house fires at Twin Lakes. Walker doubted that was a coincidence.

"I wish we'd known that before we met him."

"It gets worse," Sharpe said. "Pendle applied to be a fireman and didn't pass the exams. After that, he applied to be a cop and a deputy and crapped out there, too."

Walker sagged in his seat. Pendle might as well have shot up a flare and waved a flag that said, I'M AN ARSONIST. And they'd missed it. Now Walker was sure he knew what had really happened the night Bogert was caught stealing supplies.

"Pendle wasn't waiting for Bogert inside that house. He was in there planting bombs. It must've scared the shit out of Pendle when Bogert showed up. But when he saw Bogert was stealing building materials, Pendle found a way to turn the situation to his advantage."

"I'm sure he's still thanking God for that miracle," Sharpe said. "Not only was he saved from getting caught, he got the glory of making his first big arrest."

"But he couldn't stick around to bask in that admiration because he knew that once houses began bursting into flames, his bombs would be found," Walker said. "And everybody would've realized that he was the one person who had total access to the development at night to plant the devices."

"He'd always intended to quit," Sharpe said. "Going out a hero was an added benefit. He was counting on the fact that it'd be months before the houses blew up and by then he'd be long gone, out of sight and out of mind as a suspect."

"It worked," Walker said. "He even scored a job on the Freeway Service Patrol, where he could still play cop and have a chance at seeing the houses when they burned."

"Oh, he saw them," Sharpe said. "He told us he did. We were so intent on nailing Bogert that we missed the obvious arsonist sitting right in front of us."

"Who cares?" Walker said. "The only people who know about our mistake is the two of us."

"That doesn't make us any less stupid."

"You're not seeing the bright side."

"I thought that was the bright side."

"If we'd realized it was Pendle from the get-go, we never would have discovered that Bogert was a serial arsonist engaged in a massive insurance fraud."

"That's true," Sharpe said.

"Not only that, but in a few weeks, that crooked arson investigator Martin Graff will finally be in jail and those spineless politicians who let him walk will face a rude public reckoning." Walker stood now, lifted up by his own rhetoric. "We didn't make a mistake, Sharpe. We scored a massive win. We're heroes. We're superstars."

"That's a great way of looking at it," Sharpe said, nodding to himself, the hint of a smile on his face. "I feel much better about the whole thing."

"You should," Walker said. "It beats admitting how blind and stupid we are and that the only thing that saved our fat, ignorant asses was pure luck."

Sharpe's smile became a frown instead. "You never know when to keep your mouth shut."

"We have to work fast, before anybody else realizes how incompetent we are," Walker said. "Pendle had means and opportunity, but what was his motive for torching Twin Lakes?"

"Boredom? Too much time on his hands? I don't know. We'll have to ask him when we arrest him."

Walker sat down again, feeling the full weight of the investigation ahead on his shoulders. "How are we going to do that? We don't have any evidence, just a lot of speculation."

"I've started with less," Sharpe said.

"A stomachache."

"That's right."

"Have you ever thought about buying some Gas-X?"

"Nope," Sharpe said. "If I did that, my detective career would be over."

Fire Station 75 was in Chatsworth Lake Manor, a hardscrabble residential community tucked into a craggy, hilly, boulder-strewn patch of inhospitable land squeezed between the northwest border of the Chatsworth Nature Preserve and the southern end of Santa Susana Pass State Park.

The station looked like just another old, single-story ranch-style house along Lake Manor Road, but with a flagpole and chainsaw-sculpted wooden grizzly bear erected on the front lawn. Because that's exactly what it was. The county fire department moved into the house after the original station, up in Twin Lakes, was demolished in the late 1960s to make way for the 118 freeway.

The only things that gave the house away as a fire station, besides the sign along the roofline, were the paramedic truck parked under the carport and the fire engine visible in the open, freestanding, pitch-roofed metal garage in the back.

"Sure, I remember Warren Pendle," Captain Guyette said, standing in front of the garage and facing Walker and Sharpe. Behind him, his men were busy cleaning and polishing the fire engine. "He grew up just a few blocks away from here. The kid hung around here so much that we drafted him as a volunteer. He'd do anything we asked. To be honest, we kind of took advantage of him."

Walker said, "You made him shine the truck? Wash your laundry? Do the dishes? Clean the toilets?"

"Only alongside my guys when they were doing it, too."

"So how was that taking advantage if you were *all* doing the grunt work?"

"Because he took the one job nobody wanted."

Guyette led them inside the garage to a set of tall cabinets and opened one of the doors, revealing a coat closet. Hanging inside were the various pieces of a ferret costume: the furry head and whiskered nose, the humanlike body in a firefighter's coat, and the paw-shaped gloves and shoes.

"Warren played Fireplug the Fire Ferret when we did fire-safety presentations at community events," Guyette said.

"That's degrading," Walker said.

"It's horrible," Guyette said. "It's also hotter in that costume than it is fighting a fire. But Warren loved it. I've never seen anyone who wanted to be a firefighter more than him."

Sharpe said, "Dancing around in that ferret suit is not firefighter work."

"Actually, it is. Community relations is part of the job, but I wouldn't expect you to understand that, Shar-Pei." Guyette closed the cabinet door. "In return for going with us to schools and community picnics in that ridiculous suit, we taught Warren firefighting skills and sponsored him for the trainee program."

"But even with your help," Sharpe said, "he couldn't get in."

"I wasn't surprised. He had the enthusiasm and dedication, but not the intelligence or physical abilities . . . and he's a bit off."

"In what way?"

"His social skills," Guyette said, walking them back out to the front of the station. "He's never quite in sync with the conversation, like a dancer who can't find the beat, you know what I mean? He can also be overeager and a bit stalkerish. It gets irritating."

Walker asked, "Is that why you let him go?"

"If I booted out everyone who irritated me, the station house would be empty." Guyette stopped beside the grizzly bear sculpture. The bear was on his hind legs and reminded Walker of Larry Bogert, only without the denim shirt. "After Warren failed the entrance exam a second time, I decided we had to give his volunteer spot to someone who actually had a chance at making it as a firefighter."

"That must have broken his heart."

"You'd think so, but he begged us to let him stay, even if it meant just being Fireplug the Fire Ferret. I was tempted to let him. But it would have been cruel and humiliating for him to be in that suit, sweating to death, and watching other volunteers become firefighters. So, I told him he had to go. It obviously crushed him, but Warren has no hard feelings about it now."

Sharpe said, "How do you know?"

"Because we see him all the time."

"He still hangs around the station?"

"No, thank God," Guyette said. "We see him up on the freeway. He's always the first guy on scene whenever there's a brush fire or car accident. When we roll up, he'll be there, laying out warning cones, directing traffic, or even dousing the flames with a fire extinguisher."

Sharpe said, "Have there been a lot of fires along the freeway?"

"That's why we call it the Highway to Hell."

Walker said, "You use 'hell' to describe everything around here."

"You would, too, if you worked here," Guyette said. "Why are you two so interested in Warren?"

"He helped us catch an arsonist," Walker said.

"Really? Which one?"

"A former Twin Lakes construction worker," Walker said. "But not the guy who planted those bombs. We're still investigating that case."

"I'm glad to hear Warren was helpful. It must've made him feel great. The kid's heart is in the right place. He's just not cut out to be a firefighter."

"Or a cop," Sharpe said.

"But at least now he's got a job that gives him the sense that he's one of us."

Sharpe said, "More like Fireplug the Fire Ferret."

"You're all heart, Shar-Pei." Guyette walked away without saying another word. He'd had enough of Walter Sharpe.

But Sharpe wasn't offended. Walker knew he got exactly what he needed from the captain, facts that reinforced his belief that Pendle was their arsonist.

On the way to their Tahoe, Sharpe said to Walker, "I'll bet there's been an uptick in fires along the 118 since Pendle was hired on the Freeway Service Patrol."

"I'm sure you're right," Walker said. "I've lost track—what percentage of arsonists turn out to be the first person to either report a fire or to try and put it out?"

"Ninety percent."

"It sure takes the fun out of being a detective."

"It's not supposed to be fun."

They got into the Tahoe. Walker started up the engine, then checked the time on the dashboard clock. It was a few minutes after 10:00 a.m.

"Do you have Pendle's home address?"

"Yeah, it's on the eastern edge of Palmdale, south of the 14 freeway, off of Sand Canyon."

"Pendle is working now, even though his shift is technically over until 2:00 p.m. So, what do you say we take a swing past his house, see what we can see?"

"We don't have a search warrant," Sharpe said.

"Who said anything about a search?"

"Then what's the point?"

"You'd be surprised what you can learn about who you're chasing by looking at how they live."

"This could be the one day that Pendle decides to go home between shifts," Sharpe said.

"Even better," Walker said. "Maybe he'll invite us in."

CHAPTER TWENTY-EIGHT

Pendle's small house was in the perfect neighborhood for shooting another *Walking Dead* series, Walker thought. No set dressing would be required.

His tidy single-story house was at the end of a forgotten, dusty cul-de-sac, south of the dry Santa Clara River bed, within a partially built housing tract abandoned in the 1980s.

There was a graded, weed-choked lot on either side of his home, and the same was true for his neighbors across the crumbling asphalt street. There was also a row of three garbage cans on the street in front of each house awaiting the weekly trash pickup. One neighbor had a couch and a recliner on the street, too, but it looked like they'd been there for months.

Walker didn't know what calamity had doomed the development decades ago, but the wave of home construction sweeping through the Santa Clarita Valley wasn't touching this spot.

He pulled up the Tahoe in front of Pendle's trash cans and studied the house. Something about it screamed "cheaply built" to Walker, but otherwise it was better maintained than his own home, with fresh paint and drought-tolerant landscaping of cactuses, succulents, and African daisies amid crushed gravel.

But his eyes were drawn away from the house to the empty lots beside it. There were charred patches of dirt where fires had burned away scrub.

"Do you see what I see?" Walker asked.

"I see that and more," Sharpe said.

"I'm talking about the charred patches in the empty lots."

"You mean the obvious stuff I'd have to be blindfolded to miss," Sharpe said. "I'm talking about the burn spots on his driveway and in the asphalt in the middle of the cul-de-sac."

Walker looked at the driveway and the street. He hadn't seen those and there was no point admitting it now. "What does that mean?"

"You need glasses."

"I mean the burn spots," Walker said.

"That he's been testing out incendiary devices on the concrete and in the street, where he hopes it won't set fire to anything," Sharpe said. "Though judging by the fires in the weeds, some of his experiments went awry."

"His neighbors must love him."

Walker got out of the Tahoe, walked over to the trash can marked RECYCLABLES, and lifted the lid. It was filled with fast-food bags, Amazon boxes, junk mail, newspapers, beer cans, and empty Sparkling Ice bottles. And that was just what he could see.

Sharpe came up next to him and looked in the can. "He sure likes strawberry-kiwi Sparkling Ice."

"I wonder what other goodies might be in here." Walker wheeled the trash can to the back seat of their Tahoe and opened the door.

"You can't steal his trash can," Sharpe said.

"I'm not going to." Walker bent down, lifted the garbage can by the wheels, and emptied it onto the seat. "Just his trash."

"We don't have a warrant."

"We don't need a warrant for this. The Supreme Court said so."

Sharpe stared at the mess in their truck. "It's a good thing we have gas masks. It's a forty-minute drive back to the station."

Walker closed the door and wheeled the empty can back to its place. "Stop whining. It's not like the can was filled with rotting food, dirty diapers, and dog shit."

"It still stinks. How are you going to explain the stench to the arson investigators on the next shift who get the truck?"

"They'll think you had another gut feeling about a case."

"Very funny," Sharpe said, then looked past Walker to the cul-de-sac. "We have company."

Walker turned to see a sunburned, disheveled man in a tank top, cargo shorts, and flip-flops coming their way from the house across the street. He was in his thirties, reeked of pot, and reminded him of Shaggy, Scooby-Doo's friend in those old cartoons.

The man said, "You guys must work with Warren."

Walker said, "What makes you say that?"

"He's an arson investigator and that's what's written on the side of your truck." He pointed to the side of the Tahoe in case there was any confusion.

"Right. I forgot. We become blind to it after a while."

Pendle is pretending to be an arson investigator?

Walker introduced himself and Sharpe to the man, who said his name was Monroe Piltz.

"Warren is at work," Monroe said, using the huge jagged toenails on his right foot to scratch the dry, flaky skin on his left ankle.

"We know," Walker said, tearing his eyes away from those toenails. "We're here casing his place for a surprise party. So don't tell him you saw us or it will ruin it."

"Warren has friends?"

"Why does that shock you?"

Monroe grunted. "Come on, you've met the guy."

"He's a little awkward, sure, but you get used to that."

"Maybe you fellas can because he's not setting fires in your office or blowing things up in the parking lot."

Sharpe said, "Actually, we all do that. It's part of our job to test our theories on how a fire started."

"That's his excuse, too," Monroe said. "Except he keeps setting fire to the weeds and the explosions have made our cat so anxious, we've had to put her on meds."

"I'm sorry to hear that," Sharpe said. "What kind of stuff does he blow up?"

Monroe scratched his right ankle with the gnarly toenails of his left foot. Walker wondered how he kept his balance.

"I don't know . . . he doesn't let me get close enough to see. One time, a few months ago, it was unavoidable. He spent weeks building a shed on his property, even ran an electric line out to it. I thought it was going to be his workshop. But the first time he turned on the lights, the entire thing became a fireball, just like he wanted."

Walker said, "How do you know it wasn't an accident?"

"Two reasons," Monroe said. "Number one, because his dad was an electrician, so he knows how to wire stuff. And number two, because as soon as he turned on the lights, he stood in front of the shed, watching it with a fire hose in his hands that he'd connected to the hydrant out on the street."

"Seems reasonable to me," Sharpe said.

"You ever blow up a shed at home?" Monroe asked. Walker was curious to know the answer to that, too.

"No," Sharpe said, "but I've set fire to a car and a few trash cans— all for research, of course."

Monroe grunted again. "Sure you have. That's like saying you watch Pornhub for the cinematography. I've seen the way he looks at those fires. It's like he's getting a lap dance."

"That's not how I look at fire," Sharpe said.

"Take a video of yourself next time," Monroe said. "You might be surprised."

Walker said, "Do you have any videos of Warren setting fires?"

Monroe looked at him in mock outrage. "What kind of neighbor do you think I am?"

Walker grinned back at him. "One with a sense of humor and a taste for revenge. It'd be fun at the surprise party to show the videos and embarrass him in front of everybody."

Monroe grinned back. He obviously liked that idea. "I've got a ton of them. I could put them on a flash drive for you."

Sharpe said, "Is the shed fire on there?"

"Hell yes."

Walker looked at Sharpe. "This is going to be a great party."

"I already feel like celebrating," Sharpe said, then looked at Monroe. "How did you know that Warren's father was an electrician?"

"Warren told everybody. He's fixed a few faulty light switches, electrical outlets, and household appliances for us and the other neighbors. I suppose it's his way of apologizing for the noise and fires."

Sharpe said, "You probably haven't bought a coffee maker in years."

"Or a microwave. Or a toaster," Monroe said. "What's the party for?"

Walker said, "Employee of the Month."

They spoke for a few more minutes, then Monroe went off to get them the flash drive.

Walker shook his head, watching the man go. "God, I love nosy neighbors."

"You wouldn't feel that way if yours were watching you all the time and taking videos."

"They love me," Walker said.

"How do you know?"

"Who doesn't love having a cop on the street?"

"My neighbors," Sharpe said.

"Maybe they would if you'd stop blowing up trash cans and setting cars on fire."

"I don't do that often."

"Oh, well, then never mind," Walker said.

Monroe came back with the flash drive and promised not to say anything to Warren about their little meeting but asked to be invited to the party.

"You'll get the first invitation," Walker said, but didn't tell him it would be in the form of a subpoena to testify at Warren Pendle's trial.

They drove back to LASD headquarters and watched the videos in Sharpe's office on his laptop.

The videos were taken on Monroe's phone, through his living room window. In most of them, Pendle would set something on the driveway or in the cul-de-sac, light it with a common barbecue igniter gun, then step back a safe distance, where he had a fire extinguisher on the ground, ready to use. The object would usually flare up and die out quickly, leaving a scorch mark on the driveway or asphalt.

But in one video, Pendle put a wooden box on the ground that had a wire dangling from it. He ran the wire to a battery, and the instant he connected it, the package exploded, embers flying and setting the weeds on fire. Pendle dashed into the vacant lot with his fire extinguisher and quickly put out the blaze.

Judging by the burned patches in the lots, Walker figured this kind of accident happened frequently.

Sharpe fast-forwarded the video until they saw the shed, which was in the side yard of Pendle's Cyclone-fenced property and looked more like an outhouse than a workshop, even though it had stucco walls, a small window, and a porch light beside the door.

The structure was sloppy and lopsided and Monroe could easily see it from across the street, though he had to zoom in to get a close-up shot. Nothing about the way it was designed or built suggested to Walker that Pendle was proud of it or intended it to last.

A power cord ran from the shed to an outdoor electrical outlet on the house. Pendle flicked a switch on the wall and the porch light on the shed went on.

Pendle picked up the fire hose, pointed it at the shed, and waited. After a minute or two, the shed erupted into flames, the force of the blast shattering the window and cracking the stucco. Fire and smoke belched out toward Pendle, who doused the shed with water, drowning the flames. The shed was reduced to a pile of wet, smoking rubble.

Sharpe turned off the video and Walker said, "It sure looks to me like he was testing one of his house bombs."

"It could be argued that we're just seeing what we want to see."

"How else would you explain what he did?"

"Bad electrical work. We have no proof that he placed one of his incendiary devices in that shed. We need more."

Walker knew he was right and stood up. "Fine. Maybe there will be a confession in the trash."

The two detectives put on gloves, went to the parking lot, laid a tarp on the ground beside the Tahoe, and then emptied the trash in the back seat onto the ground.

They started by bagging some Sparkling Ice water bottles to be sent to the lab to extract DNA and fingerprints off them that could be used for comparative purposes with any evidence from the bombs. After that, they sorted through the rest of the trash. Among the newspapers, various fast-food containers, junk mail, and beer cans, they also found some bits of wire, an empty dispenser of electrical tape, and an empty bottle of lighter fluid. Although some of those items could be used to make bombs, there were legitimate reasons for having them, too.

The trash included several discarded Amazon boxes and bags that still contained the receipts, which told them that the purchased items included Sparkling Ice, Oreo Cookies, the *Chicago Fire: The Complete*

Series DVD boxed set, Cheetos, electrical tape, batteries, soldering supplies, and replacement parts for various household appliances, but no heating elements.

"He has everything he needs here to make bombs," Walker said. "But also to have a *Chicago Fire* viewing party and barbecue while he fixes toasters. There's no smoking gun."

"That's true, but all of this, combined with the video and everything else we know, may be just enough to get a search warrant with a very narrow scope."

"How narrow?"

"A peek at his Amazon purchases to see if he bought coffee-maker heating coils in bulk six months ago."

"There are lots of places he could have bought those coils."

"Yeah, but that's where you got yours and, looking at this trash, he obviously buys everything else from Amazon."

It's worth a shot, Walker thought.

While Sharpe sought the warrant, Walker photographed everything, then bagged the items in the trash he thought might be important later, which included the Amazon receipts and items that could be used to make explosives.

When that was done, he took the Tahoe to a nearby car wash and had them shampoo the interior, then went to the Carl's Jr. across the street for a late lunch.

While he ate, he went on Amazon with his phone and ordered a Wonder Woman costume in Carly's size and paid extra for overnight delivery. It would be waiting for him when they got home on Tuesday night, which was when the crime scene cleaning crew promised they'd be done with their work. It would be their first night alone in bed since Wednesday.

Walker was crossing the street to pick up the Tahoe when Sharpe called.

"Did you get the warrant?" Walker asked.

"I did and already served it on Amazon," Sharpe said. "Pendle ordered four dozen coffee-maker heating coils eight months ago."

"Wow, Amazon Prime even offers fast delivery on search warrant compliance," Walker said. "We've got him."

"Burnside isn't convinced. Pendle can explain away the coffee-maker parts by pointing to all the appliance repairs he does for his neighbors."

Walker crossed the street and sat down on a bus bench to continue the conversation. The bench advertised the services of a "Major League" lawyer who specialized in helping drunk drivers avoid jail time and keep their driver's licenses. His slogan: *I'll Fight the Woke Mob for You.*

"What about the shed video?"

"Pendle's lawyer could argue that he was being careful and responsible, waiting around after he activated the electricity in his shed to make sure it was safe . . . and when the fire started, he prevented a possible catastrophe."

"A real Boy Scout," Walker said. "Burnside doesn't believe any of that, does she?"

"She thinks he's guilty, too. She okayed the arrest, but warned me if the charges are going to stick, we'll have to break him."

"Oh, I can break him," Walker said. "Like a breadstick."

Even, he thought, if Pendle gets a major-league lawyer to fight the woke mob for him.

"How do you want to handle the arrest?" Sharpe asked.

"With finesse," Walker said.

He already had a plan for taking Pendle down fast and easy, one that wouldn't put any innocent people at risk or give him an opportunity to resist or escape.

Pendle wouldn't even see the arrest coming until he was already in handcuffs.

CHAPTER
TWENTY-NINE

Eve Ronin sat on the guardrail along the shoulder of the westbound 118 freeway on Wednesday morning, held her jacket tight around her, and stared glumly at the traffic whizzing by at high speed. Her right rear tire was flat. And the expression on her face suggested that the possibility of her being able to change the tire was as likely as her splitting an atom.

That's when a gleaming white Freeway Service Patrol truck rolled up behind her car. She regarded the vehicle with a mixture of relief and trepidation.

Officer Warren Pendle slowly opened his door, looked cautiously to his left at the oncoming traffic, and carefully stepped out as a huge big rig roared past him, creating a blast of wind that forced him to hold the brim of his cowboy hat to keep it from blowing off his head.

He walked around the front of his truck to the freeway guardrail. His uniform was military crisp, his shoes shined, and he offered Eve a big, friendly smile as he approached.

"Good morning, ma'am," he said, politely tipping the brim of his hat. "Having some troubles with your vehicle?"

Eve scowled at the Bronco, as if it intentionally offended her. "Yes, I am. Are you Triple A?"

"No, ma'am."

"That's good, because I'm not a member, which I am deeply regretting right now. I was just sitting here trying to figure out who to call for help."

"You can rest easy now. Help has arrived and it won't cost you anything."

"It won't?"

"I'm Officer Warren Pendle with the freeway service division of the California Highway Patrol." He patted the patch on his chest. "What's the problem?"

Eve gestured to her flat. "I must have run over a nail or something and I've never changed a tire in my life."

"That's nothing to be ashamed of. You'd be surprised how many men and women haven't, either. I see it every day. Do you have a spare?"

Eve got up. "I'm not sure. I hope so."

"Let me see." Pendle stepped to the rear of her SUV and, as he turned to reach for the liftgate handle, Eve came up behind him and pulled out her Glock.

"Don't move, Warren. I'm Detective Eve Ronin, with the Los Angeles County Sheriff's Department, and you're under arrest."

Pendle started to turn, but she jammed the gun in his back, and he faced forward again. "For what?"

She ignored his question. "Spread your legs, place your hands behind your head, and lace your fingers together."

He did as he was told. Eve patted him down, felt something on his right ankle, and lifted his pant leg to find a holstered gun.

"It's registered," he said. "I have the paperwork in the truck."

She removed the gun and put it in her pocket. "Why are you armed?"

"For community safety. I'm a law enforcement officer. Just like you."

"No, Warren, you're not."

Eve heard another vehicle rolling up behind Pendle's truck but she kept her focus on her prisoner. She holstered her weapon, took out her handcuffs, and cuffed Pendle's arms behind his back.

"Are you going to tell me what I'm being charged with?"

"They will." She turned him around to see Walker and Sharpe standing side by side on the freeway shoulder behind her. The color drained from Pendle's face.

"Nice hat," Walker said. He took out his phone, turned on the recording app, and read Pendle his rights. "Do you understand your rights as I have explained them to you?"

Pendle stood with his back to the Bronco, facing the three detectives, his tow truck, and the oncoming traffic. Cars sped by, sending blasts of air into the space where they stood between the two parked vehicles, threatening to blow his hat away—and he wouldn't be able to save it.

"Yes, of course I do," Pendle said. "I'm a CHP officer."

Sharpe said, "You're a tow truck driver."

"I'm wearing a badge," Pendle said.

"It's a *patch*," Sharpe said.

Pendle said, "When is somebody here going to tell me what you think I've done so we can clear up this misunderstanding?"

Walker said, "You're under arrest on so many counts of arson, we're going to need a calculator to add them all up."

"It's not me. It's unthinkable," he said. "I was a firefighter trainee until I answered the call of law enforcement."

"You weren't a trainee," Sharpe said. "You were Fireplug the Fire Ferret. We know you planted the incendiary devices at Twin Lakes. Bogert nearly caught you doing it instead of you catching him stealing supplies."

"Here's the irony," Walker said. "Bogert is an arsonist, too."

"I don't understand," Pendle said.

Eve rested her back against the grille of Pendle's truck and crossed her arms under her chest. A woman in judgment. "He sets homes on fire so he can get hired to remodel them. It's an insurance scam."

"You two could have been best buddies," Walker said. "An opportunity lost."

"Maybe not," Eve said to Walker, then looked at Pendle. "We arrested Bogert a few days ago. You two would be perfect cellmates since you're so much alike."

"We have nothing in common," Pendle said, practically spitting the words at her. "I arrested him first, remember? I enforce the law. I don't break it."

Sharpe said, "We know about all the coffee-maker heating coils you ordered from Amazon and the shed you built to test the devices that you used at Twin Lakes."

Walker added, "Your neighbor Monroe, the one with the cat you drove insane, has it all on video. We've seen it."

"You should arrest him for being a Peeping Tom," Pendle said. "I'm obviously the victim here."

"You weren't as careful as you think you were wiping forensic evidence off those gasoline-filled strawberry-kiwi Sparkling Ice bottles you used in your bombs," Walker said. "We got the empties from your trash and the lab compared them with the bottles we recovered from the unexploded devices. Guess what we found?"

"Absolutely nothing," Pendle said, shouting to be heard over a tractor trailer that charged past them in a blur. His cowboy hat blew off, but Eve caught it.

When the noise settled again into the almost surf-like ebb and flow of freeway traffic, Walker took the hat from her, stepped forward, and carefully placed it on Pendle's head.

"No DNA or fingerprints, that's true." Walker adjusted the hat so it sat just right, and he could see that Pendle was trembling.

Walker smiled at him and stepped back beside Eve. "But you didn't know there's a pollen that's unique to the weeds beside your house in Sand Canyon. It's all over the bottles and it ties you to the bombs."

It was a lie, but Walker could see that it hit Pendle like a slap in the face.

Eve saw it, too. "Ouch."

"That's not all," Sharpe said. "I'm sure when we search your truck, we're going to find your fire-setting kit, too."

Eve looked at Sharpe. "His what?"

She knew what it was.

But her question gave Sharpe the mallet to drive the wooden stake in. "It's the bag full of goodies that Warren has been using to set fires along this freeway since the day he was hired. Fireplug would be so ashamed."

Pendle flinched. "I want to see your warrant."

"We don't need one." Sharpe patted the hood. "The truck isn't yours. It belongs to the county."

Pendle looked like he was about to vomit.

The breadstick is about to break. Walker said, "The only thing we don't know, Warren, is why you did it."

Pendle glanced at the freeway, then at the hills, where Twin Lakes was nestled, then back at the three of them. He shrugged, defeated.

"Boredom. I had nothing else to do up there at night."

"And out here?"

"The same," he said. "Changing tires and towing cars is monotonous. I need excitement."

"That may be true about Twin Lakes," Sharpe said, "but it was about more on the freeway. You wanted the glory of spotting the fires and putting them out. You wanted to be a hero."

"Who doesn't?"

"Me," Sharpe said.

"Me too," Eve said.

"Me three," Walker said.

"Then why did you all become cops?"

"To catch people like you," Walker said.

"I can't go to prison," he said to Walker, one man of action to another. "You know what they do to cops in there."

"You aren't a cop."

Pendle looked past the three detectives as if he could see his bleak future ahead.

And then he could.

For Walker, it happened in the blink of an eye. Pendle was there, and then he wasn't. Gone in a snap.

Except the snap was a wet smacking sound and the horrific wailing of brakes as a Greyhound bus passed by the three of them.

The bus came to a jarring stop and nearly got rear-ended by a car, causing a chain reaction of screeching brakes that stretched back half a mile.

Something skipped across the top of the bus and landed at Eve's feet.

It was a cowboy hat, splattered with blood.

Eve ran to the front of the bus, stopped cold, then turned and looked back at Walker and Sharpe. The expression on her face said it all.

Pendle was dead.

"So much for finesse," Sharpe said.

CHAPTER THIRTY

"You can't blame yourself for this," Carly said, sitting across from Walker at their kitchen table while Cody giggled in his playpen.

"No, but the department can, and spread the blame to Sharpe and Eve while they're at it, even though I told the LT it was entirely my fault," Walker said, his spaghetti dinner untouched. "I was actually trying to minimize the chances of something going wrong."

"You also wanted to have some fun."

It was more of a psychological observation than the supportive words he would have liked, but he was used to that from Carly. She was who she was and so was he.

"Well, sure, that too. I don't get many chances for creativity in this new job."

"There are risks to creativity."

"There are risks to everything in what I do." There was an edge of anger in his voice that made Carly shift from shrink mode to wife mode. Or at least change the subject.

"Did you find the fire-setting kit in Pendle's truck?"

Walker nodded. "Sharpe nailed it, as usual. It was a toolbox stuffed with premade simple arson devices for any occasion, like matches, firecrackers, electrical tape, batteries, that kind of thing. As well as minibar bottles full of accelerants, those little flame guns for lighting candles, and bags of sawdust and wood shavings for kindling."

"I'm guessing it was all arranged in the box in a very orderly manner, like a silverware drawer."

"It was," he said.

"It fits the profile."

He looked at her. "You did a profile?"

"In my own mind, based on what you've told me about his pressed-and-starched uniform and his gleaming truck. I couldn't help myself. You also have the recording of your conversation with him before his suicide. So there's no doubt you got the right man."

"That's the one thing working in our favor."

"You have more than that going for you. You solved the crime." Carly picked up their plates and carried them back into the kitchen. "I'm sure the internal investigation will clear you all of any wrongdoing. How are Walter and Eve taking being benched?"

"Sharpe isn't worried at all. He told the LT that he's not responsible for crazy people doing crazy things, though I'm not sure if he was talking about me or Pendle. Maybe both."

"You aren't crazy." Carly stuck her empty plate in the sink.

"Is that your professional opinion?"

"Yes."

"I'd like it in writing, please. Maybe even notarized."

Carly covered his plate with plastic wrap and put it in the refrigerator. "But you are reckless."

"You can leave that part out."

"What about Eve?" Carly opened the freezer and took out a quart of chocolate chip cookie dough ice cream.

"I'm not sure how she feels. We haven't talked about it."

Carly stuck two spoons in the quart of ice cream and brought it back to the table, taking a seat beside her husband.

"The good news is that you have four days of paid leave to enjoy. You can spend more time with us . . . and finally get to some of those projects around the house that you've been wanting to do."

He didn't want to do any of them.

"Actually, I have some cop work to do."

Carly took a spoonful of ice cream. "You're on leave."

"The work is in San Diego."

"That's outside your jurisdiction."

"I've got a hunch that a guy we're chasing for an arson here will show up down there this weekend. It might be our only opportunity to catch him."

Carly took a spoonful, then: "Do your bosses know what you have in mind?"

Walker dug into the ice cream with his spoon and ate a mouthful before speaking. "I'm on leave, so it hasn't come up in conversation."

"You're going rogue."

"I'm showing some personal initiative."

"While you're under investigation for your role in a suspect's death."

"Suicide." Walker had more ice cream.

Carly set down her spoon and watched her husband eat. "This could make things worse for you."

"Or better, if I catch the guy." Walker dug around the ice cream, dislodged a big chunk of cookie dough, and ate it. "Speaking of which, did I get anything from Amazon today?"

"Two big boxes. They're by the front door."

"Excellent." Walker got up, took a box cutter from the junk drawer in the kitchen, and went over to the boxes.

Carly stood behind him as he opened one up. "What is it?"

"A cunning disguise."

He pulled out the individual pieces of a full Mandalorian suit, setting them on the floor.

"Are you going to a costume party?"

"You could say that. Help me put it on."

She did and it fit him perfectly.

The first layer was a dark-gray jumpsuit, over which they attached the metallic-looking pleather shoulder, arm, chest, and leg plates with Velcro, so he'd have to avoid wearing the outfit while defusing any bombs or undressing around any flammable gases. The cross-body bandolier came with fake ammo cartridges but could fit some real ones. The empty holster on the utility belt was a perfect fit for his Glock, which was hidden by the knee-length cape.

The final touch was the helmet, which had a built-in, tinted wraparound visor that still limited his peripheral vision, which wasn't ideal for a gunfight on earth or in outer space, unless it was a face-to-face duel.

"Trick or treat," Walker said.

"I didn't know you were into *Star Wars*."

"I'm not, but the guy I'm chasing is. There's a big science fiction fan convention in San Diego this weekend that I'm certain he won't want to miss."

"Even if he's a fugitive?"

"Nobody can see his face inside this helmet. He'll blend in, just like I will."

"So how are you going to spot him?"

Walker took off his helmet. "His Mandalorian suit is real, or perhaps I should say 'the real deal.' Up close, you can see that it has some unique wear and tear that no other suit will have."

"How many people are attending this event?"

"About twenty-five thousand."

"How many will be in Mandalorian suits?"

"I have no idea," Walker said.

"I can't picture Walter Sharpe in a Mandalorian suit or even attending a conference like this."

"Neither can I," he said. "That's why I have a backup plan."

Walker patted the unopened box.

The next morning, Walker met Eve Ronin for breakfast at Bobby's Coffee Shop in Woodland Hills, where they were less likely to be spotted by any of her colleagues at the Lost Hills station.

The restaurant opened on Ventura Boulevard in 1949 and the decades of greasy steam that soaked into the walls, through the framing, and into every fiber of insulation gave the place its comforting bacony-buttery smell even when nothing was on the grill in the open kitchen.

Eve was already in a booth when he arrived and didn't even offer him a greeting before getting right to the point.

"What did you want to talk about that couldn't be done on the phone?"

The waitress came over before he could answer. He ordered a coffee and a stack of pancakes and so did Eve.

He said, "I want to apologize for getting you into trouble."

"You didn't. Arresting bad guys is my job."

"But this wasn't your case, it was mine . . . and it didn't end well."

The waitress brought the coffees and left.

"I don't think I'm facing any career blowback," Eve said. "The captain put me on leave for a few days to deal with things."

"Deal with what?"

She looked at him, a bit astonished. "Has anyone ever killed themselves in front of you before?"

"This was the first time."

"Not for me." Eve poured a packet of sugar into her coffee and stirred it. "A deputy broke into my condo and blew his head off in front of me."

"Why?" Walker asked.

"He blamed me for destroying his career. His family sued me and the department, but the case was settled before it ever went to court."

Walker took a sip of his coffee and tried to ask his next question as casually and nonjudgmentally as he could. "Did you ruin his career?"

"He ruined it himself. I just threatened to expose what he did."

Walker brushed some nonexistent crumbs off the table. "Then you have nothing to feel guilty about . . . then or now."

"I still have to live with what I saw and my role in it."

The waitress came, set a plate of pancakes down in front of each of them, and walked away.

"You weren't responsible for what happened to Pendle." Walker slathered his stack with maple syrup. "If anybody is, it was me. I arranged the whole setup. I bullied him. You were a bystander. So let it go."

"His suicide doesn't bother you?"

Walker ate some of his pancakes. "Not one bit."

"I tell myself and other people that it doesn't bother me." She idly moved the pat of butter around the top of her pancakes with her knife. "But the truth is, it does. I'm awakened by that gunshot in my mind, my ears ringing, once or twice a month."

"How do you know it's that gunshot?"

"I just do," she said. "I wonder how this suicide will wake me up. Will it be the screech of the bus brakes? Or the awful, wet crunch of impact?"

Walker kept eating. "Maybe it will be nothing."

"I hope you're wrong. I don't want to stop feeling. I don't want to get emotional calluses."

"Calluses?"

"It's something Duncan warned me about," Eve said, and took a small bite of her pancakes, more out of going through the motions than wanting to eat. "But you didn't ask me to breakfast to check on my feelings."

"It matters to me," Walker said. "I'm a sensitive guy married to a shrink. I'm all about feelings."

Eve smiled. "Carly is. You, not so much." She pointed her fork at him. "You want something from me."

"No, I'm offering you something positive to do so you don't just sit around for days, wallowing in what happened on the freeway."

Eve laughed and had some more of her pancakes. "Spoken like a man who is all about feelings."

"We're going to catch Colin Oxley."

Walker told her his plan. By the time he was done, they'd both finished their pancakes. Somehow, having someone to chase gave them both appetites.

Eve said, "What makes you think he'll come out of hiding for this conference?"

"I'm a manhunter. I know my prey."

Walker took out his phone, pulled up one of the photographs she took at Oxley's house, and zoomed in on the framed SciCon posters. He showed it to her.

"He's never missed a SciCon in his adult life," he said. "On top of that, they're screening a big new *Star Wars* movie and the entire cast will be there. But even without all that, he's not going to pass up the chance to preen around in his Mandalorian suit. It will be a taste of freedom for him after days of living in his van somewhere."

She handed the phone back to Walker. "What if he also brings his vial of plague?"

"He probably will. It's too risky to leave it behind where somebody might stumble on it and remove the cork."

"He might do it himself in the middle of the convention center."

"One more very good reason to take him down," Walker said.

Eve pushed the empty plate away and sat back in her seat. "Thousands of people could die if this goes wrong."

He leaned forward, resting his arms on the table. "Thousands of people could be saved if this goes right."

"The responsible thing to do would be to notify the FBI about your theory," she said. "They can secure the conference center and have a hazardous materials unit on standby."

"That would be the *irresponsible* thing to do."

Now she leaned forward. "How do you figure that?"

"FBI agents and cops will stand out like neon signs in that crowd. When Oxley spots them, and he will, it could provoke him into doing something crazy, like releasing the virus. But he will never see us coming."

"Have you got a Mandalorian suit for me, too?"

"One of us needs to have unobstructed peripheral vision." Walker leaned back and smiled. "A Wonder Woman suit will work for you."

"He's seen my face, Walker."

"If you're wearing a low-cut red-and-gold corset and a star-spangled miniskirt, I guarantee you that he won't be looking at your face."

"You already got me the Wonder Woman suit, didn't you?"

"And the Lasso of Truth." Walker jerked a thumb over his shoulder. "It's in my truck."

She leaned back and smiled, too. "You're convinced that I'll say yes."

"It's not a big risk. You're the same size as Carly," he said. "My birthday is coming up and she will look great in it."

"That was more than I needed to hear," Eve said. "Do you have tickets to the conference?"

Walker held up his badge. "This is our ticket. We'll tell security that we're chasing a fugitive wanted for multiple homicides."

"So, we *will* be notifying the local law, just not until we get there."

"When it will be too late for them to bring in reinforcements and screw things up."

"But they will be just a radio call away if we get into trouble."

"We won't," Walker said. "The odds of us spotting Oxley among the tens of thousands of geeks in costumes are low anyway."

"Good," she said. "Because if we make an arrest as the Mandalorian and Wonder Woman, we will never live it down. When do we leave?"

"Right now," he said.

CHAPTER THIRTY-ONE

Walker followed Eve to her house in a guard-gated community of Spanish-Mediterranean McMansions on a ridge in Calabasas.

TV pays well, he thought as he parked in front of her huge one-story house that overlooked a canyon.

They changed into their costumes in her house, which was too large for one person and only sparsely furnished. She went to her room, and he used a bathroom.

He put on everything except the helmet, clipped his badge to his belt, put some extra ammo cartridges into the loops of his bandolier, and slipped his Glock into the holster.

Eve put on her entire Wonder Woman suit, including the tiara, golden wrist plates, and Lasso of Truth. The miniskirt was just long enough to hide a belt holding her badge and a small Glock if she didn't do any spinning.

"It's a good look for you," Walker said.

"You look naked without your Stetson."

"We all have to make sacrifices for justice."

They got into his pickup truck and headed for San Diego. Walker kept the speedometer at ninety most of the way and used near-empty toll roads to get through Orange County. Luck was on their side and they didn't get pulled over by the CHP for speeding. They made the three-hour drive in a little over two.

Walker and Eve killed the time talking about her TV series and the challenges she faced balancing her real life with her fictional one, even though she wasn't playing herself on-screen. But she felt pressured to be that character and feared that maybe, unconsciously, she was already trying to match her fantasy image. To make things worse, the show was shot in and around Calabasas, even outside the Lost Hills station, so she often ran into her fantasy self while doing her real job.

"It's dizzying," she said.

"You may want to see my wife," Walker said.

"You think I'm losing my mind?"

"Not yet," he said. "But a little prevention couldn't hurt."

"It could if word got out in the department that I was seeing a shrink."

"Meet her at Bobby's or the Coffee Bean," he said. "You'll look like two friends getting together."

"I'm not sure anybody would believe that," she said. "I have a family, and a lover, but I don't have friends."

"You have me," he said, and that made her smile.

The San Diego Convention Center was a 2.6-million-square-foot complex shaped vaguely like a docked ocean liner with symbolic sails along the top. It was located on the downtown waterfront, facing the Embarcadero marina directly below and, across the bay, Coronado and the naval air station.

Walker tried not to hit any people as he navigated streets packed solid with costumed attendees representing the *Star Wars*, *Star Trek*, DC, and Marvel universes, but few from our own. He pulled up to the gate of a restricted parking area on the north end of the center and lowered his window to talk to the uniformed San Diego police officer on duty.

"We're law enforcement." Walker introduced himself and Eve, then flashed his badge and Eve flashed hers.

The officer smirked at the badges. "You expect me to believe those are real?"

"Why wouldn't they be?"

"Have you looked in the mirror, pal?" the officer said.

"We're undercover," Walker said. "Point us to the security office. They can verify our IDs. If we're frauds, they'll arrest us."

The officer figured that was a safe alternative and he pointed them to a parking spot. They got out of the truck and approached an AUTHORIZED PERSONNEL ONLY security door, where they were buzzed in and escorted by a guard through employee-only corridors to the security office.

Walker held his helmet under his arm and willed himself not to be self-conscious about how ridiculous he looked, but that wasn't easy to do while wearing a cape. He figured it was even harder for Eve, showing so much skin and wearing a tiara, though when he glanced at her, she projected pure confidence and authority in her stature and her walk. She *was* Wonder Woman.

The security office was windowless and lined with rows of computer consoles facing a vast video wall that showed hundreds of live images in individual squares from cameras all over the convention center. Each console was manned by someone with a headset talking to ground personnel and facing a monitor focused on a handful of the squares up on the big screen.

Walker and Eve were met by Georgette Flaherty, the center's head of security, and Manny Santos, an openly skeptical San Diego police detective.

"This is a first," Santos said, making a show of giving them both the once-over. "You say you're cops?"

"We are," Walker said. They produced their badges, Walker introduced them both, and then he said, "We're pursuing a fugitive wanted for multiple homicides. We think he's here right now."

Flaherty cocked a perfectly tweezed eyebrow at Eve. "You're Eve Ronin? The cop with the TV show?"

"That's me," she said.

"It's not enough for you? Now you want to play Wonder Woman, too?"

"It's a disguise," she said. "And I don't play Eve, I am Eve."

Santos said, "Do my bosses know you're here?"

"This was a fast-developing situation," Walker said. "We didn't have time to notify anybody."

"But you had time to get those getups."

"They aren't hard to find in San Diego today. You can buy your own across the street."

The skepticism deepened on Santos' face. "I'm not into cosplay and you're way out of your jurisdiction. I've got to let my captain know about this."

"Fine, but while you're doing that, give us rovers and we'll start looking for our man."

"What's he look like?"

"Me," Walker said. "Only with the helmet on."

Flaherty said, "Do you know how many guys out there are dressed like you?" She pointed to the giant wall screen and all the video feeds that it contained. "Hundreds."

She was right. He could see Mandalorians everywhere. But at least some of them were female versions, or had armor or helmets with different designs that stood apart from Oxley's. That gave him a shred of hope.

"I know they are scattered everywhere," Eve said, "but are there some places the Mandalorians are more likely to be?"

"Lining up hours early for the *Star Wars* premiere outside of Ballroom 6 upstairs or at the various *Star Wars* booths in Exhibit Halls A through C on the ground floor. Does this fugitive have a name?"

"Colin Oxley," Walker said.

"Every attendee has to wear a registration name tag around their neck or clipped to their clothing. It has an RFID chip embedded inside that's scanned at all entrances and exits." Flaherty leaned over a nearby computer keyboard and hit some keys, then read the screen. "His tag was scanned at the main entrance six hours ago and nowhere else, so he's here and hasn't left, unless he's swapped IDs with someone else."

"Shit," Santos said. "If this guy is a killer, why weren't we alerted ahead of time? We could have grabbed him when he walked through the door."

"*If* that was him wearing his tag," Walker said. "He could have given his ID to someone else just to see if it was safe for him to come in or if we were waiting at the door to grab him. That's what I would do."

"That doesn't answer my question," Santos said.

"We were playing a hunch," Eve said. "We didn't know if it would pay off."

"You're playing more than that, Wonder Woman," Santos said. "Have you two got a hotel room here?"

"This is strictly professional," she said.

"Yeah, I can see that," Santos said. "Are the attendees at risk from this guy?"

Walker wasn't ready to tell him that Oxley could be carrying a vial of a highly infectious weaponized virus that could kill everyone in the convention center . . . and thousands more if any infected people were allowed to leave. He chose his next words carefully.

"He's not a mass shooter, if that's what you're asking. His killings in LA were personal."

Eve turned to Flaherty. "Can you tell us where Oxley is right now by tracking his ID badge?"

"We could if he was one of our employees," Flaherty said. "But we don't track our twenty-five thousand guests. The optics would be terrible and the fans wouldn't tolerate it. They'd never step in here again, for this event or any other, and the city would lose tens of millions of dollars in convention spending."

Santos said, "How are you going to tell Oxley apart from every other Mandalorian? He already took a huge risk walking into the center. He'd be a fool to still be wearing a name tag around his neck."

"He's got some distinctive scratches and burns on his suit," Walker said.

"Scratches and burns. Shit," Santos said. "You're looking for a grain of basmati rice in a box of Rice-A-Roni."

Flaherty handed them each a map of the center and explained that SciCon was using only the north half of the facility.

On the ground floor, Exhibit Halls A and C were for people selling DVDs, comic books, models, books, action figures, jewelry, and countless other science fiction and fantasy paraphernalia. Exhibit Hall B was set aside for elaborate displays by movie studios promoting their new and upcoming releases. The studios would also be hosting giveaways, displaying props and costumes, and staging celebrity photo ops, all guaranteed to generate fan frenzies.

On the second floor, the grand ballroom would be screening one movie or TV show premiere or sneak preview after another, while panel discussions on various subjects would be held in the surrounding meeting rooms.

And every inch of the place would be jammed with thousands of costumed attendees. Walker wondered how many other fugitives besides Oxley were wandering among the crowds, feeling completely secure in their anonymity and relishing their freedom.

Santos walked over to a wall where dozens of rovers were charging. He handed Walker and Eve one each, and a set of earbuds to go with them, then instructed the detectives on how to talk only to each other and how to reach him.

Walker clipped the rover to his belt, under his cape, and inserted his earbuds. Eve did the same under her skirt, which didn't quite cover the radio.

Santos poked a finger at Walker's chest plate. "In the unlikely event that you spot Oxley, you call us and we'll take him down, swiftly and quietly. Is that understood?"

"Gotcha," Walker said.

"And if I find out you're bullshitting me, that you're off the reservation, I'll arrest you both and drag your asses out of here."

"I'm half-Cherokee," Walker said. "Do you have any idea how offensive the term 'off the reservation' is to me?"

Santos blushed. "I'm sorry, I wasn't aware of that. I meant no offense."

"How would you like it if I said you'll be making burritos at Taco Bell if Oxley escapes because you got in our way?"

"Point taken," Santos said. "I'll alert guards at every exit to double-check the IDs of any Mandalorian leaving the center."

"That'd be a dumb move," Walker said. "If Oxley sees that extra attention being given to Mandalorians, he'll know we're onto him, and he'll find another way out. He's not a stupid man. We want to catch him by surprise. Just pretend we were never here and do whatever it is you usually do."

Walker marched out of the room. Eve followed him.

Once they were in the hallway, Eve whispered, "Are you really half-Cherokee?"

"Nope. I just hate it when people poke me in the chest," Walker said. "Let's take another good look at Oxley's suit."

Walker and Eve took out their phones, pulled up their photos of the Mandalorian suit, and discussed the distinctive markings on it.

"I'll recognize it," Eve said. "Particularly that one slash across the chest, even from a distance."

"Me too." Walker pocketed his phone. "Okay, let's start by walking the *Star Wars* movie line outside of the upstairs ballroom. I'll come up from the back, you go down from the front, and we'll meet in the middle. If he's not there, we'll do a grid pattern in Exhibit Hall B, aisle by aisle, each of us working from a different end."

"Works for me," Eve said.

Walker put the Mandalorian helmet over his head and, in a deep voice, said, "That is the way."

CHAPTER
THIRTY-TWO

It took them an hour to search the *Star Wars* line and half of Exhibit Hall B, and they still had two more exhibit halls to go, not counting the meeting rooms and lobbies.

And when that was done, Walker knew that they'd have to do it all again, because people constantly moved through the building, except while they were watching a screening or listening to a panel discussion.

But Walker was so physically uncomfortable that he was ready to tear off his suit and give up. The crotch plate pinched his scrotum, the jumpsuit itched the cuts on his back, and his breath fogged up his visor. If that wasn't enough, his peripheral vision was terrible, so he kept banging into people, who angrily hurled profanities at him, though he didn't understand the ones in Jawaese, Klingon, and Dothraki.

He was also dispirited by the futility of their search. There had been a few Mandalorians that looked like Oxley from a distance, but once Walker and Eve closed in on them, it was obvious they were mistaken. It wasn't just the markings on the armor that didn't match, but the physical quality of the suits themselves. The body armor often looked like tinfoil or painted Styrofoam. Oxley's suit was more substantial, made with better materials and sharper attention to detail, than those worn by any of the Mandalorians they'd seen so far.

And they'd seen at least a hundred of them.

Walker was beginning to accept how foolhardy this search was and to fear that, by not alerting the FBI days ago that Oxley might show up at SciCon, he may have squandered the one real shot they had of apprehending the killer and securing the vial of plague.

And for what? Because he was bored and wanted to catch Oxley himself.

Walker was nearing the end of an aisle, passing a movie studio display dedicated to the hyped-up, tricked-out cars from a series of postapocalypse science fiction films, when he noticed some activity at one of the ballroom exits directly in front of him.

Two uniformed San Diego police officers were confronting a Mandalorian. One of the officers asked the Mandalorian to remove his helmet so they could see his face.

"I can't," the Mandalorian shouted. "It is the way."

"We won't ask twice," the cop said.

Oh shit, Walker thought. He looked anxiously to his left, at several other exits, and saw more uniformed police officers either getting into position or already in place, creating checkpoints to confront any Mandalorians who passed through.

He looked to his right and saw the same thing happening there, too, then looked back at the scene playing out in front of him with dread.

One cop suddenly grabbed the Mandalorian's arms from behind while the other simultaneously yanked off the man's helmet.

It wasn't Oxley in the suit, and the greasy-haired, sweaty man wearing it was outraged. "You've seen my face. Now to redeem myself, I'll have to bathe in the Living Waters of Mandalore!"

"Taking a bath would be a very good idea," the cop said, and put the helmet back on the man's head. "And maybe try some deodorant, too."

Eve's voice crackled in Walker's ear.

"I'm in the central aisle, right where it cuts through the middle of aisle 14. I can see cops at the north exit confronting people in Mandalorian suits."

"They're doing the same thing at the multiple exits leading to the lobby."

"Is Santos insane?"

"He must be." Walker reached for his rover and switched to Santos' channel. "Santos, this is Walker. What the hell are you doing? I see cops rousting Mandalorians. You might as well get on a loudspeaker and tell Oxley that we know he's here. You're going to scare him off."

"No, Walker, I'm going to flush him out."

Or push him into unleashing the zombie apocalypse.

"You have to pull the cops out of here before it's too late," Walker said. "The consequences could be catastrophic, on an epic scale, if you don't listen to me."

"That's a good description of what you're facing. You didn't mention that there's a national BOLO out for Oxley, or that you and Ronin have gone rogue," Santos said. "The FBI is demanding your immediate detention and the navy is sending armed marines across the bay right now to secure this facility. What has Oxley got on him? A fucking nuclear bomb?"

"If he does, do you think spooking him is the best way to keep him from setting it off?"

"What I think, and especially what *you* think, doesn't matter. The Feds are in charge. Turn yourselves over to the first officers you see or we'll come drag you out in cuffs."

Walker switched to Eve's channel. "We've been burned. They are coming for Oxley and for us."

"This is going to end badly."

Walker turned and rushed back down the aisle, toward the west end of the hall, talking to Eve in a flurry as he was on the move.

"If I were Oxley, and I was in this hall, and I would be because of all the *Star Wars* stuff here, and I saw the cops stopping every Mandalorian, I would ditch the suit, head for the food concessions, put on an apron and cap to blend in as a worker, and try to get out through the kitchens."

"He'll never ditch the suit."

She was right. But Walker said, "I'd still go for the kitchens and hope I could find a way to get out before they put cops on the loading docks and the fire exits."

Walker found himself in the middle of a huge, sandy display meant to replicate the dunes of Tatooine and where several full-scale landspeeder hover vehicles were displayed as selfie bait. Fans dressed as Princess Leia, C-3PO, Luke Skywalker, Rebel pilots, and even a few Groots and blond-haired Targaryens were posing for selfies in front of the models.

He weaved around them, unintentionally photobombing their shots, and found himself in the center aisle, right in the path of a Mandalorian marching his way, a man on a mission. It was a Mandalorian whose scratched and scorched armor told a story of many brutal battles fought and won, thanks to his combat skills and the awesome resilience of beskar steel.

Walker froze just for an instant, registering the sight of the Mandalorian and realizing who it was, but it was an instant too long.

The Mandalorian saw him and intuitively detected recognition somehow in Walker's body language.

So much for taking Oxley by surprise.

"I've found him," Walker said to Eve. "He's in the center aisle, near the Tatooine display. He's made me."

"I'm on my way."

"Come up behind him and to one side," he said. "His peripheral vision is shit."

Walker moved purposefully down the aisle toward Oxley, who stopped and whipped back his cape to reveal the blaster in his holster.

"Stay where you are," Oxley said, drawing his weapon. It was a real Taser gun.

But Walker kept coming. "I'm the law and you're a renegade. You need to redeem yourself in the Living Waters of Mandalore."

Whatever the hell that means.

Walker whipped back his cape so Oxley could see the badge clipped to his belt but mostly to distract him from Wonder Woman Eve, who was working her way up behind him, off to his right side, about ten yards back.

"Take one more step and I'll fry you with fifty thousand volts," Oxley said.

"Not from where you're standing. Your Taser has a range of fifteen feet. I don't have a tape measure on me, but I'm pretty sure you're too far." Walker casually rested his hand on the grip of his holstered Glock. "This has an effective range of fifty yards."

With his left hand, Oxley took an ammo cartridge from his bandolier and stuck his arm out horizontally at his side. He held the cartridge lengthwise between his index finger and thumb so Walker could get a good look at it.

"The range of this weapon is infinite," Oxley said. "I think you know that, whoever you are."

It was the vial.

Most of the *Star Wars*–costumed people around Walker and Oxley were totally oblivious to the showdown. The few that had noticed them were smiling, amused by their improvised playacting. But Walker knew that would change the instant the cops swarmed in. He had to end this fast and without killing twenty-five thousand people.

No pressure.

Walker spoke quietly, so only Eve could hear him over the rover. "He's got the vial in his left hand."

"I see it."

"You're going to have to take it."

"*Take* it?"

"Or catch it," Walker said. "You'll know when."

"I will?"

Walker now addressed himself to Oxley, who was still pointing the Taser at him while holding out the vial with his other hand. "Is that really how you want to die? It's going to be horrible."

"Not as horrible as the suffering I've already endured, that *all* of us have."

"All of us? Not me, pal." Walker took off his helmet and held it in his left hand, down at his side. "You just mean the losers who can't get laid."

"I'll become a martyr, and the deaths of all these people, and millions of others when this virus sweeps the globe, will incite the incel revolution. We will rise and give humanity a fresh start."

"I don't see how that's going to work."

Walker began absently swinging his left arm, as if it were a nervous tic. Maybe it was. He felt better doing it. Eve was getting closer, but so were the cops. In his peripheral vision, he could see uniformed police officers coming down the aisles on both sides of them, guns drawn. It would be over in seconds, one way or another.

"This is my Infinity Stone." Oxley raised his left arm to emphasize the vial that he held between his two fingers. "The natural balance will be restored. Desirable women will no longer be able to deny men their bodies, nor will the rich, selfish, and handsome be able to hoard the world's sexual wealth and control the reproductive future of mankind to further their own genetic line."

C-3PO, Groot, and Chewbacca clapped enthusiastically at that. Walker ignored them, focusing on Oxley.

"How do you know it'll be the desperately horny who survive the zombie apocalypse and not all of us handsome studs?" Walker said. "It sounds to me like you really haven't thought this through."

There was a commotion. All the costumed characters around them turned to their right to see police officers rushing through the Tatooine display toward the center aisle. Oxley quickly turned his head each way to see the cops coming on both sides of him.

"Uh-oh," Walker said.

If Oxley saw Eve at all in his limited peripheral vision, Walker hoped she was just another costumed attendee in the blurred background, presenting no threat to him, unlike the cops who were closing in.

Oxley faced Walker again and held up his arm. "I'll do it, Walker. Tell them to back off."

"Including the guy above you?"

Oxley looked up. Walker pitched his helmet like a softball at Oxley's crotch.

As Oxley instinctively twisted to avoid the impact, Walker drew his Glock and shot Oxley in the left shoulder.

Oxley screamed, involuntarily dropping the vial.

Eve dived for it.

Time slowed to a crawl for Walker. The people fleeing, the cops rushing in, and Oxley tumbling backward all became a blur to him. All he saw, with absolute clarity, was the fragile vial falling, and Eve diving, her arms outstretched, both palms up, to form a cup. She was Wonder Woman, flying through the air, trying to catch a raindrop.

And then time abruptly restarted, and everything moved very fast.

Eve hit the floor hard. Walker couldn't see if she'd caught the vial or not, because at that same instant, he was tackled by a cop.

As he fell, another scenario flashed across his mind—Eve getting under Oxley's arm a split second too soon, the vial missing her palm and shattering on her golden wrist plates.

What a sick joke that would be.

Whatever happened had happened. It couldn't be changed now.

With one cheek pressed into the floor, and an officer wrenching his arms behind his back, Walker looked at Eve, who was face down on the floor, her arms out in front of her, her hands closed.

Eve lifted her head, her nose broken and bleeding, and looked anxiously at Walker as she slowly opened her hands, just enough for them both to see if she held death or salvation.

The vial was in the palm of her hand and it was intact.

There would be no martyrs today.

CHAPTER THIRTY-THREE

Eve Ronin got all of the media attention for Oxley's arrest and Walker certainly understood why. He was just a guy in a costume, but she was the hot celebrity cop in the Wonder Woman suit, a stunning vision of cleavage, legs, patriotism, and hard-boiled attitude. The badge, Glock, and Lasso of Truth on her hips didn't hurt, either.

A bystander's Instagram video of Eve in her Wonder Woman suit marching Oxley out of the convention center in handcuffs went viral, increasing her popularity with the public and reigniting the smoldering animosity of her fellow deputies.

Eve blamed Walker for this and didn't speak to him, or acknowledge his apologetic emails, for weeks.

◆ ◆ ◆

Shortly after the shooting at SciCon, the FBI held a joint press conference outside the convention center with Los Angeles County sheriff Richard Lansing and San Diego police officials.

The FBI announced that their agents, working closely with local law enforcement, had thwarted a potential "homegrown terrorist attack" by a single demented individual, a member of the radical incel movement who was wanted in Los Angeles for two arson-related homicides. No

mention was made of Triax Biotech or that Oxley was carrying a weaponized virus that, if things had gone wrong, could have wiped out
nearly everyone in San Diego within days, the state within weeks, and
the nation within months. That news might have upset people.

Sheriff Lansing filled in the backstory, but only in broad strokes,
and without mentioning the names of those impacted by the crimes.
He said that Oxley had killed the lover of a woman who'd spurned his
sexual advances and then he'd tried to fake his own death by abducting
a man off the street, killing him in his home, and burning it down.
From there, Oxley fled to San Diego in an attempt to martyr himself.

Lansing praised Walker and Eve for their "relentless pursuit of
justice" and for choosing to reduce the risk of any SciCon attendees
being harmed by "entering the convention undercover" to locate and
capture the terrorist. Their inventive approach worked, resulting in an
arrest that didn't injure anyone except the suspect, who was in stable
condition at a local hospital. The sheriff characterized the "flawless,
meticulously planned operation" as a perfect example of what "smooth
interagency cooperation" can achieve in law enforcement.

Walker and Eve were not present at the press conference and they
both declined to comment when reporters personally contacted them.
The two detectives were not reprimanded, nor disciplined in any way,
for their involvement in Colin Oxley's arrest, nor for the suicide of
Warren Pendle. They returned to active duty the following week.

Special Agent Donna Leyland also wasn't present at the press conference and her name wasn't mentioned. She was on a flight to her new
posting at the FBI field office in Fairbanks, Alaska.

◆ ◆ ◆

Three Months Later

Martin Graff was enjoying the vigorous German massage performed
by the driver's seat of his leased Kalahari Gold Metallic Mercedes S 500

265

as he left the Braemar Country Club in the hills above Tarzana and headed home.

The older and fatter Graff became, the more golf aggravated his sciatica, sending shooting pain from his right butt cheek to his heel, where his chronic plantar fasciitis was also giving him grief. Unfortunately, Mercedes hadn't yet devised a calf-massage feature or he'd be using it, too.

He kept playing golf, despite the pain, for the social benefit of hanging out with investment bankers, Hollywood talent agents, and famous TV actors. It made him feel like a big *macher*, as his Yiddish-speaking Jewish grandfather used to say, and that was worth a little discomfort.

If only his grandfather could see him now. The old man wouldn't approve of him driving a "Hitler-mobile," but he'd appreciate that Graff could afford a $125K car. He'd also be impressed by Graff's Rolex, his alligator-skin shoes, and his large house in Sherman Oaks with a valley view.

His luxurious lifestyle wouldn't have been possible on the piti-ful salary Graff previously earned as an arson investigator for the San Bernardino County Sheriff's Department. So, all things considered, his humiliating problems there, which had once seemed so dire and cat-astrophic, turned out to be the best thing that ever happened to him. And yet, there were some aspects of the old job that he missed, like setting a wildfire that became so intense and powerful it generated its own thunderstorm. It was awesome to see, and sometimes he physically ached to experience it again.

The "Check Engine" warning light flashed on his 12.3-inch 3D dig-ital instrument cluster. He would have ignored it, but then his coolant, battery, and ABS system warning lights also began flashing. It could be nothing, he thought, or it could mean imminent, catastrophic engine failure, or that the vehicle's computer system was about to become sen-tient, shout "Heil, Hitler," and drive him into a wall. Luckily, he'd be passing the Mercedes dealership on Ventura Boulevard on his way home, so he could stop in and avoid that fate.

Graff drove his S 500 into the dealership's garage five minutes later, where the eager-to-please service adviser told him he'd have their limo driver take him home, and if it turned out the repair would take longer than an hour or so, they'd gladly deliver a loaner S-Class to him. That was fine with Graff, because the VIP treatment was more evidence that he truly was a big *macher*.

Two minutes later, Graff was on the road, heading home again, eastbound on Ventura Boulevard, in the back seat of an S-Class with reclining air-cooled seats and a back-massage feature. He was adjusting the massager settings to his liking when the driver spoke to him.

"Sore back?"

Graff glanced up at the sliver of the man's face that was visible in the rearview mirror. Actor Walter Matthau had come back from the dead to put on a Mercedes-branded polo shirt and give him a lift. "Yeah, as a matter of fact."

"That's an occupational hazard in our business, all that crouching, bending over, and squatting we have to do, especially if you're packing some pounds in the middle," the driver said as they crossed under the 405 freeway. "Bet you have the plantar fasciitis, too."

"A coworker sent me to his podiatrist for insoles, but they haven't worked for me." Graff got the massager just right and closed his eyes to enjoy the rollers grinding into his back. Now, if only Mercedes engineers could figure out how to give him a happy ending, the massage would be perfect and he'd never have to visit one of those Vietnamese "nail salons" in Canoga Park again. Then he remembered a throwaway comment the driver had made and he opened his eyes. "Did you just call me fat?"

"I was speaking in general about how the job impacts a man's body, yours and mine," he said. "I don't want to think about what it's doing to our lungs."

"You don't have to worry about the air in here. It's not like you're breathing exhaust." Graff closed his eyes again and settled back into the embrace of rich Nappa leather. "This S-Class has an air-purification system that uses charcoal filters and ionizers. You won't get fresher air unless you're standing in the Alps."

"Huh. I didn't know that."

"Isn't it your business to know?"

"The only time I've been in a car like this, it was torched by someone who couldn't afford the payments. You know how it is. At that point, you don't notice the luxury features."

Graff opened his eyes, and was about to ask him about that strange comment, when he noticed the driver was making a left-hand turn onto Van Nuys Boulevard. "Hey, you're going the wrong direction. I live south of the boulevard."

"I think those days are over, Marty."

Graff's heart started pounding. Something was very, very wrong here. He thought about their conversation and realized he'd skated past some things.

"What did you mean before, when you were talking about our jobs?"

"We're in the same line of work except that, unlike you, I'm honest and very good at what I do."

"I'm a fire investigator, not a driver."

"Me too," the man said, and Graff felt his intestines twisting. "My name is Walter Sharpe. Does that mean anything to you?"

"No, should it?"

"We've never met, but I'm the guy who caught you before, down in San Bernardino. This time, though, you're not wriggling free."

"What are you talking about?"

"Prison, Marty." Sharpe came to a stop at a red light and held up his badge to the rearview mirror. "You're under arrest."

Graff reached for the door and tried to open it, but it wouldn't budge. It was locked. He desperately yanked at the latch and threw his shoulder into the door.

"Child locks are another great feature this car has. Guess you didn't know about that one," Sharpe said casually, and eased into the intersection as the light turned green. "You might also want to look behind you."

Graff twisted his body to see, sending a sharp jolt of pain down his sciatic nerve, from his butt to the tips of his toes, and it made him wince. When he opened his eyes, he saw an LAPD patrol car following them. He very slowly and tentatively turned around again, trying not to irritate his back.

"Where are you taking me?" he asked, wishing it were to a chiropractor and not where he thought it was.

"A few blocks up to the LAPD station at the Van Nuys Government Center," Sharpe said. That's what Graff was afraid of. "It's where we're processing the three dozen people we swept up today in simultaneous arrests conducted all over the San Fernando Valley as part of Operation Fire Hose."

"What is that?"

"The multiagency task force investigating Larry Bogert's insurance fraud scheme. We've got the homeowners, the adjusters, everybody."

Graff could see the Los Angeles County courthouse looming ahead and his own bleak future. But he'd seen that future of shame, imprisonment, and communal showers before and ended up on the manicured fairways at Braemar instead. If he did it once, he could do it again.

"I'll testify against them all in exchange for immunity or probation," Graff said. "I'll stay at home and wear one of those ankle bracelets."

"We don't want or need anything from you," Sharpe said, pulling into the parking lot, where a crowd of somber handcuffed people were being led from police cars and paddy wagons into the police station. Graff recognized every one of them. "A homeowner gave up Bogert, and he gave up the rest of you. Bogert even got you to incriminate yourself on camera. You've basically hung yourself already."

Graff settled back into his leather seat to feel those magic German fingers one last time and he sobbed.

◆　◆　◆

Sharpe got out of the Mercedes and turned to the two officers emerging from the patrol car that had been following him. "Do you guys mind cuffing Graff and taking him in for booking?"

One of the officers nodded. Sharpe thanked him and spotted Walker leaning against their Tahoe, arms crossed under his chest, watching the scene unfold.

"We could have arrested Graff at the country club," Walker said as Sharpe approached. "It would have been a lot easier than rigging his Mercedes to malfunction, using an over-the-air update of his operating system to do it, just so you could play chauffeur."

"That's true," Sharpe said, "but this was much more fun and I get to keep this nice Mercedes shirt as a souvenir."

Walker smiled, stepped forward, and put his arm around his partner's shoulders. "I'm proud of you, Sharpe. You've made enormous progress under my tutelage. I think we're almost ready to move on to the next lesson."

"What's that?"

"How to look badass in a Mandalorian suit."

AUTHOR'S NOTE

This book is entirely a work of fiction, but I was inspired by the cases investigated by Ed Nordskog, a highly respected former Los Angeles County Sheriff's Department arson and explosives detective, that are chronicled in his books *Fireraisers, Freaks, and Fiends*, *"Torchered" Minds: Case Histories of Notorious Serial Arsonists*, and *The Arsonist Profiles: Analyzing Arson Motives and Behavior*. I also relied heavily upon his books *Incendiary Devices: Investigation and Analysis* and *Fire Death Scene Investigation: A Field Guide for Homicide, Coroner, and Arson Investigators* (coauthored with Joe Konefal) for background on investigative procedure. On top of all that, he kindly and patiently answered all of my dumb emailed questions with extensively detailed, anecdote-rich replies.

I don't think it's possible to write about arson investigation without frequently referring to *Kirk's Fire Investigation, Eighth Edition* by David J. Icove and Gerald A. Haynes, *NFPA 921: Guide for Fire and Explosion Investigations* 2021 (National Fire Protection Association), *Fire Investigator: Principles and Practice to NPFA 921 and 1033, Fifth Edition* (Jones & Bartlett Learning), and *A Guide for Investigating Fire and Arson* (National Institute of Justice). It seems like those books were constantly open on my desk or anywhere else that I was writing (which is why one book is stained with BBQ sauce and another is soiled with suntan lotion and salt water).

I'm certain all of the authors that I've just acknowledged will cringe at everything I got wrong about arson investigation in this book. Most of those mistakes, whatever they may be, are due to my ignorance, sloppiness, or misunderstanding. But some of them were undoubtedly made on purpose, because the truth just wasn't as much fun as the fiction. Please don't blame the authors of those fine nonfiction books for any of that. It's all on me. I don't let facts get in the way of telling a good story.

I'm also grateful to private investigator Tom Simon, a retired FBI special agent and a big fan of vintage crime fiction, for his technical and practical advice on hunting fugitives.

A lot of the places in this book actually exist, others are figments of my imagination, and others are a mix of the two (for example, Twin Lakes is real, but not the housing tract). I've also taken a few minor liberties with geography to suit my storytelling needs. So, if you try to use Google Earth to follow Sharpe and Walker as they investigate, like some of my readers do, you may hit some snags.

Finally, I want to thank my wonderful publisher Gracie Doyle, my insightful and supportive editors Megha Parekh and Charlotte Herscher, my dedicated literary agent Amy Tannenbaum, and most of all, my wife Valerie and my daughter Madison for giving me their love, their enthusiasm, and occasionally a bite of their desserts.

About the Author

Photo © 2013 Roland Scarpa

Lee Goldberg is a two-time Edgar Award and two-time Shamus Award finalist and the #1 *New York Times* bestselling author of more than sixty novels, including the Eve Ronin series, the Ian Ludlow series, the Sharpe & Walker series, and seven books in the Fox & O'Hare series, which he coauthored with Janet Evanovich. He has also written and/or produced many TV shows, including *Diagnosis Murder*, *SeaQuest*, and *Monk*, and is the cocreator of the Hallmark movie series *Mystery 101*. As an international television consultant, he has advised networks and studios in Canada, France, Germany, Spain, China, Sweden, and the Netherlands on the creation, writing, and production of episodic series. For more information, visit www.leegoldberg.com.